Down at Jika Jika Tavern

The Poacher's Moon Crime Series

Also by Ashling McCarthy

The Poacher's Moon Crime Series:
The Leopard in the Lala (Book 2). 2023

Down at Jika Jika Tavern

The Poacher's Moon Crime Series

Book 1

Ashling McCarthy

To my beautiful mom, how I wish you still walked this earth with us.

And, to my own Nonhle: may you grow to be strong, and brave, and true to yourself.

How to pronounce the name Nonhle

isiZulu is full of beautiful sounding words and names, but sometimes, the untrained tongue can get a bit tied up. Because names are so important, I'm going to help you pronounce the name Nonhle, which means Mother of Beauty.

Imagine it's late, and the bush fire you've been standing around needs to be put out before you can go to bed. You throw a jug of water over the hot coals, which hiss with relief as they cool. That's what ***hle*** sounds like! Non-***hle***.

Or, press your tongue flat against your back molars, and breathe out to make the h sound, whilst adding a long sounding le at the end.

Glossary

Words and phrases in languages, such as isiZulu and Afrikaans, have been *italicised* and can be found in the glossary at the back of the book.

A terrible mistake
29th November 2012

The driver parked the old Nissan Sentra in an informal layby between the dirt road and the railway lines; the cut of the tracks, thin and bright, in the dark fabric of the night. A sudden gust of wind blew in through the open windows but did little to mask the varying odours of unexpressed emotion inside. For within the shoddy interior, two men, and a boy on the cusp of manhood, prepared themselves for the dangerous task ahead.

The boy, Mandla, watched as the man in the passenger seat pulled out a battered water bottle filled with muddy brown liquid. A string of tiny red and white beads on a thin white thread hung from the bottle's neck, a talisman of luck. Bheki untwisted the cap, sniffed the contents, and recoiled with a grimace; but then, after a deep breath, he pinched his nose between two fingers and let the bitter brew run down his throat.

Bheki's attempt to pass the bottle to the man in the driver's seat resulted in the rolling of the man's eyes and an adolescent turn of his head. Bheki clicked his tongue against his teeth in irritation and handed the bottle to Mandla. Mandla hesitated. He'd never drunk *muthi* before, but he didn't want to offend the ancestors and create bad luck for himself.

He took a tentative sip and then glugged down as much of the liquid as he could manage. And then he waited. After a minute or two, his bottom lip – which tasted like he'd licked the floor of a cattle *kraal*

– protruded in disappointment.

'*Hawu*, Bheki,' he whined. 'I can still see you; can you see me?'

Bheki's serious face lit up and he roared with laughter, smacking the driver's arm with delight as if Mandla was joking.

'That's good, little man. But it's not me you should be worried about. It's the men with the big guns and the dogs that you need to hide from!'

Mandla felt the blood drain right out of his head, and a whimper escaped his lips.

At the sound, the man in the driver's seat finally spoke. '*Wena!*' he scolded Bheki.

'Don't listen to him, Mandla,' Nkosi said, twisting in his seat to glare at Mandla.

Mandla sat up immediately. He knew that Nkosi had taken a big risk bringing him on this excursion. It was his chance to prove himself, and perhaps get the opportunity to join Nkosi's team, permanently.

When Nkosi finally indicated that it was time, the three quickly emerged from the vehicle. They set about covering its dusty body with acacia branches, which they'd ferried in the boot of the vehicle, from Nkosi's village. It was a necessary precaution as a small copse of trees missing branches, near a game reserve, might alert a patrolling security company to illegal activity going on. Out of the boot came tatty backpacks and gear, which they shouldered according to their rank and role. They ran up the slope into the dark and began the thirty-minute walk along the railway line, headed towards a large marula tree, which marked their entry point. When the tree was in sight, Nkosi swore and stopped dead in his tracks. Mandla, who had been trotting to keep up with the two men, bumped into the back of Bheki who had pulled up alongside Nkosi. The majestic marula tree had been chosen as their entry point because it had a large, solid limb that stretched over the fence into the reserve. Nkosi had planned for them to scale the tree and drop to the other side from the low hanging branch. But now, that branch was gone, only a stub coated in bleeding sap was left of the freshly hacked limb.

Mandla felt a wave of worry wash over him, and he immediately reached for his lip, his fingers plucking at the thin skin. Nkosi, who had been staring at the tree, suddenly came to life. He spun Mandla around so that he could access Mandla's backpack. Out came a wire cutter, and in less than a minute, an opening was created, allowing all three to leopard crawl through and melt into the tall grass of the open veld.

It was not a big reserve, and Nkosi guided them through the unknown terrain, walking to a set of coordinates he'd tapped into a Garmin. The veld, lit up like a soccer pitch at night by the glow of a full moon, was dotted with acacias and ant mounds. Mandla felt cold fingers caress his neck; the oddly shaped ant mounds looked like children frozen in play and old women bent with age. He jumped as a movement to their left brought the trio to a halt. A ghostly journey of giraffe cruised slowly through the trees, like a ship in the Zululand night, charting a course to the nearest dam. As they waited for the giants to pass, Nkosi consulted his Garmin and then veered north, leading the group into a stand of luminous fever trees.

Mandla shivered as the moon disappeared from view and the darkness wrapped itself around them. The bush went still, the constant chirp of frogs and crickets, the persistent call of a fiery-necked nightjar, silenced. In the trees, amongst the shrubs, on the game paths, fur bristled, ears pricked, and noses twitched. Then, abruptly, the bush came alive as an alpha baboon let forth a volley of barks, upsetting birds that had roosted for the night, and sending animals crashing through the undergrowth. Mandla yelled out in terror. His first thought was to run. Run as fast as he could back to the fence, back to safety. Before his brain was able to engage his feet, Nkosi grabbed him by the back of the neck, pulling him further into the shadows. He found a tree and shoved Mandla against it.

'Don't move,' he hissed. 'Or I'll kill you.'

Mandla listened as the two men went over the information they had. According to the SMS that Nkosi had received a couple of hours before, the rhino was not too deep into the reserve. The large solitary bull had camped out at a waterhole earlier that day, making no signs of moving off. He would be a perfect target if he were still stretched out in the mud. But there was a possibility that the rhino had become hungry and ventured out in search of food. Nkosi signalled to the others to pick up their gear and they continued north, eyes peering through the bush, seeking out any potential threat, whether animal or human. Mandla hurried to keep up with them. As it was his first mission, he'd been given the lowly task of carrying the bag with a few supplies. If, and he hoped this would not be the case, things didn't go as planned and they couldn't reach the fence, they would have enough food to get them through a night in the reserve. Mandla's fear grew by the second; his body was rigid, and his legs made jerky oversized steps. His eyes swivelled in their sockets as he sought out the slightest movements around him.

A short while later, Nkosi dropped to his knees, motioning for the others to join him under a large tree. The water hole was in sight. They quietly placed their gear on the ground, and Bheki drew out an axe and unstrapped a hunting knife, from the bags. Nkosi double-checked his hunting rifle and took aim at an imaginary rhino, with a soft bam-bam. As the men disappeared into the night, Mandla leant against the large tree. He wrapped his arms around his skinny frame to keep the tremors he couldn't seem to control from consuming his body. His only job was to look after the gear, while Bheki and Nkosi went in search of the bull. With the two men gone, he finally allowed a tear to escape down his dusty cheek. He'd made a terrible mistake, but there was no turning back now. Though the moon was bright out there in the veld, there was less light under the canopy, and he had no idea how to get back the way they'd come. He'd just have to sit still and wait for the men to return.

Except he couldn't sit still. He sat bolt upright at a deep throaty grunting that sounded like a large animal ready to charge but seemed to come from the tree above him. The grunting stopped, and he heard the faint ruffle of feathers as a large bird shook itself, before launching from the branch above, on silent wings. Mandla sat back and tried to relax, but then came the faint crackling of dry wood and leaves behind him. He made himself as small as possible, held his breath, and kept one eye open. A flash of white made his heart leap in his chest, then he sighed with relief as a large buck picked its way slowly through the undergrowth. Then the slow crawl of a thousand legs tickled his neck. He managed to stifle a scream but leapt to his feet in a dance of fear as he swept the unwelcome guest onto the floor. He brushed the area around the tree furiously with his shoe, then threw himself at the trunk as if it could protect him from the bone-chilling wail of a terrified child, which shattered the silence. It was the sound of a child trying to escape from the hard fists of an angry uncle. A sound Mandla knew too well. *Waow, waow … waow, waow.* A sound so traumatising that Mandla, no longer able to control himself, released a warm river of urine, which flowed down his leg and into his shoe.

1: It is so good to see you
25th November 2012

When the taxi dropped Nonhle Ngubane off on the side of the road, she was covered in a fine coating of red dust. Her once glossy black weave, bought especially for her December homecoming, was now a burnished copper, set alight by the afternoon sun falling across the veld. This was usually her favourite time of day, out here, away from the city. Magic light suffused the veld, the tips of the long grass ablaze, tiny winged insects dancing across their fuzzy tops. A lone zebra cut a path through the toothless fire, on its way towards some unknown spot on the horizon. Nonhle, however, was completely uninterested in the magic light; she slouched in a wrinkled heap, too tired to pick up her oversized suitcase packed with clothes and gifts for her family.

She sighed and attempted to reorganise the scowl that the trip had induced. She'd spent much of it in a passive-aggressive war with the enormous mama behind her as they fought for control of the window they shared. Nonhle, who was desperate to retain some of the glamour she'd worked so hard to create before boarding the taxi, wanted the window closed. The mama, hemmed in on all sides, her large posterior glued to the fake leather seat, was equally keen on keeping it open so that the funnel of air – currently disorganising Nonhle's weave – could blow over her sweaty form.

The battle had gone on for a good portion of the trip; the window shoved forwards by the mama's meaty elbow, and backwards with Nonhle's hand. After passing through the last toll plaza, the taxi driver had swerved to a stop and threatened to leave them on the side of the freeway, if they continued slamming his precious window back and forth. A mortified silence had filled the interior of the taxi until passengers started *eh-he'ing* and *mm-hmm'ing* in agreement. Since the window had been open at this point, Nonhle had been forced to sit in a furious sulk for the rest of the journey, while the mama relaxed in glorious contentment as the cool air brought down the dangerously high temperature of her inner core.

Nonhle stood in the dying light, trying to rid herself of the irritation that continued to course through her body. Inhaling deeply, she welcomed the spice and honey fragrance of the veld, into her lungs. It was a scent she had longed for while studying in Durban. There was a pureness in the air out here, rich with the starchiness of the African potato, and the pungent aroma of wild garlic. Of course, Durban had its own unique scents, and by the end of her two-month break at home, she'd be longing for them. Depending on where you were in the city, the clean scent of the ocean would wash over you, or the unmistakable aroma of curry and biryani would cling to hair and clothes. Her mouth watered as her brain conjured up the acidic tang of white vinegar doused liberally over a plate of hot, greasy chips, then smothered in glossy red tomato sauce. The sudden flow of saliva nudged her out of her contemplation, and she bent down to pick up the handle of her new purchase.

It was a travel suitcase with wheels, a polished beetle-red case with a hard exterior. Just before she was due home, she'd gone shopping, and once presents for her parents had been bought, she used the remainder of her hard-earned money to purchase the case. She'd almost screamed at the taxi driver when he'd unceremoniously tossed it into the trailer and covered it with the bags of the other passengers. When she'd asked him, through gritted teeth, why he insisted it go at the bottom, he looked at her as if she was simple.

'Because, *sisi*, it is hard, like a stone.'

With that, he continued to cover it with bags of fruit, vegetables and luggage made of soft material containing the worldly goods of the other passengers. She couldn't argue with that fact. Instead, she'd gone and found herself a seat in the taxi.

Location-wise, the ideal seat was the middle row, next to a window. Sitting at the back made her motion-sick, while on a short trip, sitting in the front meant she'd constantly be moving her knees and handbag aside to let passengers on and off. If she were early enough, she could be strategic in her choice of seat. Firstly, she would survey the passengers who would be on the same trip, and single out individuals that she did not want to sit next to for a few hours. On this journey, it included a young man who had the distinct look of a *tsotsi* as well as the large mama she'd ended up warring silently with over the window. So, she'd let a few passengers board, knowing it was likely that it would be the young man and the large mama who would push their way to the front. Once they'd boarded, she'd quickly jumped in, ensuring that she didn't sit next to either of them. She sighed now as she thought of the futility of her plan. She looked down at her suitcase, its once lustrous surface covered with a crosshatch of scratches.

The taxi had dropped her at the T-junction, some way from the compound where her parents lived. As she crossed over the railway line that traversed the country, the wheels of her case proved useless in navigating the 4x4 course of steel rails and concrete sleepers. With two hands, she hefted it to chest height and tottered across the line to the safety of the other side, banging it down hard, as her arms finally gave out. She was exhausted. She contemplated turning the case on its side so that she could sit on it until someone drove by and offered her a lift. But she knew that she might sit for some time, and the darkness of night would steal the last remnants of light from the sky, while she waited. Instead, she squared her shoulders, grabbed the handle of the suitcase, and began her long walk home, the little wheels rattling and jerking over stones and ruts in the road.

About a kilometre into her walk, a khaki coloured Land Cruiser pulled up next to her. Her eyes took in the large logo of a rhino's head, encircled by the words Umkhombe Anti-Poaching Unit, before settling on the face of the driver. To her irritation, she found her lips turning up spontaneously into a wide smile.

'*Sawubona,* sisi,' said the driver, his sunglasses masking whether the faint smile on his lips extended to his eyes. 'Can I give you a lift?'

While he opened his door and hoisted her suitcase onto the back seat, she realised that she was still grinning foolishly at him. He slammed the door shut and folded himself into the driver's seat, so she ran around the front of the vehicle to the passenger side and swung the heavy door open.

'*Ngiyabonga,*' she said, putting on her seat belt at his gesture.

'It's not too far, but I'm glad you stopped.'

'No problem,' he said, his fingers tapping the steering wheel. 'Where are you going?'

It was obvious he wasn't from around here; she could tell immediately. Even though he spoke isiZulu, he had a distinct accent, much like her own. One cultivated in response to the type of school she'd attended. She wondered if, when back home with certain people, he was also made to feel guilty about it.

'I'm going home,' she said, with a sigh of happiness as she sank into the leather seat. 'It's the compound for The Last Outpost lodge. You know it?' she asked, looking at him expectantly.

The half-smile disappeared, his forehead crinkling before smoothing out just as quickly.

Definitely not from around here, Nonhle thought. She pointed at the windscreen at the road ahead, 'It's about four-kilometres —"

'I know where it is,' he said abruptly, turning the key in the ignition, and pulled out into the road.

Nonhle closed her mouth and wondered what his problem was. His eyes were fixed ahead, his lips a long flat line. Uncomfortable with the silence, she forced a brightness she didn't feel, into her voice. 'So,' she ventured, choosing a less prickly subject to engage in, 'you're not from Mevamhlope. Where's home for you?'

'What makes you think I'm from somewhere else?' he said, his tone even less amiable than before.

Flummoxed that she'd somehow managed to upset him further, she looked out the window in embarrassment. How had she managed to irritate him twice in such a short space of time? Before she knew it, he'd pulled to the side of the road outside the workers' compound. The once white walls were covered in splashes of vibrant fuchsia bougainvillea, and patches of blue, revealed by peeling paint.

She turned to thank him, but her words addressed his empty seat; he'd already opened his door, to swing her suitcase easily to the floor. He pulled out the handle and passed it over to her, their hands touching briefly in the exchange. He was a tall man and good looking. Very good looking, she thought. Pity about his personality. He was looking past her, his eyes scanning the compound.

'How long have you lived here?' he asked, his expression grim.

'All my life. My parents have worked for the lodge for about twenty-five years now,' she said, surprised at this interest.

'Has it changed much?'

She faced the compound and gave it a quick once over. 'A little,' she mused, 'but not much.'

He clicked his tongue against his teeth in disgust and turned back to his vehicle. He got in and without saying a word, lifted his hand curtly in her direction.

Well. That went well, she mocked herself as she watched a cloud of red dust chase after him. She snatched the handle of her suitcase and dragged it through the gate towards home. The familiar scent of wood smoke and home cooking wafted down the path towards her, and her stomach gurgled in anticipation of what her mother would have been preparing for her first night home. A loud ululation pierced the air. Nonhle lifted her head and caught sight of her mother, Thuli, walking up the path between the houses. Nonhle laughed at the delight on her mother's face. Her mother was a small, slim woman; a reed had more substance. She was graceful, her steps deliberate as if testing the earth with her heel, before committing her foot to the full action of walking.

'My girl,' said Mama, grasping Nonhle in a tight hug. 'It is so good to see you. I thought you had missed the taxi from Durban. It's so late!' she admonished.

'Sorry, Mama. You know how it is, they won't leave the rank until the taxi is full.' She leant into her mother, feeling the need for additional support.

'Mama,' whispered Nonhle, breathing in her mother's familiar scent of Lifebouy soap and Vaseline. 'I am so happy to be home.'

When Nonhle released her mother from her embrace, she saw that she'd transferred some of the red dust she'd accumulated on her travels onto Thuli's white blouse. She shook her head, and a flurry of dust motes danced around her, then floated gently to the floor.

'I'm a mess!' she wailed. She must be mad to think that any man, never mind the one who'd dropped her off, might find her attractive in her current state. 'Dirtier than one of those boys,' she muttered as the whoop of soccer-playing children reached them.

'There's hot water for you to wash with. I'm sorry you can't shower,' Mama said. She gazed up into the sky. 'The rain has not come, and the borehole water is low. Baba's cattle are getting thinner every day.' She shook her head sadly, then took her daughter by the hand. 'I put a basin and washcloth in your room.'

Nonhle sighed; she'd forgotten about the drought.

'Thanks, Mama,' she said as they entered the small house.

She pulled her case into the room she had once shared with her cousin, now a grown woman living some way away in another village, with four children and a useless boyfriend.

'And Nonhle.'

'Yes, Mama.'

'Take off those eyelashes before Baba sees you.'

***

Later that evening, Nonhle's father, Samson Ngubane, walked up the path towards the house. The light from his torch guided his steps, then cast leaping shadows as he swung it across the darkness. As he looked up from his inspection of the path, he saw his only child – like a divine being encircled by light – launch off the top step, to skip down to meet him.

For some reason, this child of his often made him want to weep. He was in awe of her; she was the first person in the family to attend university. Her mother was smart, but between them, they had never been any match for Nonhle's curious mind and truth-seeking enquiries. She had done nothing but make him proud. He was dreading the day when she would be too busy to come home for the holidays; the responsibilities of whatever big job in Durban she took, overriding her obligation to come home. He hoped that she would choose to stay in Durban, rather than head off to Johannesburg or Cape Town. Since leaving for university, she only came home for a visit in July, and then worked at the lodge in December. Those times were the highlight of his year.

'Sawubona, Baba," she greeted, her hand resting lightly on his shoulders.

'Come, let me look at you,' he said, leading her back towards the kitchen stairs, and into the light.

'My daughter,' he smiled, eyes roaming her face, 'you are growing into a fine woman.' He was sad to see that she had finally lost the soft layer she'd gained when she'd moved to Durban three years ago. But she had on a new weave. Her once short hair now swept across her forehead and came to rest below her earlobes. 'Let me remind you of the *sjambok* that lies under my bed. I am not too old to come to Durban and use it on any boy who thinks you are as easy as a baby impala to hunt,' he grinned, displaying large white mielie sized teeth.

She gave him a mirthless laugh. 'Don't worry, Baba. I don't seem to have any problem scaring them off, myself.'

Samson nodded, pleased at her admission. 'You make me proud, Nonhle. Just make sure you don't get too clever though; the boys won't know what to do with you.' He shook his head sadly at the prospect of an unmarried daughter.

They walked up the stairs and Samson settled himself onto a kitchen chair, just as Thuli placed a mug of tea in front of him. He briefly squeezed his wife's hand, which she'd placed on his shoulder.

'My child,' he said, continuing with the thought that caused him much concern. He worried that in their pursuit to ensure their daughter had the best chance of success, he had allowed her to become too modern. 'I do not know one man who likes to look stupid in front of a woman. There is an old saying: *kuhlonishwa kabili*. If we want to be respected, we must also be respectful. And men, we like to be respected.'

'Yes, Baba,' said Nonhle, turning away, but not before he heard her murmur, 'And so do we.'

Thuli, who had come home from work an hour before him, returned to the task of peeling potatoes, shredding spinach, and chopping tomatoes for the evening meal. Samson felt his heart grow full at the sight of the two women in his life. Now that they were all home together, he could truly relax. He also worried about Nonhle down in Durban. She was a smart girl, but there were many tsotsis waiting to take advantage, and she had a soft heart, his daughter. Soft like her mother's.

As they sat down for their first family dinner in many months, Baba watched Nonhle as she shared the stories she'd accumulated since they'd last seen her. She was a hoarder, his child. In her youth, she'd collected feathers, placing each one gently in a box; a clear lid allowing her to gaze proudly at her collection but keeping the mites and the dust, out. As she shared each story, her face was radiant with the experiences his wife and himself would never have. He was so grateful that she had found a way to step outside of this rural life that was both beautiful and harsh; for it was limiting, for a woman like her, in so many ways.

They would probably never know life outside the dust and the ivory-coloured veld. They would always be surrounded by acacia thorn, with a longing for rain, and the smell of wood smoke. Even when Nonhle – because Samson knew it was a case of 'when' and not 'if' – found a good job and earned decent money, he could never leave this place of his birth. His heart was firmly rooted in the red soil of Zululand, where he lived with one side of his face seeing but never tasting the wealth of the lives of local and foreign guests, and the other confronted with the poverty and the hopelessness felt by those who lived in communities on the outskirts of The Last Outpost Lodge.

2: You are being very dramatic
Three months prior

The figure, hurrying along the narrow path running across the ridge of Intaba Yemikhovu, kept looking back over his shoulder. He could feel them now, the hot breath of a thousand ghosts pushing him on. Usually, he avoided this route, but it was the quickest and in the terrifying shadow of the night, he'd take his chances. Tonight, he was luckier than usual, the path alight with a lunar glow. He often wondered if, in another form, he might have the strength to reach up and unseat the moon from its resting place. He'd like to watch it roll down the mountain, clearing a path through trees and bushes, then finally coming to rest in the waters of Lake Jozini. As it sat basking in the warm waters, he imagined schools of tiger fish drawn to its light, like moths to a flame. He laughed softly at the ridiculous thought. If the stories were true, then he believed that there was only one man who had the ability to shift heaven and earth in such a way. The traveller's route would take him past the man's home, and, as was his custom, he threw up countless prayers of protection to the ancestors he knew to be listening.

He slowed his gait as a tiny flicker of light appeared some way up the path. Already the air had taken on a peculiar quality, a density that vibrated around him, compressing the previously unhindered movement of his chest. The wind carried the sounds of a hypnotic wail; human or spirit, he couldn't be sure. The sound became vines that looped around his neck and body, trying to draw him down the path towards the light. His heart began to expand and contract at such a rate, that he felt it might burst through the wall of muscle and skin.

As he rounded the bend, a structure became visible – a rondavel made of packed mud; long beams of light pierced through crumbling sections of wall. Smoke escaped the thatched roof, creating a ghostly shroud; a perfect setting for the otherworldly activity that went on inside. As he turned to flee in the direction he'd come, the wailing stopped. The vibration in the air subsided and then, like a mighty wind that ceases to blow, the night became still. He remained where he was for some time. He'd been fooled before, tricked into thinking the scene unfolding inside had come to an end. He'd hurried down the path in front of the rondavel and as he'd crossed the rectangle of light cast by the doorway, a scream had rent the air. He'd practically cartwheeled down the mountain, legs whirring as his torso strained forward, the momentum so great, that his body had finally overtaken his feet and he'd landed in a dusty heap someway down the incline.

***

Inside the rondavel, Mthunzi Mnguni knelt on a reed mat. A fug of smoke, produced by the burning of *imphepho* to help him communicate with the ancestors, settled around him. A band of hyena skin circled his head, and the long black wig of braids he wore, was adorned with white beads. With the windows closed, it was hot and hazy, and he'd discarded his shirt at some point during the night. The walls were lined with shelves holding bottles and containers of all shapes and sizes. Some clear, others opaque, but each filled with some form of organic material, plant or animal, that would be used to concoct muthi for the multitude of people that sought him out. The skins of honey badger and a leopard hung from the rafters, and small baskets of pangolin scales, vulture heads, teeth, claws and other parts from animals and birds, lined the walls. Those that came looking for Mthunzi Mnguni, were looking for healing, for love, for luck, and often, for revenge.

A fierce conversation was in progress. An argument really, about how best to proceed with a plan that had been simmering in Mthunzi's heart and mind for years. Mthunzi clenched his fists in frustration. They'd reached an impasse; everyone needed to agree to go ahead, but as usual, MaNoxolo was spoiling the vote.

'Really, Ma,' said Zenzile, a small shrew of a woman. 'You must accept that you cannot win this fight. Why can you not accept that Mthunzi must do this?'

MaNoxolo shook visibly with indignation. 'Zenzile, I will never agree to this! It is not in line with Mthunzi's true calling as *isangoma* – which is to *heal*,' she reminded them.

Mthunzi cast a thunderous look in her direction. 'Ma, you seem to have forgotten that this man ruined my life. Cast me out into the wilderness. Destroyed my reputation!'

'Mthunzi, my child,' she turned to look at him, her gentle eyes searching his. 'You are being very dramatic. He was right to do what he did. I know, deep inside you, that you know you have been very wrong. That is why you have done nothing to him, so far.'

She was right. He *had* done nothing at all. It had been years since, what he liked to call 'The Great Betrayal', had occurred. He was perfectly capable of ensuring that the man he'd once called his friend suffered for his treacherous act. But Mthunzi hadn't acted. He hadn't even called in the services of another isangoma, so that his own hands remained clean. Why was that, he wondered? He stared hard at MaNoxolo through the fog of imphepho. *It was her fault.*

He closed his eyes and tried very hard to control his growing rage. This infuriating woman was doing her best to prevent him from what the other ancestors kept assuring him would be his greatest triumph. For years they'd been talking about getting revenge, and she'd sat there like a hippopotamus on a grass mat, always with the counterargument of his true calling. Yes. It was true. He had willingly moved in another direction, one that was far from the purpose he was destined to fulfil. She had been sent as his *idlozi*, his ancestor, to carry out the mission of healing, and he had complied. For years he had done his very best. And how had he been rewarded? He had not. It was so clear to him now. He had been tricked into carrying out her mission, one which had led him into poverty. So, when the other ancestors had arrived unexpectedly, promising financial freedom, he could not resist. Oh, he had tried. The hours spent attempting to convince MaNoxolo that he could do both had been unproductive. Neither would bend, and it had created a great gulf between them. But she would not leave. She chose to stay by his side, like a great big thorn, attempting to steer him in the right direction. Mthunzi knew full well that the two *amadlozi*, Zenzile and Mzamo, were spiteful and selfish ancestors. They were here to redress the life of poverty they'd been forced to endure in human form on earth, many moons ago. They had been thrilled when they found Mthunzi, up on his mountain, with only MaNoxolo by his side.

'Ma!' bellowed Mzamo, causing Mthunzi's eyes to fly open. 'Enough is enough. You need to admit that you are a failure, a completely useless idlozi who has failed at her mission in this life. Mthunzi does not need you. We do not want you.' He flew across the room, striking MaNoxolo, who had no time to defend the blow.

A collective inhalation brought the activity in the room to a momentary standstill. MaNoxolo moved a shaking hand to her face, which crumpled in on itself as large tears navigated a course over her cheeks, tentatively clinging to her chin, before flinging themselves onto her mammoth chest.

While Mthunzi's body failed to defend her, his conscience sprang to life. His beloved MaNoxolo! He had brought this humiliation on her. Deep within him, he knew that he was wrong. A thin tendril of shame unfurled, desperately seeking the light of his truth. He managed to prise one foot from the floor and made to move towards her. But one look at Mzamo's face and both his foot and the tendril withdrew.

'Now,' said Mzamo, his voice cold and calculating. 'Take a look at the bones again, Mthunzi. They are going to tell us what to do next.

'Zenzile, her tiny frame perched like a sparrow on the stool, beckoned him towards the mat. On it lay Mthunzi's set of bones. An assortment of precious items MaNoxolo had revealed to him in his dreams, during his training. Each had to be collected from the various locations he'd visited in his somnolent state. The tooth of a caracal he'd found lying in the bed of the animal's bones; an ammonite found on the shores of False Bay; a chunk of petrified tree; a small tin snuff box; a brass button; among other items, all of which helped him to divine the future. He swept the bones into a bag, held the mouth closed, and rattled them about. With a practised flick of his wrist, he threw the bag, and the bones tumbled out onto the mat in front of him.

They all leaned forward to assess the scene, and as the sweat ran down the rolling hills of Mthunzi's chest and belly, a great sigh escaped each of them. One of the bones rolled to the outskirts of the mat. It was a woman's earring, a cheap gold hoop that Mthunzi had found encircling the thin branch of a fever tree. It seemed an insignificant symbol to signify that years of patient planning were over and that retribution was near. Mthunzi sat back on his heels. He had to admit he didn't feel as excited as he'd expected, but he was sure that would change as the plan began to unfold. He could feel Zenzile and Mzamo looking at him with anticipation. He gave them a hesitant smile, and picked up the earring, pinching it firmly between thumb and forefinger.

Outside, the moon began its descent behind the ridge. The slow breathing of the night began to accelerate, accompanied by the sounds of wakening creatures – the dawn chorus of shrikes and weavers, and the high-pitched yawn of a hunting dog. MaNoxolo had moved to the door of the house. She leant her large form against the frame and closed her eyes. How weary she felt, like a mother burdened by a wayward son who simply could not see the man he had become. For years she had remained by his side in this toxic environment, and she would remain for a further twenty-five years until he remembered who he was.

Her head turned at the sound of the tentative movement of the man outside, who had been rooted in place, like an ancient tree. The slow release from the grip of fear encouraged his feet to move, taking him on past the rondavel and towards his homestead, where sleeping forms were slowly stirring.

3: A series of disappointments
Three months prior

The old man watched as the woman came marching furiously up the path towards him. He could hear her laboured breathing and muttered curses as she navigated the steep climb. He always wondered why the isangoma had chosen such an out of the way location. For that must be who she was visiting, there being no other reason for the direction she was heading. He chuckled as she came closer. Her mouth turned down at each corner as if an invisible line of string connected them to the movement of her feet.

Zodwa Shezi didn't stop when she greeted the old man sitting alongside the path, his cattle scattered across the hill behind him. She was in a rush and her mind was consumed with her reason for seeking out the expensive services of Mthunzi Mnguni. It had been a long time since she had walked this route. Back then it had been a different mission altogether. No doubt planned by her aunt, she thought acidly. Oh, they had pretended it was out of concern, out of love. Love, she snorted. Zodwa had learnt from a young age that love didn't really exist. It might for some, she conceded, but not for her.

She felt that her life had been one of great hardship and abuse, a life so unfair, that in the constant revisiting of it, it was a wonder she was able to move forward at all. Zodwa had been born into a small village, a collection of rondavel huts in a sea of grass, where the earth met the sky on a lonely hilltop. In winter, the mornings were cold and misty until the sun gained strength with each passing hour. She had run wild as a child, content with the freedom she'd been given to traverse the hills and the valleys, until she'd noticed that the other girls did not. Because the other girls had mothers. Mothers who had called them home when the sun dipped behind the hills. Mothers who had laughed and smiled at their silly ways. She didn't have a mother like that, but she did have her *Gogo*, her mother's mother. And she smiled briefly at the thought.

When Zodwa was four, her mother had packed a bag and walked down the mountain, never to return. Gogo and Zodwa watched her disappear, then Gogo took Zodwa's hand, and together they walked back into their hut. With Mama gone, the arguments stopped, Gogo took control, and life began to change. Gogo made her attend school, a one-roomed classroom with broken windows and a brick for a chair, some kilometres away. And it was in that small room, at the age of eight, that she learnt her Gogo, her only friend in the world, had died. Gogo had been bitten by a black mamba searching for rats in the dark corners of the storeroom. By the time the neighbours reached the local clinic, Gogo was dead.

No-one in the village could afford to take on another mouth to feed. Her mother could not be found; she'd lied when she told Gogo she'd be living with a relative in Durban. So, Zodwa had been sent to live with her mother's brother on the other side of the reserve, with his wife and their small child. It had all gone wrong the moment she'd arrived. Her uncle, carrying two plastic bags with all her belongings, had opened the kitchen door to a sick, screaming toddler and an exhausted wife. Zodwa's aunt had taken one look at her and then walked into the bedroom, closing the door softly behind her. From that moment on, Zodwa created a barrier around herself, like the thorny acacia branches protecting the cattle in their neighbour's kraal. She promised herself that she would never let anyone disappoint her again. She had failed, of course. Zodwa's life had been a series of disappointments, which was why she'd come in search of Mthunzi Mnguni.

By the time she had reached Mthunzi's home, she was furious. She wanted to undo the years of bad luck that seemed to follow her like a great, skulking marabou stork, her personal omen of doom. Who better to choose than the very isangoma who had once held such an important position in the life of her uncle?

Before she could call out a greeting, a booming voice bade her, '*Ngena*. Come in.'

She bent to enter the low doorway, a curtain of cowrie shells clicking against each other as they parted to admit her. Zodwa fell to her knees before the mat in respect and was transported back in time to a somewhat different interior. Back then, she had entered the *isigodlo*, a room where the isangoma practised the art of healing. It had been dark in a comforting way, the scent of herbs soaked into the walls and the floor. Pinpricks of light fell across the pale reed mat on the floor and the kind face of a younger Mthunzi had greeted her. Now, though the room was still dark, it smelt rancid; the copper tang of dried blood coated her throat as she chose to breathe through her nose. She cast her eyes around in the gloom, and as she lifted them to survey the ceiling, she came face-to-face with the frozen sneer of a leopard, hanging from the beams.

Leaping to her feet, she wailed in fright, kicking over a bucket of pangolin scales. While most of the scales came to rest between the buckets and boxes that lined the wall, one skidded across the floor towards the open door as if attempting to escape. The isangoma's mouth twitched, and then he released a great bellow of laughter as he took in the face of the terrified woman. Zodwa looked up at the unmoving moth-eaten leopard skin. A few teeth were missing, no doubt knocked out by young men much braver than she. She glared at Mthunzi, whose face ran with tears as he struggled to control himself.

'Hee-hee-hee,' he wheezed, wiping his face with a threadbare facecloth. 'That was very mischievous of me. Don't be afraid *ndodakazi*. Old *ingwe* cannot hurt you now.'

Zodwa was not amused. This visit was costing her dearly; she'd spent many months stealing small amounts from her boyfriend, and now this supposedly great man was playing games like a child. When he finally gathered himself, she had returned to her position on her knees, eyes averted as was customary. She had stolen a look at him while his entire body shook with laughter; he had aged in the passing years, but he was not an old man. A few grey hairs and a softer body, but he did not appear as terrifying as his reputation, although perhaps this was not a good time to judge.

'What brings you to request my help, ndodakazi?' he asked, his demeanour once again professional.

'*Makhosi*,' she addressed him respectfully, clapping her hands. 'It was many years ago now that we last saw each other, but I am sure that you will remember me ...'

A look of surprise crossed the isangoma's face. Zodwa frowned. Surely, he had not forgotten her. Of course, she had changed. She was much older and wider; back then she'd been a reed of a girl in clothing, while not fancy, had at least matched. Now, she wore whatever second-hand pieces she could find at the pension day markets. She looked down at her skirt and top, a clash of colours and patterns, which did her heavyset frame no favours.

Zodwa felt herself grow annoyed, embarrassed even. Surely the ancestors would have told him of her arrival. She was certain that Mthunzi would have known she was coming. Isn't that how these things worked? Unable to control her annoyance, she glared at the isangoma disrespectfully. 'It has been a long time; I was a girl. I am Zodwa Shezi, the relative of —'.

'Yoh! ' Mthunzi's face lit up with delight. He swivelled his head slowly from side to side, recognition dawning. Zodwa followed his gaze as his eyes left her face to stare intently at a spot off to the left of her. He nodded and focused his attention on her again.

Zodwa's face softened. This was better. He did remember her. Perhaps he would give her a discount, since she was, in fact, a repeat customer. She remembered that he had not been able to help them back then, so technically, he owed her.

'Well, well, well,' Mthunzi said, genuine interest transforming his face. 'How is my old friend doing these days?'

Zodwa scowled. 'Haah, Makhosi. I don't see them much. I moved out a long time ago.'

'Ah.' Disappointment replaced delight, and the isangoma's body slumped slightly. 'That is unfortunate,' he said, fiddling with the cloth bag that held his bones. 'I have not seen him myself now for many, many years.'

'Oh no, Makhosi,' Zodwa hurried to clarify. 'It is a good thing. I was not happy.'

The isangoma looked at her, questioningly. 'You were not happy? But he took you in when no one else would.'

Zodwa lowered her head and stared at her hands. She took in a few deep breaths to calm the rage that made it hard to breathe. The smell of dried blood and herbs was overpowering, and she longed to move outside into the light and air.

Her voice rose, close to hysteria. 'That does not mean they loved me, Makhosi. Or treated me well. And it is all her fault!'

'Her?' he said, his fingers no longer plucking at the fabric. 'I thought you were talking about your uncle?'

'No,' Zodwa cried, shaking her fists in exasperation. '*You* were talking about my uncle. *I* am talking about his wife!'

As Mthunzi sat back on his haunches, Zodwa leant towards him, her body hung suspended over the mat. 'Makhosi,' she whispered. 'My aunt ... she has bewitched me!'

'Haah,' he exhaled in disbelief. 'That is a big accusation to make. Do you have evidence to prove it?'

'Evidence?' she wailed. 'My whole life is the evidence! One person cannot have suffered so much unless *someone* had bewitched them!'

Mthunzi was not sympathetic. 'Sometimes, child, the state of our lives is not the fault of others, but rather our own.' He continued to frown at her. 'But come, tell me more before I throw the bones.'

'Zodwa never failed to seize an opportunity to complain about her miserable upbringing and launched into a monologue that lasted quite some time. She was so engrossed in her tale of woe, that she only realised that Mthunzi had gone somewhere inside his head when a silence stretched out between them. Her knees began to burn in protest and the heat in the room became unbearable.

Just as she thought she should remind him that she was sitting there, he sighed deeply, rattled the bag, called out and threw the bones onto the mat. He watched them fall, his eyebrows rising in anticipation, at what the bones might reveal.

He made a series of sounds, his tongue flicking off his teeth. Then he shook his head slowly in disbelief.

'Yoh! My child. It seems you are right.' He rested his sad eyes upon her. 'Your aunt has indeed bewitched you, but it appears that she does not work alone.' He looked closely at the bones, his eyes tracking where and how they had fallen. Suddenly, he reared back in shock. 'No! It cannot be!'

Zodwa leant forward, eyes skimming over the small items, seeking out the offending object. 'What, Makhosi? What do you see?'

'Oh, my child! It is not good. But I am sorry to say that I am not surprised.' He shook his head sorrowfully; the beads in his hair tapping together. 'Child, it is not your aunt … it is your uncle!'

Zodwa deflated as her arms gave way, and she sat back onto her knees. 'Baba,' she whispered, for he was the only father she had ever known. She could not believe it. Zodwa suddenly found it difficult to breathe, and her dismay quickly turned to anger. No more! No more would this family betray her. It was time for revenge. Time to take back her life and ensure that she would never suffer at their hands again.

'Yes,' said the isangoma, wiping a trickle of sweat from his forehead. 'The bones tell me that your uncle is not who he seems. He has a darkness about him, which he hides behind a curtain of light. But,' he added softly, 'we knew that already, didn't we?'

'What about my aunt?' Zodwa demanded, refusing to be distracted from the focus of her quest. 'What do the bones say about her?'

The isangoma pointed to a long, flexible goat's tendon. 'This one here, tells me that he uses her, twists and bends her to his will.' He picked it up and wound it around one large finger. 'The curse was your uncle's idea; your aunt simply does his bidding,' he said, before placing it gently back on the mat.

She felt his words like a physical presence. Hot and penetrating, they pierced through the layers of protection she'd wrapped herself in, over the years. They settled like thorns; an uncomfortable presence that needed to be removed.

Her pre-occupation was broken by the sound of the bones as he swept them into their bag. 'The curse is strong,' he said. 'We have much work to do in undoing it.'

'Yes, Makhosi,' she agreed fervently; her heart and mind open and ready to receive the directives that Mthunzi had to offer.

Zodwa was as ready as she'd ever be to see her aunt and uncle suffer from the effects of whatever terrifying curse Mthunzi had the power to concoct. She would do whatever he asked, but she closed her eyes and prayed that she would not be the one to bring him a human part. A neighbour in her village had suffered terrible luck for years. She'd been to every isangoma she could find to determine the source of the bad luck. Until finally, after losing four children in the womb, and then her husband to a heart attack, she found an isangoma who was able to help her. He came to her home and had dug up an assortment of strange and random objects; the most terrifying of which was what appeared to be the body part of a small child. Zodwa did not think she had the stomach for that.

***

Mthunzi began to sing, calling out to his ancestors. His body shook, and his arms flew into the air as if completely out of his control. The smallest ancestor, Zenzile, coughed from across the room, giving him a small frown. Mthunzi toned down his theatrics and slowly came back into the present. He lifted his gaze to meet Zodwa's eyes, but he saw that they were closed. He watched her. Discontent settled on her face until its planes became as unreadable as the granite rocks that hung over the river course below his house.

He knew now that the time had finally come, and it had come in the form of a hateful, spiteful woman, who would carry out his plan under the misguided notion that she was getting her revenge for a bewitchment that didn't even exist. The ancestors had foretold her coming in the form of an earring, but not the specifics of its unfolding. Never would he have imagined that it would involve the woman seated in front of him. The relative of his greatest enemy seeking retribution for a miserable life caused largely by her actions. Mthunzi smiled. She was perfect.

He waited for some time, allowing Zodwa to marinate in the lie. He wanted her to soak in it, until it became a living, breathing beast that rode upon her back, dictating her every move. Mthunzi lifted his nose to the air around him, like a hunting dog searching out the scent of a bushbuck. When a person was so filled with anxiety, fear, or hatred, Mthunzi could smell it. Over the years, he had become particularly attuned to the change in body odour of his clients, and at this moment, the odour steaming off Zodwa let him know that something had shifted within her, and she was ready.

He cleared his throat to get her attention. 'Child, the amadlozi have spoken. I will contact you when the time is right, and we are ready to move forward. Be patient, and prepare yourself, it will require great strength. And you have the money, of course? It will not be cheap, but it will be worth it, that, I promise.'

The woman rose from her kneeling position. She moved slowly, like someone in a dream state. Mthunzi wrote her number down in a notebook containing the many ways he'd planned, over the years, to pay back his once closest friend.

He watched her begin her descent down the mountain path. Secure that she believed that the plan, which had wrapped itself around her heart and mind, was for her alone. Created by the ancestors, and facilitated by Mthunzi, in response to her great need. He was sure that by the time she left, a small spark had lit the kindling, which had lain brittle in her chest for all these years.

4: Cheeup-chup-toops, chizza-chizza
26th November 2012

As the night crept back into the crevices and burrows it had emerged from ten hours before, the emerald-spotted wood dove began its lonesome call from the flame tree outside Nonhle's window. She stretched and turned, the light sheet that had covered her during the night, falling to the floor. Summer nights in Zululand were humid, and the walls of their small house seemed to absorb the heat during the day and release it internally throughout the long night. The old rusted fan in the corner of her room turned lazily, blowing hot air in her direction.

Today was Nonhle's first day back at work at The Last Outpost Lodge. She was looking forward to seeing familiar faces and catching up on their news. Over the next two months, until a new academic year began, she would assist at reception, fielding calls and dealing with guests. She had been strategic in landing herself that position. Her very first position at the lodge had been as a cleaner. It had been an experience she hoped never to repeat. A whole year at university and they'd tasked her with making beds and cleaning toilets. She had been amazed at just how disgusting people could be when they knew that someone else was going to clean up after them. After one particularly traumatic toilet incident, she'd vowed to make herself indispensable in ways that would ensure she moved up the ladder as quickly as possible.

Nonhle lay staring blankly at the ceiling as she relived yesterday's encounter with the man in the Land Cruiser. She walked herself through the short timeline of their conversation and tried to pinpoint exactly how she could have annoyed him. She was surprised by how upset she was. The moment he'd stopped to offer her a lift and she'd caught a glimpse of his face, she'd felt hopeful, a sudden sense of possibility overcame her. She huffed scornfully at her silliness. Hopeful for what? Hopeful that she might meet someone worthwhile over the summer holidays? Hopeful that a man as tall and good looking as him might be interested in someone like her? *'Pathetic!'* she rebuked herself. *'You don't even know his name.'*

She heard movement in the kitchen. By now Baba would have been up for an hour at least, readying himself for the day ahead; a habit ingrained so deeply that she was sure that when he retired, it would continue, regardless. It was a quality she envied in her father. When her alarm sounded, she mostly felt cheated by a night that had gone too quickly. She was a night-owl, preferring the cocoon-like shelter that the night provided as she sat reading a book, or working on a class assignment. She found the sudden brightness of morning, and the happy chatter of birds, a little too enthusiastic so early in the day. Samson would say that she wasn't rising early enough. An hour earlier, before the sun had risen, the morning light would wash over her in soft waves, readying her for the intense light of a Zululand day. Nonhle stretched one last time, then boosted herself up in one athletic move, knowing that half the battle was won as soon as her feet hit the floor.

She stepped out of her room and went straight into the kitchen; her weave still wrapped up in its scarlet headscarf.

'Morning Mama, Baba,' she said, laying a hand on each one's shoulder as she moved over to the kettle. Her parents were seated at a simple pine table, steaming bowls of maize porridge doused in brown sugar and milk, in front of them.

'There's more on the stove, my child,' said Mama, tapping her spoon against her bowl, then indicated that a pot of tea was already on the table.

Baba had to be at the lodge at 5.30 a.m., to ready the vehicle for the first game drive of the day. Unlike many of the game rangers, mostly in their early to late-twenties, Baba did not have the luxury of rolling out of bed and into his vehicle. The youngsters stayed together in shared accommodation on the lodge's property and were a short walk away from their vehicles.

The Ngubanes had been living in this small house for nea
five years, when The Last Outpost had five rooms, and
vehicle. Baba and Mama had been as much part of its histo
owner, William McKenzie. It had taken many years before t
had reached its capacity of 120 guests, who would fly in from countries
like America and France. Back then, all the black staff members had
lived in the compound, away from the lodge, and were ferried in each
morning and out each evening. After apartheid fell and the lodge
expanded, additional staff quarters for all had been added to the lodge,
but her parents had chosen to remain where they were. It was quieter
here, far from the youngsters and the loud music. Nonhle didn't mind
the quiet. She had been away at school for most of her teenage years,
and by the end of each term, she had longed for the solitude of her own
room.

Baba greeted her with a big grin, then stood up from the table.
'Morning, *ngane yami*. I see we have not yet learnt to embrace the
beauty of the dawn?'

Nonhle yawned in response, lifting the mug of tea her mother had
poured, to her lips. She thought with longing about a strong cappuccino
from the campus café, topped with thick cream. She missed home
when she was away, but she also missed the small luxuries that she
could access easily while living in Durban.

Baba, who had opened the kitchen door, turned back to look at her.
'Come outside with me before I leave, Nonhle.'

Nonhle followed him, taking her mug with her. He stood on the last
step before the path began. His eyes were closed, face lifted towards the
sky. She took a sip of tea, and while she waited, she studied his face. His
dark hair was greying at the temples and the sun had etched another line
on his forehead. He was a good-looking man and in excellent shape.
Despite the long years of work, worry about money, drought, and his
'too clever' daughter, he had the appearance of a man happy with his
lot in life. As her eyes travelled the lines of his face, he breathed deeply,
opened one eye to stare at her, and told her to close both of hers.

'Really, Baba?' she said, the roll of her eyes softened by the smile on
her lips.

She loved that she could count on her father to bring certainty to
her life. Right from when she was able to give meaning to the words

she sounded out, Baba had included her in his favourite game. At first, it was a game between Mama and himself, but when Nonhle finally understood what was being asked of her, Mama had quietly slipped away, giving Nonhle and Baba something special to bond over. She was twenty-three now, and Baba still made time for them to play it, whenever she returned.

Nonhle stood with her hands clasping her mug and turned her face towards the canopy of the flame tree that stretched over their house. She closed her eyes and relied only on her ears to tell her the story of the life going on within the tree. She heard the flutter of wings, and the rustle of leaves, as birds flitted between the branches. She separated out the *zik-ziks* from the *dee-dee-deedeicks*, the *cheeup-chup-toops* from the *chizza-chizzas*. Each sound as clear to her as the voices of family and friends. The birds shouted over each other, just like her group of friends did at university, each vying to outdo each other with their tales and jokes. From somewhere behind the tree, out in the veld, she picked out the cascade of *doo-doo-doos* of a Burchell's Coucal. She pictured it calling out, giving a final shake of its body as the last *doo* left its throat. When she was younger, she would often get confused between the coucal and the dove. Then Baba told her to think of the dove as the sad lover who had lost his only love to the gleeful chuckle of the coucal. She could completely imagine the rakish looking coucal as a smug thief of hearts and could picture the despondent wood dove, sitting on his branch, lamenting the loss of his one true love. She called out the names of the birds she could identify, and Baba *mmh-ed* in agreement at each one.

Just before she opened her eyes, a different sound caught her ear. 'That's one I haven't heard in a long time, Baba,' she said, her ears straining to identify the chipping and chirping that sounded from the tree.

He gave her a little time before asking, 'What do you think?'

She hazarded a guess. 'A Little Bee-eater?' She opened her eyes to scan the branches of the tree, finally locating the tiny colourful bird, high in the branches. 'Yes!' she gloated. 'You can take the girl out of the bush, but not the bush out of the girl!' She was amused at the look on her father's face. He thought he had her with that one. Nonhle laughed. 'I'll let you in on a little secret, Baba. I downloaded an app onto my phone that lets me look up birds. It's like a bird-library. You can see its picture, listen to its call, and read a description. You should get one,' she encouraged him. 'It would make life easier with all those know-it-all guests!'

Samson stared at his daughter. 'What's an app?' he asked, incomprehension clouding his features.

***

Nonhle arrived at The Last Outpost in one of the khaki-green game vehicles that traversed the reserve daily. She'd caught a ride with Mama, and the rest of the staff from the compound, who were on day duty. She loved driving up in the big game vehicle. There was a sense of freedom that came with riding in a truck, its sides open from midway up, so that they had an unhindered view of the passing veld. But the wind played havoc with her hair, and she could feel the dust coating her skin, so she was glad when the vehicle skidded to a halt, in the parking lot.

She nimbly descended the steel ladder on the side of the vehicle, and after helping Mama down, she turned to assist a bulky woman who was tentatively trying to descend. The stairs, which had to be climbed facing the vehicle, whether getting in or out, could be disastrous. She'd once witnessed an elderly British guest miss the last step, tumble backwards, and come to rest at the base of an acacia tree a few metres away. There had been a minor panic at the prospect of the guest suing the lodge, but she had taken it in her stride, remarking that no holiday was complete without some minor adjustment to one's physical condition. That week, Mr McKenzie built a concrete loading island for easy access onto the vehicles, but currently, game vehicles were parked on either side of it.

For Nonhle, the lodge was an oasis in a sun-sucked land. Much of her childhood had been spent between the compound and the local school that she attended. The compound was a study in natural hues – the red ochre of the soil, the rows of light brown homes, all surrounded by tall ivory coloured grass. The flame tree outside her bedroom window, a dark leafy green in summer with vibrant orange flowers, the only nod to colourful flamboyance. Her school had been painted brown and cream, split horizontally as if it could be zipped open and the children inside revealed – rows of light brown to ebony-skinned children in yellow and black tunics – seated at pine desks. Every time she entered the lodge, she saw it through the eyes of the guests, and felt a sense of excitement for them. From the time they drove through the gates in the airport-to-lodge shuttle, they were welcomed by sentries of mountain aloe on the journey up to reception. The aloes, tall dry-leafed bodies topped with spears of red-hot flowers, signalled the way like daytime torchbearers.

When the guests descended from the shuttle, stretching tired backs and legs, their first view of the lodge would conjure up every romantic notion they'd ever had about holidaying in mysterious, and potentially dangerous, Africa. Thatching of pale gold topped the reception's roof, spreading out backwards like a canopy over the various buildings and rooms that lay beyond the entrance. On either side of the large wooden doors, thrown wide in welcome, water fountains – home to large, bulbous bull-frogs – serenaded the guests. Inside, the peculiar oily aroma of tamboti wood scented the air, every piece of furniture carved from the indigenous tree. Large dark grey granite tiles offered up cool respite from the heat of the day. Nonhle loved entering those front doors.

'*Sanibonani!*' she greeted the staff behind the front desk, clapping her hands in glee.

'Nonhle!' cried Sizah, her face breaking out into a great toothy grin. 'Sisi, we have missed you,' she said, rushing around the counter to hug Nonhle. She let Nonhle go and took on a defiant stance. 'Please, girl! You *must* be done in Durban? We need you *here!*'

'Did you just stamp your foot, Sizah?' Nonhle laughed, and Sizah giggled as she pulled her friend close for another hug. A series of pointed coughs from a guest at the front desk broke the moment. 'Anyway,' Nonhle whispered in her friend's ear before letting her go, 'I don't think my long-term plans include dealing with impatient guests.'

Nonhle took herself off to the staff room to drop her bag and make herself a cup of coffee before the day began. She helped herself to a couple of biscuits and ran her eyes over the work schedule for the coming weeks. Several weddings would be taking place in the run-up to Christmas.

Must be foreigners, she thought. *Who in their right mind would choose to get married in forty-degree heat?*

The lodge would host a New Year's Eve party, which involved a huge amount of work. Every year they did their best to outdo the previous year's efforts. The door opened and Sizah darted in. Her friend, a few years older, had a head full of short braids, that she'd swirled around her scalp. Sizah was excellent at her job; she had the unusual ability of telling someone off firmly, without devastating the recipient.

'Come on,' Sizah said, 'before I start to boss you around. I'll make a quick cup of tea, and you can fill me in on your love life.' Sizah reached into the cupboard for a mug and teabags, and once the kettle was boiling, she gave her friend her full attention. 'So,' she pressed. 'Anything you want to tell me?' She waggled her eyebrows suggestively.

'You ask me that every year, and you're always disappointed,' Nonhle laughed.

'Haah, Nonhle! Come on,' she said, lifting her hands to rest on her hips in mock irritation. 'Not even one?' She clicked her tongue, 'You're boring, man.' She poured hot water into her cup and stirred the teabag for precisely three seconds, then fished it out.

'Actually,' said Nonhle, scrutinising her fingernails. 'I did meet someone yesterday.'

Sizah whipped around, raising her teaspoon like a conductor's baton. 'Yesterday? When? On the taxi?'

'No,' laughed Nonhle at Sizah's enthusiasm. 'On the road. He saw me walking and gave me a lift home.'

'And?' Sizah made encouraging swirls mid-air with the teaspoon.

'I didn't get his name. Tall guy with perfect teeth. He works for Umkhombe Anti-Poaching Unit.'

'*Hehe!*' Sizah crowed as she took in Nonhle's expression. 'Join the club. Every woman from here to Pongola has eyes for *u*Senzo Mdletshe.'

'Oh,' said Nonhle, attempting to look disinterested. 'I thought he was really rude, actually.'

Sizah laughed. 'Exactly. And that's why he's so fascinating. Nothing like a mean man to keep us girls interested.'

Taking one look at the wistful expression on her friend's face, she said, 'Listen, dear. Don't waste your time. No one, and I mean, no one,' she gave Nonhle a knowing look, 'has had any luck in that department.'

5: Just pretend you're doing research
26th November 2012

Nonhle's feet ached and she felt strangely empty. She had forgotten how physically and mentally tiring dealing with guests could be, both those arriving and leaving. She had drawn the short straw when it came to the reconciliation of the bill of a departing American couple. The staff, and numerous guests, could not wait to see the back of them. The man, who had spent every possible opportunity informing people of how well off he was, had haggled over the final invoice as if his livelihood depended on it. Sizah had eventually intervened, giving Nonhle a chance to escape to the kitchen, to calm her frayed nerves.

By the time she'd packed her things together and headed out to the parking lot, Nonhle realised that she'd missed the staff transport. She stood there for a moment, listening to the wind shuffle through the lala palms. As she turned back towards reception in search of a lift, the tall figure of Thomas McKenzie, the lodge owner's son, strode down the path towards her.

'Nonhle,' he said, his face lighting up at the sight of her. 'When did you get back?'

Nonhle felt herself blush. Ever since she began working at the lodge, one December a few years ago, she'd had a crush on him. Though she often longed for home and her parents, he was one of the reasons she happily returned each year, putting up with the awkward hours and demanding guests. She recalled the first time she had officially met Thomas. It was her first day of work, and she was in a khaki pinafore with a doek on her head, a mop in hand and a bucket at her feet.

Samson, facing her, had his hands on her shoulders and was giving one of his speeches about integrity, honesty, and hard work. Samson eyed Thomas walking through the aloe garden and waved him over.

'Thomas,' her father had called, his face beaming with pride, 'this is my daughter, Nonhle. She's studying in Durban to be an anth …'

'Anthropologist,' Nonhle offered as Baba stumbled over the word. Her face had been hot with shame at meeting the boss's son in such a humiliating outfit.

'This is her holiday job,' Baba stated, with a wink at Thomas.

Thomas had laughed at her expression. 'An anthropologist, hey. Just pretend you're doing research … exploring the fascinating lives of domestic workers.' He'd given her a quick once-over. 'All you're missing is a notebook.' She'd tapped a pocket and he'd burst out laughing. 'Then you'll be fine,' he said, giving Samson a clap on the back, before heading to reception.

Over the intervening years, he'd always taken the time to ask her how her degree was progressing. She'd felt singled out, special. But now as he asked her again, she acknowledged that's all they'd ever really talked about. Nothing personal. Just work and studies. Which was fine. She would be starting her master's programme next year and she was thinking about conducting her research at the lodge. She was certain of her topic but hadn't finalised anything yet.

'Are you leaving?' she said hopefully, pointing at the keys in his hand.

He nodded. 'Jump in. I'll give you a lift down.'

They thundered down the dirt road, the vehicle making such a racket that they were unable to talk. Instead, she focused on keeping each breast squashed under a hand to stop them from jiggling out of her bra. Halfway to the main gate, the radio crackled into life. Thomas slowed down to listen, then snatched the radio off the hook, to respond.

'Change of plan,' he said, his usually sunny disposition, now grim. 'This won't take long.'

Nonhle grabbed the door handle to keep from toppling over as Thomas swung the old Landy onto a road with deep tracks. The dry grass between the wheel tracks brushed the underside of the vehicle like a dry cough. The turning wheels crushed grass and plants beneath them, releasing the reassuringly familiar scent of the earth. Though she could see no markers, Thomas, like her father, had the ability of reading every tree, bush, stone, and indentation in the earth as a route marker. He quickly made his way towards the spot where two security guards and the veld manager were waiting. There was little in this section of the reserve that was manmade, only the fence that ran around the perimeter. The vegetation held the rights to the land; its mange-like appearance created by the drought, and hungry grazers, revealed the deep red of the soil. The fence had been breached recently and the walking security team had located a significant number of snares planted by people poaching for the pot. The area was mostly untraversed by the rangers, as a small community who lived nearby, were visible from the fence line. Foreign guests on safari didn't like to see impoverished communities living so close to luxury. They wanted a wild and untamed landscape that extended as far as the eye could see.

Thomas jumped out of the vehicle and strode over to the waiting men. 'How many?' he said, by way of introduction.

'Eleven,' replied the veld manager, turning to show Thomas a pile of coiled wire. A few were shiny and new, but most were rusted and well used. 'They must have been laid recently. We only found that poor bugger,' he said, pointing to the motionless body of a banded mongoose.

Thomas stared at the pile of snares with disgust. He addressed the two security guards, harshly, in isiZulu. 'What happened to the community liaison officer? I thought we'd come to an agreement about poaching. If they stop, we'll provide them with game meat every quarter.'

'Ah, boss,' said Phineas, a small man whose uniform seemed to overwhelm him. 'That man, he no longer lives in that village. He found a job in *eGoli.*'

Thomas's eyes swivelled between the two guards. 'What! When? Why am I only hearing about this now?' He gave them a hard, calculating glare. Phineas merely shrugged, looking down at his boots. The second guard looked away; his expression completely devoid of emotion.

From the vehicle, Nonhle watched Thomas turn his back on the two men. She could see that he was furious, his body blocking them from further conversation as he addressed the veld manager.

'We need to get back into the community. Identify a new person to act as our liaison officer. Waste of bloody time, apparently, but let's move on it quickly. December 15th is around the corner. Guys are going to go *bossies* out here getting ready for Christmas and New Year celebrations.'

Nonhle noticed the confidence and the authority that Thomas and the veld manager naturally exuded, while the two security guards were an interesting mix of inferiority and indifference. Their indifference, and the fact that they had access to information, which the other two men did not, inadvertently cast them in a position of power. It was clear that Thomas and the veld manager were completely unaware of this.

Nonhle felt her heart quicken. While she'd settled on a topic for her masters, it hadn't filled her with excitement. She'd chosen it because she'd witnessed it time and again while working at the lodge: cultural transference as a two-way process in the tourism industry. Guests thought they were coming to South Africa to experience the culture, not to impart it. But they did, and Nonhle was interested in documenting its effect on people who worked at the lodge. However, she was still struggling to figure out its relevance in the grand scheme of applied anthropology. But now, watching the interaction between the men, her mind began to race. Perhaps her topic could focus on cultural and local knowledge shared, or in this case, unshared between lodges and communities. The passionate voice of her anthropology lecturer came back to her clearly: *research is meaningless if it never leaves the shelf.* She knew for certain that this research could be applied – if certain people were willing to listen.

Once Thomas had given final instructions to the veld manager, he climbed back into the Landy. Nonhle was eager to share her revelation with him, but he didn't even look at her. He drove off in silence, his thoughts obviously on what needed to take place next, to curb the poaching.

Thomas navigated the Landy onto a well-worn road, the change of texture under the wheels a welcome relief. With the drought, the animals were scarce, choosing to remain in areas where sustenance was available. Although the reserve was not as badly off as others, the remaining grass was dry and brittle. On the odd occasion that rain fell, small green shoots disappeared as quickly as they'd emerged, hoovered up by herds of impala. They drove alongside a large water hole and

Nonhle couldn't help but exclaim in excitement. Two large white rhino and a group of warthogs jockeyed for position at the feeding lot. Thomas brought the vehicle to a stop next to the water's edge. A buffet of grass and salt licks had been laid out as no rain had been predicted for the foreseeable future. One of the rhino kept four warthogs at bay by lowering its giant head, giving it a good shake in their direction. The warthogs danced and darted between the two, grabbing mouthfuls where they could.

Thomas gestured for Nonhle to get out. She gave him a pained look, then remembered, with relief, her skirt and heels.

'Okay,' he said, with a grin as she pointed apologetically at her shoes, 'well, at least open the door!'

As she hesitantly pushed it open, one of the rhino lunged at a warthog, and it back-pedalled with an indignant squeal. The door was pulled swiftly shut and Thomas laughed at her panicked expression.

'I thought you were the daughter of Samson Ngubane, best game ranger this reserve has ever had.'

Nonhle shot him a look, but the door remained closed.

'Relax,' he said. 'We're completely fine, I promise. They're only interested in feeding themselves. And, I have it on good authority, that the elephants are sucking the reservoir dry on the other side of the reserve.'

'Thomas,' she said, encouraged by his change in mood. 'I need your advice. Next year is my master's year. I had a really clear idea of what I wanted to research, but after what happened back there, I think I've changed my mind.'

He leant forward and rested his arms on the frame of the open window. The wind caught a curl of his hair, making her think of a long-crested eagle.

'Back there?' he asked. 'You mean with the poaching problem?'

'Yes!' she said, her voice high with enthusiasm. 'It hit me that something really important might be missing in terms of cross-cultural understanding between lodges and communities, and how —'

'Of course!' Thomas interrupted, smacking a fist against the metal frame of the door. 'You could find out why communities just can't seem to appreciate that some cultural practices, like poaching for the pot, have to stop, for the greater good!'

Nonhle's face fell. 'Um … that's not where I was going, at all. I was thinking —'

'But why not?' he exclaimed. 'It's perfect! Anthropology's about cultural practices, right? So, if we focus on eliminating negative cultural practices, we might actually win this war.'

'Well,' she said, slowly. 'I guess that's probably part of the problem. Maybe if they felt included in what was going on around them, on land that used to be theirs, they might be more likely to buy into this concept of the *greater good*. I mean, what does that even mean? The 'greater good'?' she said, annoyed now at this man and his arrogance as if he knew best.

Thomas immediately became defensive. 'You know,' he said, folding his arms across his chest, 'we actually do great stuff for the community. We built a local crèche, which means more children are getting some form of early childhood development. And we've done some other projects that management thought the community would love.'

He frowned. 'Not that they were very successful. Within a month of our guys handing it over to the community, they abandoned it, which was really disappointing; it wasn't a cheap exercise. Makes you not want to help out at all, to be honest. I mean look at the situation back there. We should just arrest every poacher, at the very least destroy their hunting dogs, but instead, we offer them game meat every quarter. That's more than most!'

Nonhle felt her breathing grow shallow. *What a self-righteous moron. Who was this man?* She looked out across the dry water hole. The rhino had moved off and the warthog were happily inhaling fodder as quickly as possible.

Once she'd composed herself, she gave him a frank stare. 'Out of interest, did you ever ask the community what they wanted? Was it a discussion?'

Thomas laughed. 'Come on, Nonhle. If we were to ask the community what they wanted, we'd been providing everything under the sun! There is a serious sense of entitlement out there.'

'Or,' she said, her face rigid with anger, 'you'd be providing them with what they actually need. Who are you to tell a community what's best for them?'

'What I mean,' said Thomas, surprise at her tone registering on his face, 'is that surely we know better.' His eyes scrunched closed as the words tripped off his tongue. 'I didn't mean it like that! It's just that we have access to knowledge and information that they don't! I can just go online and see what's worked in other communities, other countries! Surely that makes sense to you?'

Nonhle realised that at one point in her life, she might have agreed. It made perfect sense; why wouldn't you assume that those with more education and experience than you, would know better and would have the answers. But the last four years she'd spent studying had changed that perception.

'Thomas,' she said, in irritation. 'You have no idea how people live, the problems they face, what they hope for, what they want for their children. You think because you drive past these communities, sometimes go into them, that makes you an expert on life inside them? That what you think is the need, is actually the need?'

Before Thomas could respond, a colony of hadeda ibis swooped in, creating a terrible din overhead as they came into roost for the night. The distraction gave Nonhle a chance to gather her thoughts.

'Do you ever think about how people on the outside of the reserve feel about being on the outside? People once had access to all of this land, and now they don't.'

She saw he was cross now. His cheeks were ruddy, and he'd stuffed his hands into his pockets. 'Oh, come on, Nonhle! That was decades ago. We've had this reserve for coming on thirty years now. There was nothing on this land before that. It wasn't being farmed, even for subsistence crops. Surely people can learn to move on. I mean, if people can adopt various aspects of Western culture that are convenient for them, why not this? It's not just about poaching for the pot. That's just the starting point for poaching bigger animals.'

'I agree,' she countered, 'but how much do people in these communities benefit from the reserves? There are jobs, yes, but only basic ones for people with poor education. Poaching for the pot provides them with meat they'd have to buy with money they don't have.

'And,' she said, giving him an accusatory glare, 'wild animals that breach the fence kill cattle. So, not only are people unable to hunt for meat, but their livestock is destroyed?'

Thomas looked at her scornfully. 'I can just imagine the textbook you got that out of. You're only looking at it from one point of view. Without these conservation areas, there would be no wildlife left in South Africa. Within a few years, all this,' he gestured expansively towards the animals, the cluster of fever trees – their yellow bark glowing in the late afternoon light – 'would be gone. There would be no wildlife, no trees, the tourists wouldn't come, and the economy in these backyard places would disappear. Communities would suffer far worse than they are now.'

Nonhle looked out over the veld, annoyed at the conflicting thoughts, which seemed to swing her from one direction to the other. She would hate to live in a world without wild spaces. While she too had grown up on the outside of a reserve, living vicariously through the tales of her parents, she now had an opportunity to step inside and she didn't want to waste that. She knew that there were examples of successful relationships being built between communities and lodges, and there was no reason it couldn't work here too, at The Last Outpost Lodge.

'Can I make a suggestion,' she offered, knowing that peace between them was essential. 'If you want people to respect something, you need to make them feel like they have a reason to. I've lived next to this reserve my whole life. My father works in it! And the first time I saw an elephant, out in the open, without a fence in front of it, was when I started working here. I was nineteen! Thomas,' she turned to him, her voice sharp with pain. 'Do you even understand how wrong that is?'

6: Loss of identity
26th November 2012

The drive to Nonhle's home was devoid of conversation; they allowed instead the bush to whisper its unfathomable secrets, as it tolerated their passage. Thomas knew he'd become defensive back there. He thought about what she'd said at the water hole about knowing what life was like inside the communities surrounding the lodge. He'd always felt that he did know *them*. He knew their language, he understood as many of the customs that an outsider could know, but even he could admit that there was an invisible force between them. He didn't move in and out of their lives, like some of them moved in and out of his.

From the time he was a small boy, there had always been a Zulu in his life: the cook, the cleaner, the gardener. They were as much a part of his story as the lodge itself. Each had offered him something of value, all of which, had shaped him. Thomas thought especially of Nonhle's father, Samson Ngubane. That man had offered Thomas much more than he was entitled to. Thomas had been an only child, and, because he was the only baby to have survived birth, his mother treated him like a priceless doll, until the day she'd unexpectedly died. When he'd longed to explore the scrubby bush, she had held him back. She was terrified he'd be gored by a warthog or snatched by a leopard. Instead, he'd stand with his small set of binoculars on the veranda, eyes scanning the reserve in search of life.

Once in a while, he'd have a school friend come and stay for a few days during the holidays, but mostly, he was left to his own devices. Since the workers' children stayed on the compound, he couldn't play with any of them either. So, Samson, not yet a senior ranger, had taken pity on the young boy and taught Thomas everything he thought a boy should know about the veld. Thomas hung around Samson like a small cloud attached by an invisible thread, bobbing and weaving in the wind. By the age of twelve, Thomas knew two things: how to speak isiZulu like a Zulu, and that when he grew up, he wanted to be a game ranger, just like Baba Ngubane.

He stole a quick look at Nonhle. He wondered if she had any idea how generous her father had been to him as a child. And what had he offered Samson, or any of the others? As a child; mess, disrespect, and perhaps laughter. As an adult; wages and a fleeting interest in the story of their lives. The truth was, he didn't want to get too close. Closeness meant understanding and understanding usually meant that action was required. Animals and veld were far easier; they didn't bring their problems to the table. And God knew, just being a South African meant that you had more problems to contend with than you were ever prepared for; land ownership being one such problem. Although it hadn't been a big part of their conversation at the water hole, Nonhle had alluded to it, and it struck him at the very heart of his fear. That smouldering coal was beginning to flame, and it was only time before it became a raging fire, and it terrified him.

Talk of land became talk of belonging – about those who belonged here, and those who did not. It was not that Thomas entertained these feelings of dread within himself as he went about his day. But rather, it was in the social gatherings of friends and family, of farmers and colleagues, that fear glided in like a vulture. It either stood on the fringes waiting its turn to pick and tear at the body of their concern, or it stuck its head straight in, seeking out their collective heart. On those occasions, Thomas chose to remove himself, as fear turned to hate, and their future in South Africa died in their mouths.

As he focused on the road ahead of him, his eyes tracked his surroundings. He loved this place. He loved the freedom of driving through the bush, the horizon unmarred by buildings and pollution. He loved the sudden silent appearance of an elephant, the roadblocks of rotating dung beetles, and skittish zebra. He loved the night sky, with its swathe of milky way, and falling stars. He loved the way he felt in this place, who he was in this place. The talk of land made him anxious; a sense of impending loss overwhelmed him. Not just the loss of land necessarily, but the loss of identity. Who would he be if he weren't here? He could not visualise himself in another country. Being white did not make him Scottish, Irish, or German, any more than being black meant Nonhle could transport herself to Tanzania or the Congo and feel at home there. He was aware that his history was different. He didn't care that he could trace his lineage back to Scotland over three generations; it was irrelevant. It was not his home. His blood would not sing in response to a call that would never come. He would be a refugee in a strange land, his heart embittered by his unwanted displacement from home. It was the slow insidious feeling of being erased from this land, of no longer being needed, or even required, that squeezed the lightness of being from his spirit.

***

Nonhle too knew exactly what it felt like to be on the outside of a circle; more than one circle, in fact. Circles she longed to be welcomed back into, and those, she did not. The day she'd gone off to a new school in town was the day she was baptised into the world of otherness. This *otherness* was not self-inflicted but rather constructed by much-loved childhood friends. Friends who'd fast become enemies when the line of the haves and the have-nots was drawn. It was constructed by the white girls at school, who hadn't yet come to understand that there is more that makes us similar, than that which sets us apart.

Nonhle had recognised the opportunity of a lifetime, the day her mother had come home, hope streaming from her in invisible waves. She was being offered a future that her mother had been denied, and Nonhle wanted to set aside any childish pursuits, to grasp it with both hands.

Nonhle knew that her mother had had bigger dreams for herself. Working as a senior waitress at the lodge restaurant at her age had not been part of the plan. As Nonhle grew older, she came to realise what had kept her mother back; it was time and confidence. As the years went by, more and more young people arrived with their qualifications and degrees, and their superior knowledge of seemingly everything. As competent as Mama was, she could not compete with their enthusiastic smiles, and radiating self-assurance.

Mama's confidence had been eroded as a teenager, and Nonhle thought with sadness, that her mother was unlikely to ever get it back. To her frustration, her mother still carried the weight of those humiliating years of girlhood on her shoulders and deferred to what she perceived to be the greater knowledge of the graduates. They'd spoken of it once when Nonhle had battled with her own sense of identity.

As a teenager, Mama had spent hours teaching herself to speak English. Like Nonhle, she too had dreams of a life, a far cry, from the one she had lived these past twenty-five years. Oh, she was happy with her life, she reassured Nonhle. She knew she was more privileged than many of her relatives who remained in the family homestead. But, back then, she'd longed for a job in a city. She attempted to teach herself to speak English, without the accent that would give away her identity as a girl from rural Zululand. Each morning she'd listen to Springbok Radio on her father's small wind-up radio, and she'd read whatever English text she could get her hands on, from newspapers to words on the back of tinned food. It was hard work, and the other girls would follow her around, laughing like a flock of *hlekabafazi* as they mimicked her attempts to pronounce 'determine' instead of 'determine', and other such puzzling pronunciations. But she'd never got the chance to leave the village and move to the city. A year after meeting her first boyfriend, now husband, she fell pregnant and knew her life would not change in the way she had hoped. Instead, she had focused on Nonhle, and tried to fill the gap created by poor quality education in rural schools.

When Nonhle still attended the local school, waiting for Mama to return home from work, felt endless. Nonhle would sit on the stairs leading up to the kitchen, watching for the vehicle that would drop Mama back home. Mama would kiss Nonhle's head, then disappear straight into the bedroom to change out of her work clothes. Then, before she focused on the task of preparing dinner, the two of them would sit at the worn table in their tiny kitchen. In summer, when the sun still spilled through the window, Nonhle would watch tiny particles of dust and plant matter orbit their heads, until finally settling on the surface of their steaming mugs of tea. First Mama would ask about Nonhle's day; a full description of the day's events, starting with

Nonhle's journey to school, was required. Only once this was delivered in English, would Mama begin preparing dinner, and tell the stories that she'd heard during her shift. She wanted Nonhle to know that there was life beyond Mevamhlope, and one day, if she worked hard enough (and didn't have babies too soon), she would be free to explore it.

Mama's gentle and quiet nature lent itself to observation and listening. She told Nonhle about the tall, friendly Americans with their strident voices; voices that would serve them well if they ever found themselves stranded on the top of the Lubombo mountains. They arrived with complicated cameras and safari outfits adorned with a seemingly endless array of pockets, full of strange paraphernalia, that appeared to have no purpose whatsoever. She described the red-faced Englishmen and women, who were fearful of the small pale geckos that walked up and down walls on tiny sticky feet. These little lizards left tiny pellets of poo on clean white linen – a smudge of dark brown topped with a chalky white dollop – like an ice-cream cone from the Wimpy in town.

Most of all she loved to share with Nonhle the conversations she overheard, because, like most tourists, they forgot about the servers who waited patiently in the background, ready to clear away plates of half-eaten food and top up empty wine glasses.

No, Nonhle, she laughed at her clever daughter, *when hovering close to guests to better serve them, overhearing was not quite the same as eavesdropping.*

Sometimes, depending on the guest, she was included in the show of photographs from other trips. She absorbed them in wonder, while fellow diners eventually moved on to other conversations, having had the same experience, less than a year before.

On those sunny afternoons, Nonhle would listen spellbound as her mother painted a picture of giant ruins, which sat at the top of a thousand stairs above the Sacred Valley in Peru, and of the Great Barrier Reef, its water bluer than the wings and chest of a European Roller, swarming with all manner of marine life and coral. Mama stuck out her tongue in disgust as she revealed that some of the guests craved raw fish wrapped inside rice and seaweed, and were disappointed that succulent, juicy nyala steak was on the menu again. Her face softened as she talked of the children sent to expensive boarding schools, so that they could earn degrees and make money, and have all the things that their parents never had when they were young. Every night Mama brought home another world and painted another picture to inspire Nonhle to dream of something bigger. Because, even if there was no money to send her to a good school, one day, things might change.

And then, like any other day, Mama had welcomed a new table of guests to lunch. They'd arrived from Texas early that morning and were at varying stages of exhaustion, except for one guest. She looked crisp and cool in a light cotton blouse; dark braids coiled high on her head. As Mama placed a glass of peach iced-tea in front of her, the woman took her hand. She gave it a squeeze and looked into Thuli's eyes.

'I'm home, sisi,' she whispered. *'Finally, home.'*

This was not the first guest that had shared this sentiment with Mama. She'd even been witness to prone bodies; lips planted firmly onto the red soil in gratitude. As the lunch progressed, there was something beneath the American veneer that was beginning to surface, and Mama suddenly knew, with great certainty, that Thenji was not American, but had once come from these very parts. During the week as the other guests rested between game drives, Thenji would wander down to the restaurant, seeking out Thuli. She'd order coffee, then settle down in a quiet corner, an often-unopened book in her lap.

As Mama laid out the coffee tray, Thenji would strike up a conversation. They were tentative at first, two women circling the great divide between them, but as often is the case, stories of children and family narrowed the gap. Thenji was protective of her story, and it wasn't until the day before her departure that she offered Thuli the first scenes of the tale of her life. Thenji Aldridge, formerly Thenjiwe Xulu, was a daughter of the green hills that lay to the right of Mevamhlope. She was also a daughter of a family in exile; having fled from South Africa, by way of Lesotho, arriving in London, and finally settling in Texas. And although Thenji's physical connection to this place had been cut like an umbilical cord at birth, her spiritual connection had never been severed.

Thenji left on the early shuttle to the airport the next day, and Mama had been surprised to find she felt saddened by the loss of that daily encounter with the woman. But it was the nature of the industry, guests came and went, with regular frequency. Some absences were missed, others, celebrated. So, it was with great joy that Mama found Thenji sitting in her favourite spot, a year later. Next to her sat a child of eight, fiddling with a camera. By the end of the trip, Thenji had introduced Thuli to the concept of pen-pals. Nonhle, although she had never met the girl, was encouraged to write monthly letters. It was on her third trip that Thenji handed Thuli a letter of her own. A letter that would change Nonhle's path, sending her on a journey that would ensure she fulfilled her mother's dream of becoming more than a waitress.

It was a journey that would set Nonhle apart. A journey that she had known would be difficult because she had to catch up to the other girls; girls who had attended well-resourced schools, while she had to share her books with many other learners. But Nonhle had not imagined the difficulty of leaving behind her school friends in their worn and faded uniforms. Of being excluded from the close-knit circle created through everyday interaction and shared experiences. And worse, of being treated like an outsider in her new school for longer than she had expected as they all grappled to come to terms with each other's unfamiliar ways of being. Because even though apartheid had fallen in theory, she knew now, that it had not yet been deconstructed in the mind. Small towns with closed communities found it hard to let go of entrenched beliefs, and outsiders, Nonhle knew, were few and far between in a private school priced well beyond the means of most rural households.

However, acceptance and friendship had finally come around. Not with everyone, of course, but Thuli reminded her that in life, it was rare to have something in common with everyone. Nonhle only had to look at her own family to acknowledge the truth in that.

But now she sat next to a man whom she'd wanted to believe was standing on the inside of the same circle as her, but their polar views had pushed him out of her circle, and she was trying to work out if he'd ever find his way back in.

7: A win-win situation
30th November 2012

It was a triumphant cavalcade that pulled into the courtyard of the police station in the early hours of the morning. In the back of the van, sat the three unsuccessful poachers, each in a world of his own. For Detective Karel du Randt, the operation had been a huge success. The tip-off the anti-poaching unit had received had allowed them to move quickly. The road had been blocked off, with police positioned at the offramp to the N2 freeway, and at the only other road, the poachers could use as an escape route. The tip-off had been unusually precise, so they were able to catch the poachers wiggling their way out of the reserve, through the cut fence. For Karel, the biggest success of the operation was that no fresh rhino horn had been found on the men. The gun the poachers were using had no silencer, so it was safely assumed that because no gunshots had rung out into the night, that no rhino had been shot and abandoned to die. The reserve would send out a patrol at first light, to double-check, but for now, Karel felt relieved. The drive back from the fence line of The Last Outpost Lodge had given his team and the anti-poaching unit good insight into the trio they'd captured. Once the men had been booked and fingerprinted, and the trembling boy given into the care of an officer, Karel observed the two men. He picked out the group leader immediately; Nkosi was a picture of indifferent calm, while his 'colleague', Bheki, was a sweaty, jittery mess. The man's fingers feverishly stroked a small pouch hanging from a long leather thong around his neck. Although it might appear that the sweating poacher would easily crack under slight pressure,

Karel knew that a poacher who believed in the power of a witchdoctor was unlikely to give up information easily. Added to that, the poacher's fear of retribution from 'the boss' and other poachers, was far greater than time spent in prison.

They all knew that the boss in the area was a man named Lucky Mhlongo. Of that, Karel was certain, but, to his frustration, they had nothing concrete to pin on him. Since he did none of the dirty work himself, and paid his men well, the poachers would say nothing to implicate him; and, to Karel's utter rage, once the poachers were passed over to the local courts, they were usually let go after a small fine was paid. Or, if they ended up in jail, they always managed to be released in record time. Karel had yet to find out exactly who in the police force was being paid off by Lucky, but he had his suspicions. If he could get one of these two poachers to grass on Lucky, Karel would be a happy man.

Karel watched Bheki, who kept his eyes firmly on the pouch. Karel knew that the pouch held a little collection of organic and inorganic matter that had some sort of spell attached to it. He knew that the poachers wore them for protection. He couldn't help but laugh. His colleagues often accused him of being unwise in mocking something he couldn't possibly understand. He understood perfectly well … wasn't the evidence of its ineffectiveness sitting right in front of him?

The pouch got him thinking though. Maybe Lucky had a witchdoctor as an accomplice. The man would provide muthi and blessings for poaching expeditions. If Karel could get to the witchdoctor, maybe he could find something he could use to implicate Lucky, once and for all. Or, he thought, was the witchdoctor the kingpin, and Lucky, his assistant? It wouldn't be the first time. Either way, he needed to figure it out, and soon. It sickened Karel that these so-called 'healers' were doing everything but healing. It was like a priest claiming to be celibate while messing with the choirboys. *Disgusting.*

Karel looked between the two poachers, then focused on Nkosi – the shuttered stare, the low slouch in the chair, feet sprawled so others had to step over him. Karel wanted to hit him. Instead, he motioned to Detective Joseph Dlamini that he'd handle the sullen poacher, while Dlamini could figure out how to get Bheki to rat on the witchdoctor.

***

Nkosi laughed to himself as the red-headed policeman pushed him roughly onto a chair. The detective gave him a hard stare, nodded to the police officer standing against the wall, then left the room. Though the sun was not yet up, the room was hot and stuffy, and apart from the table and two chairs (and silent police officer), it was empty. The once green walls were dirty with hand smudges and shoe prints. For some reason, it was the prints that made him feel nervous. It reminded him of the corridor outside the principal's office at school, where a line of naughty boys had to wait their turn to feel the sting of the principal's cane against their thighs and bums. There had been a lot of kicking at the wall as they prepared themselves for what was to come. He let out a shuddering breath, focusing on what his boss had told him to do, should he end up in this situation. But talking about what to do was very different from doing it. Nkosi didn't want to mess this up. He'd been making good money, and his horizons were beginning to expand. He'd do exactly what he'd been told to do, and the boss would do the rest. Of that he was sure. There was no way that Nkosi Zungu would be sharing any information with these *ziduphunga.*

While he waited for the detective to return, Nkosi thought about the night he'd first met the boss. He'd made his way from his tiny, rural home in KwaBhengu, just south of the Mozambican border, to a similar village. The same scrubby bush, the same sandy roads, the same moth-eaten huts. But between those huts, new homes were springing up. Homes made of concrete, with plaster ceilings, and white moldings. Homes with glass windows, and a parking bay for a car. Homes with a TV, a shiny silver double-door fridge-freezer, and a DSTV satellite dish.

Nkosi was visiting a friend. A man who had once been a boy in a pair of worn-out red shorts, and a ripped faded blue t-shirt. The same outfit, worn day in and day out, eventually gave up the fight, just in time for the next generation of hand-me-downs. But now, Nkosi saw that Philani's clothes were his own; clothes not exactly suited to the dust and heat, but they let everyone know just how well he was doing. He'd finally become a man with status. Nkosi could remember how jealous he had been of Philani and all the nice things he had. It wasn't fair! He was smarter than Philani, who'd left school in Grade 10. Nkosi's teachers had high hopes that he'd make it to university. From the time he was twelve, Nkosi had wanted to become a lawyer. He hadn't known exactly what becoming a lawyer required, but he knew he'd get to drive a fast car, wear fancy suits, and when he talked, people would listen. But there was no place at university because there was no money. He couldn't even find a job in the nearest town; there were too many kids who'd finished school, and not enough work for them all.

When Philani had invited Nkosi to the village he was now living and working in, Nkosi had been excited. There'd been a look of promise in Philani's eyes, and Nkosi wanted to know what lay behind it. They spent the day reminiscing about their youth and watching TV while drinking ice-cold beers from the fridge. Night fell and the moon, bright as a new five-rand coin, hung over the village as they made their way to the local tavern. Suddenly, the quiet was disrupted by an explosion of revving, hooting, and triumphant roars. The doors of huts and houses flew open, and people flooded out to join those already standing under the night sky. Philani grabbed Nkosi by the sleeve of his shirt, and with a manic grin, pulled him towards the celebration.

A convoy of shiny 4x4 bakkies with their blinding spotlights, came to a standstill, music blaring through expensive speakers. Young men jumped out and threw down the tailgates, pulling crates of quarts and coolers of meat from the back. There were calls to get the fires started, and the crates and coolers were ferried to tables provided by community members. The poachers had returned from a successful hunt, and the boss wanted everyone to celebrate.

A win for the boss, is a win for all, said Philani with a wink.

In the middle of the confusion of sights and sounds, Nkosi's eyes came to rest on the figure of a man; he stood out from the group of young men in their branded clothing and designer shoes. This man's confidence didn't come from his clothing, his shoes, or the flash of gold in his mouth, but from the way in which everyone leapt to do his bidding. The man simply watched while everyone else got on with the tasks allocated to them. When the white-grey smoke of recently lit fires began to waft into the air, and quarts of Black Label were passed around, he sat down with the men and laughed as the story of the hunt was brought to life.

The next day, Philani introduced Nkosi to the man everyone referred to as, *'ndunankulu'*, the big boss. It was the same man he'd seen the night before. Up close, the man was leaner and wirier than his confidence had led Nkosi to believe. He had a slow, easy smile but eyes like a hungry child; they took in everything as if looking for something to devour. The boss, Lucky Mhlongo, was offering him a job. Nothing fancy to start with, but it would give Lucky a chance to see what Nkosi was made of. And Nkosi, who had never had a job, agreed immediately without asking any questions. That was two years ago and Nkosi was amazed at how his life, like Philani's, had changed in such a short time.

To his annoyance and confusion, his very first experience in the working world was to learn to identify and collect plants. The specimens would eventually make their way to the muthi markets of Durban and Johannesburg. Nkosi wanted to be out there in the bush, like Philani, with a rifle on his shoulder, and big money in his pocket. Instead, he was given over to a man called Samkele, who seemed to know everything there was to know about plants.

Within a few months, Nkosi had outshone every other recruit Samkele had trained. Samkele told the boss that Nkosi had an eye for detail and a remarkable memory. Sooner than expected, Nkosi was taken on his first hunting trip. He was given the lowly, yet important, task of carrying the supplies for the duration of the trip. And in time, he was heading up some of those trips. He had come to realise that he was an excellent navigator, his sense of direction impressive in the shadowy confusion of the bush at night. The job of looking for shy plants in the blazing sun had long since been removed from his responsibilities. His skill tracking rhino was more profitable for Lucky, and Nkosi loved his job. He loved how it made him feel, and he loved how it made other people feel about him. His confidence had grown, and soon he'd begun to feel that he wasn't appreciated as much as he should be. Wasn't he the one who made it all possible? Did all the dangerous work and came back with the prize? Yet, he received such a small portion of the money. It wasn't fair. There was no chance of moving any further up the ladder. Lucky had been clear about that.

Soon Nkosi started to think of ways to ensure that his future wasn't dependent on what *he* could do out in the bush. He had no intention of working for someone else for the rest of his life. He wanted a small business of his own. He'd gained so much knowledge that it would be a shame to let it go to waste. On a visit to a friend on the opposite side of the Hluhluwe-Imfolozi reserve, he'd come across a herd boy, an orphan. It wasn't hard to sell the boy the dream of a different life. Nkosi was familiar with the situation; there were many orphans who were not well looked after and were made to work for their keep; even in his village. He couldn't deny it.

He took the opportunity to share in detail the stories that he had heard Lucky tell, repeatedly, to every new recruit. Mandla's eyes were as big as hubcaps as he listened to Nkosi. For a boy who'd had nothing for so long, even the smallest reward was accepted with cupped palms and a dip of the knees. Nkosi decided to teach Mandla about plants, exactly as he'd been taught. Nkosi found his own clients and sold them his stock of poached plants. And if Lucky were ever to hear of Mandla, the herd boy turned plant poacher? Well, wasn't Mandla perfectly positioned to monitor the fence line of KwaZulu-Natal's biggest game reserve, for sightings of rhino. He would pass on any vital information to Nkosi, who in turn would alert the boss. A win-win situation for them both, Nkosi felt.

He wasn't sure when the idea first came to him. Perhaps it was on one of those lazy days, the air swollen with humidity, and the promise of rain. Or, in the dark, just before midnight, when one small mosquito made sleep impossible. Nonetheless, the idea had opened the door and settled in, content to overstay its welcome. After a successful hunt one night, on his way to drop off the horn to the transporter, he skimmed a thin disk from the base of the horn with his saw. He smeared the base with the blood and dirt that still covered the horn. Nkosi hid his treasure away in a pocket he'd sliced into the upholstery of the car seat. He waited two weeks before making a trip to one of the many China Malls springing up all over the rural areas and he was careful to avoid any of Lucky's contacts. His new venture had been going on for a few months, and Nkosi's funds were growing. The man at the China Mall had proved to be a rewarding partner, and with each trip, the slices of horn became fatter.

Nkosi's head jerked towards the door. He could hear the dull thump of footsteps coming down the passageway towards him. He settled his face into a blank, glassy-eyed stare, and waited for the door to swing open. The footsteps died, and low conversation slipped in through the keyhole. Nkosi's practiced dead stare flickered to life as the detective entered the room, for in his hand was a clear bag containing a small horn, which he placed on the table. Nkosi willed himself to remain calm and uninterested by its presence. They hadn't even seen a rhino last night. No way were they going to pin this one on him! *Ngeke!* His arms crossed his body, and he sank lower in his seat.

***

Karel sat down across the table, placing his laptop – bought with his own *bladdy* money, thank you very much – in front of him. Last night, once the poachers were secure in the back of the police vehicle, the car had been searched. The horn was small, pathetic in comparison to some of the specimens Karel had recovered before, but it was still valuable. Karel thought about the recent case with the baby rhino; its small face mashed to a pulp. The tiny nub of growing horn hacked out to join the larger curved horns of its mother. He clenched his fists under the table as the anger welled up within him. He hated these bastards.

Karel watched Nkosi's face as he pushed the horn towards the poacher. A brief flicker of concern played across the poacher's eyes, before returning to its blank stare.

'Your boss isn't going to be happy,' Karel said, with a disappointed shake of his head. 'He was expecting at least three horns, and now he gets none.' Karel took in the impassive face before him. 'We're happy though,' he continued, lips curling into a smirk. 'We've got you with a horn *and* with intent to illegally obtain another.'

'What?' Nkosi cried, comprehension dawning. 'That's not mine! You can't—'

'Oh, but I think you'll find that I can,' said Karel, with satisfaction. He turned the laptop to face Nkosi. He watched the poacher take in the sequence of images. Either this guy was an excellent actor, or he truly had no idea that the horn was in the boot. The photos showed the car from last night, the open boot, the spare wheel being hauled out, and inside the empty well, a bundle of dirty hessian sacking. Then, the sacking on the floor, open to expose a small rhino horn.

'You planted it!' shouted Nkosi, his body heaving in anger.

'Thought you'd say that,' said Karel. He quickly took the machine back, opened another file, and brought up a video.

'That,' he said, pointing to a spot behind the car, 'is you.'

Nkosi threw himself back into his chair, sweat pouring down his face. 'It's not mine,' he repeated, his voice belligerent.

'Maybe not technically,' said Karel with a slow smile, 'but it was hidden in your vehicle. Guilty until proven innocent, my boy. Guilty by association. All three of you.'

'So,' said Karel. 'Let's see what we've got you for.' He opened a folder and pulled out a sheet of paper. 'The charges against you and your 'colleagues': intentional cutting/damage of a fence; trespassing with intent to commit a crime; conspiracy to commit a crime; carrying of an illegal firearm. And now, illegal possession of a rhino horn.' Karel's freckled face wagged from side to side. 'Not looking good, is it?'

Karel watched in irritation as the look of fear on Nkosi's face quite quickly made way for a smug turn of the mouth. He did not like the relaxing of Nkosi's posture. This boy thought he was above the law. Karel had a fairly good idea of what was going on in Nkosi's head: everything was going to be fine because the boss would 'make it go away'.

Karel tapped the table sharply. 'You know, we're a pretty clever lot these days. Did you know there's a database full of DNA samples from rhino horn? You can match it to a carcass. It tells us where the animal was butchered. Gives us a location, helps us narrow down a place, and locate informants who are always happy to talk, when a bit of this,' he said, rubbing his thumb against the fingers of his left hand, 'is being handed out.'

Of course, the chances were slim to none that this would happen in this case. The database was a great idea, but Karel reckoned it would be years before it would be working properly. Regardless, he observed with satisfaction the subtle signs of concern that flitted across Nkosi's features. *Not so clever now, hey, my boy,* he thought.

'That's not all,' Karel continued, gleefully. 'We can also match your car, and your footprints, to other poaching scenes and that lets us build a bit of a case against you, and not only you, your friend, too. I'm sure this isn't the first time you've worked together.' Karel sat back, folding his arms across his chest, pinning the poacher with a frank stare. 'Do you think Lucky Mhlongo actually cares about you, Nkosi? If we can link you both to more than one of these cases, I know for certain he won't bother saving you. He'd see you as a liability; plenty more guys waiting to take your place.' Nkosi didn't even blink at the mention of Lucky's name.

Karel sighed. He leant forward, resting his elbows on the metal tabletop. 'You know,' he said, looking at the wall to his left. 'Detective Joseph Dlamini's having a nice chat with your friend. I wonder if Bheki will be as loyal as you are.'

8: Into the veld to search for supper
30th November 2012

In the room next door to Karel, Detective Joseph Dlamini, pushed Bheki onto a chair. It was one of those old chairs with wooden slats. The central slat was broken in exactly the right place. Joseph knew that within a few minutes, Bheki would begin shifting about to find some relief. He'd find none, of course. Bheki's shirt was patterned with dark blue sweat patches. His hands, now handcuffed at the front of his body, kept nervously reaching for the pouch hanging from his neck. He kept forgetting that it had been removed earlier and placed in a box with his shoes and belt. Joseph had handled the muthi pouch carefully, making sure that the bare skin of his hands didn't touch it at all – just in case. It might not have worked for Bheki, but Joseph didn't want to take any chances. While the muthi might be a blessing for the rightful owner, it might hold a curse for anyone wrongfully touching the bag.

Last night, Joseph had recognised Bheki when the anti-poaching unit spotlight had scanned across the three poachers, down on their knees in the grass. When Joseph had first met him, Bheki had been younger and thinner, with a pack of skinny hunting dogs panting at his feet. They'd caught him trespassing on a private farm, his dogs on the hunt for cane rat and duiker. If Joseph had been on his own, he'd have let the man go free. He'd grown up with hunting dogs. If there was meat in his bowl at night, it was only because his father took the dogs into the veld to search for supper. There was no money for frozen chicken parts from Spar when he was a boy. But Joseph hadn't been on his own that day. He was with an enthusiastic detective called Karel du

Randt, who had recently joined the station to head up wildlife crime in the area. Karel had made a big impression the day he'd arrived, and not a good one. He'd made it clear to them all that they would no longer be turning a blind eye to poaching, *of any kind.*

'*Ngibukeka njenge silima?*' Karel had roared, his face almost matching the colour of his hair.

Joseph knew that his colleagues didn't think Karel was stupid, just irrelevant. Some of the officers, who owned hunting dogs, had sneered at the *umlungu* who thought he could change decades of tradition with one passionate speech. The look on their faces when they registered that Karel was fluent in isiZulu had been amusing to watch. While it was appreciated that a white person had made the effort to learn isiZulu, it wasn't so funny that Karel could understand absolutely everything that was being said. Things would be different at the station from now on.

It had been two years since Joseph and Karel had begun working together. At first, they'd kept their distance. Joseph focusing on important matters, like murder, while Karel spent most of his time in the field, forming relationships with the local APU teams, private and government reserves, and anyone doing something to tackle poaching. At first, Joseph had been furious. As far as he could see, Karel was being paid to chat and drink cold beers, while he was knee-deep in blood, guts, and the usual unbelievable arguments that led people to murder their family members. Eventually, their paths began to cross more often as poachers and APU rangers clashed in the veld.

Over this time, Joseph had come to appreciate the difference between poaching for the pot and poaching for an international crime syndicate. He became interested in finding out the complicated inner workings of the syndicates; and Karel, grudgingly, began to understand that his colleague's lack of interest and urgency regarding poaching was a result of growing up in communities surrounding reserves. Community members remembered minimal jobs on offer at the lodges, the survivalist living conditions, and the lack of support from the reserves themselves. They remembered each of their cattle that been lost to an escaped lion, or a roaming leopard. And how often had they been compensated … rarely! Karel and Joseph had finally formed an unlikely alliance.

'*Yah! Madoda,*' Joseph said to Bheki, with a shake of his head. 'You should have stuck to poaching for the pot. Now things are going to be difficult for you.'

Bheki wiped his face with his hand, and then rubbed both hands along the length of his thighs. He finally pinned them between his knees, which refused to stay still.

It had been decided that Joseph would focus on the muthi they'd found in the car, and who had provided it, in the hopes that they might find a connection between the sangoma and Lucky Mhlongo. Joseph was glad that Karel had taken the interview with Nkosi; Karel was unable to put himself in the shoes of those who believed wholeheartedly in the power of muthi.

There had been cases up near Kruger involving more than one isangoma, and a poaching incident on a private reserve about forty minutes from the Mevamhlope town, a year ago. One of the poachers had admitted to buying muthi to make him invisible to the APU teams operating in the area. The isangoma, who had been revealed surprisingly quickly by the poacher, had denied any knowledge that the intended purpose for protection was for rhino poaching. He claimed the man had requested it so that he could become invisible when his wife came looking for him on pay day. That had produced a good laugh from the other policemen, but Karel's lips had remained thin.

Joseph picked up the evidence bag containing the muthi bottle. It was a regular 500ml water bottle that could be bought from any shop; the plastic label boasting clean, clear spring water. But wound around its neck was a string of red and white beads.

'Who did you buy it from?' he asked, swinging the bag in Bheki's direction.

Bheki's eyes widened, then his gaze shifted back to his hands.

'I don't know,' he mumbled.

'You don't know?' laughed Joseph. Bheki was a terrible liar.

'No,' said Bheki, his voice surprisingly firm.

Without a courteous knock, the door swung open and Karel marched in. Joseph folded his arms. Just once he'd like to take an entire session of questioning on his own, without Karel interfering.

'And?' said Karel, eyeing Bheki beadily.

'He says he doesn't know who he got it from.'

'Rubbish,' cried Karel. 'You think we're stupid? You just drank some muthi that someone gave you? How'd you know what was in the bottle? It could've been *rooibos* tea and battery acid, for all you know!'

'No,' said Bheki indignantly; the insult encouraging his animated response. 'It's good. Look!' He pointed at the bottle. 'The beads,' he said, in triumph. 'Look! The beads are always the same.'

Karel snorted. 'You're a bladdy idiot, man,' he said to the poacher. 'Anyone can stick a few beads on a bottle.'

Joseph observed Bheki's stricken face as it swivelled between Joseph and the bottle.

'*Eish, mfo,*' said Joseph, with pity. 'If it was "good", then why didn't it work?'

Karel had manoeuvred himself onto the table, next to Bheki. His leg nudged Bheki's arm as he leant conspiringly towards the poacher.

'You know what, hey. I think your witchdoctor's gone a bit kak. I think the ancestors he talks to have been in the soil a bit too long, hey. Maybe, he can't hear them very well with all that earth covering them,' he said, winking at Bheki, then burst out laughing at his joke.

Joseph and Bheki shared a brief look of mutual disbelief at the use of such a disrespectful name for an isangoma.

'You say you always use this isangoma's muthi, but now it hasn't worked?' Joseph looked at Bheki sympathetically. 'That doesn't sound right, mfo. If he's so powerful, maybe he didn't want it to work … for a reason.'

Karel patted Bheki's shoulder in a fatherly gesture. 'Know what I think? I think your witchdoctor isn't very powerful at all. All this time you've been scared of him for no good reason. He's probably some skinny old man with no teeth.' Once again, Karel's eyes began to crinkle with mirth as a laugh escaped him.

Then he looked at Bheki seriously. 'Here's what I'm going to do for you, Bheki,' he said. 'You give us the name of your witchdoctor, and I'll make sure that we get a more powerful witchdoctor to reverse whatever curse that might be put on you. What do you think?' Karel looked at the mute poacher as if accepting was the only option.

'Really? Not keen, hey? Well, while you're thinking about that … why don't you think about Lucky Mhlongo and whether you're ready to sacrifice your freedom for his.'

***

Back in Karel's office, Joseph asked Karel which isangoma he was thinking of approaching to help Bheki.

Karel roared with laughter. 'Ag, man! Don't be stupid. I'll find some old *khehla*, pay him a hundred bucks to dress up in some skins, and throw a few bones on the floor. Bheki won't know the difference. I'll even throw in a wildebeest tail – you know, for *authenticity*.'

Joseph shook his head, clicking his tongue in disgust as the tears streamed down Karel's face, his body heaving in delight. Joseph closed the door behind him and decided to go and check on the youngest poacher. The boy claimed not to know his uncle's number by heart, but Joseph had seen genuine fear in the boy's face when he said the man's name.

9: The whispering wind
30th November 2012

The traumatised figure of Mandla Mtshali took up hardly any space in the tiny windowless room in which they'd left him. His fingers continued to worry away at the stubborn piece of skin on his lip. He'd managed to work most of it loose, but he was stuck at a tender section and didn't have the courage to tear it off. He'd been sitting alone for what felt like an eternity. Mandla wasn't used to sitting inside; he felt trapped, scared. It was easy to tell the time of day out there in the hills. But in here, there was nothing to give him a clue.

The night had been a terrifying blur of sights and sounds – flashing lights, men screaming commands in a language he didn't understand – guns waving and jabbing until he felt the warm flow of urine run down his leg for the second time that night.

Nkosi, who Mandla had come to trust and consider the big brother he'd never had, no longer made him feel certain of his future. All three had been pushed to their knees, forced onto their stomachs and hands tied behind their backs, as the police collected their evidence. The ride to the station had been terrifying, as the vehicle had fishtailed its way along the dirt roads. Neither Nkosi or Bheki would speak to him, beyond telling him to shut his mouth and say nothing.

'The boss', said Nkosi, 'will sort it out.'

The boss? frowned Mandla in confusion. *Aren't you the boss?*

Now, in this airless room, Mandla thought about how he'd come to be out in the bushveld, in the middle of the night.

It had all begun months ago. He'd been sitting on his favourite rock, at the top of the ridge, overlooking his village. The sun beat down cruelly, but he gave thanks for the bit of shade offered by the acacia tree under which he sat. It was his favourite place; the rock smoothed perfectly to cup his skinny bum. He liked to believe that it was his bum that had worn away the stone through the years as he sat and tended the goats belonging to his uncle.

On the one side of the ridge, down in the valley, was the village in which he'd been born, and no doubt he thought sadly, in which he would die. On the other side lay the vast expanse of the Hluhluwe-Imfolozi Game Reserve. Mandla had lived all his life on the fence line of this great reserve but had never set foot inside it. It was quiet up on the ridge, the only sound to be heard, the whispering wind and the tinkle of bells attached to some of the goats. He was growing bored and restless. Each day was exactly the same as the one before it, and he was desperate for change.

Mandla was an orphan; his parents had died some eight years before. First went his father, from the disease that killed so many in South Africa. Then a year later, his beautiful, gentle mother had followed. He was eight years old when he stood at her open grave and let hot, silent tears of grief roll down his cheeks until they plopped onto the thirsty soil at his feet. Then, before he was ready, his uncle, the older brother of his mother, came to collect him. He gave Mandla a few minutes to gather his belongings from the small family hut before slamming the door on the only home he'd ever known.

His shoulders slumped as he thought of his uncle, a big meaty man with a voice like thunder and a hand that struck like lightning. Mandla had been on the receiving end of that hand for eight long years and had learnt to anticipate when it was likely to strike. He had perfected a body jerking move that ensured the impact of the hand was at its lowest when it finally reached his head. To repay the generosity of his uncle for taking him in, Mandla had been set to work for the family. Each afternoon he lit the fire for dinner, and every morning he'd wake early to clean the grey ash from the floor and light the fire for breakfast. He'd prepare a breakfast of *amasi*; a filling meal made of sour milk and maize meal, for the family, and then get dressed for school.

He'd cried the day his uncle informed him that his school days were over. There were more important things for Mandla to be getting on with, like herding the tribe of goats – a prize possession of his uncle – into the hills surrounding the village. Now each morning, instead of dressing for school, he'd slip from the house and make his way to the goat kraal. First, he'd look over the fence and count each goat. Then, he'd unhook the gate, and Mandla and the goats would make their way hopping and skipping into the open spaces and quiet hills.

The loud *kok-kok-kok* of a large bird jolted Mandla from his thoughts. Its red coloured underwings flashed as it soared over the reserve fence and into the trees on the other side. He was so intent on tracking the flight of the bird that he jumped clear off his seat when a human voice greeted him, 'Sawubona, *mfana.*'

In front of him stood a stranger; a young man with a chewed-up matchstick protruding from a confident grin. The man was leaning forward, one foot on a rock, and his elbow resting on his raised knee as if this were the most natural place for him to be.

Mandla looked around. *Where had he come from?*

'Are you lost?' he asked, tentatively.

The stranger looked offended, clicking his tongue at the suggestion. 'Lost? Never! I've been staying with some friends from down there,' he said, pointing at Mandla's village. 'I watch you come up here every day, so I wanted to see for myself what was so interesting.'

He took the matchstick out of his mouth, investigated it closely, and once satisfied he'd flattened it completely, flicked it over Mandla's head. There wasn't much to see, in Mandla's opinion, but it was quite nice to have another person up here with him on his ridge. He leapt nimbly from his rock and joined the stranger at the fence. Nkosi introduced himself to Mandla with a complicated handshake. Then they both looked out over the green vegetation of the reserve and chatted about this and that for some time. Nkosi never stopped talking. He had so much to share, from the latest soccer scores to tales of fast living in the big cities of South Africa.

Mandla learnt that Nkosi had lived in Durban and the sprawling city of Johannesburg. He'd worked as a driver for a transport company and travelled the country from left to right and north to south. There was nothing Nkosi didn't know about. He spoke about the city lights and how, even in the dead of night, with no moon in sight, there was still enough light to walk down the street, looking for girls or for an opportunity to relieve someone of a handbag or a car of its radio. Mandla was shocked when Nkosi casually mentioned his adventures in crime, but he didn't want Nkosi to think that he was a silly child, so he nodded his head and tried to look impressed. Nkosi explained that stealing small things like bags and radios was no big deal really. Mandla felt very stupid. All he did was sit on this ridge watching the goats and he didn't even get paid.

'In the city, there's plenty to go around. It's not wrong to take from the rich to give to the poor. And in this case, I'm the poor!' Nkosi said with a sarcastic laugh, his hand travelling the length of his body; his branded clothing catching Mandla's eye.

It was the terrified bleating of a goat that snapped Mandla out of his examination of Nkosi's clothes. By the time he located the sound, the body of a baby goat lay jerking under the electric fence that had given it a shock.

'Eish!' wailed Mandla in fear and frustration. 'My uncle …' He let the sentence hang in the air; the man's reaction was not worth thinking about.

'What happens now?' asked Nkosi, scrunching his nose at the smell of burnt hair.

Mandla prodded the little body. Although it was alive, it didn't look like it was going to survive. This didn't happen often; goats weren't as stupid as they looked. Mandla noticed the tasty looking clump of grass on the other side that the goat must have been aiming for.

He sighed. 'If it dies, I have to pay for it.'

Nkosi sucked his teeth in sympathy. 'Yoh! Do you have the cash?'

Mandla gave a sad laugh. 'He doesn't pay me any money. I just owe him more time.'

'I don't understand,' Nkosi said, popping another matchstick between his teeth.

Mandla watched the body of the tiny goat as it breathed its last breath. 'Oh,' he said with feeling. 'I liked that goat.' He turned to face Nkosi. 'I watch my uncle's goats, and he gives me somewhere to live, and something to eat.'

'Ah,' said Nkosi, looking at the boy with interest. 'Well,' he said. 'It is a good thing I found you.'

'Why?' asked Mandla, hopefully. 'Are you going to pay for the goat?'

'No, my friend,' said Nkosi, his teeth flashing in the sun. 'I am going to teach you how to make money. And,' he said with a knowing look, 'you don't even have to move from this hill.'

Mandla smiled politely. *Was the man blind?* 'I don't understand?' he said, looking pointedly at the empty landscape surrounding him.

Nkosi rubbed his hands together in glee. 'Yes, keep looking, my friend. There's big money right here. You just can't see it yet.'

Mandla wasn't sure if Nkosi was just very stupid, or if that sweet-smelling tobacco he was rolling into a thin cigarette, was affecting his vision. Mandla knew that there was no money to be made up here. There wasn't a single thing in the hills that he could think of that anyone would want or need. He hadn't made one cent while sitting on this rocky outcrop.

Nkosi slowly turned in a circle, his eyes scanning the environment. 'What's that over there?' he asked Mandla, pointing in the direction of a smallish bush with long stems and leaves shaped like clapping hands.

Mandla shrugged his skinny shoulders.

'And this?' Nkosi demanded, rapping his knuckles against the tree next to him.

Again, his shoulders went up, and Mandla's lower lip protruded. He honestly had no idea what they were, they'd always just been there.

Nkosi smacked the trunk of the tree with excitement. 'I'll tell you what they are! Money! Everywhere you look, nearly every tree and plant you see, can be used by *inyanga* or isangoma. Lots of these plants are hard to come by; people like to use them, but not to plant them. They take too long to grow. You, my friend, are sitting on a gold mine. Trust me!'

Mandla looked around him, counting how many different types of plants and trees he could see from where he stood. He didn't know most of their names, but he could at least tell them apart. Of course, *izinyanga* and *izangoma* were used all the time by people in his village. There was no doctor for miles around and Mandla knew people trusted traditional medicine more than they did doctors at the hospital.

'Will I make enough money to buy a pair of Converse, like yours?' asked Mandla, eyeing out Nkosi's beautiful red canvas shoes.

'Enough to buy a pair for every week in the year,' said Nkosi, giving Mandla an encouraging slap between the shoulder blades.

Now, as the walls leaned in on him, Mandla closed his eyes to see if he could bring the rolling hills, the touch of the wind, and the scent of the earth, into the room, but he could not. Instead, a great sob escaped him. Within moments, the door creaked open, and the muscular frame of a policeman came into view.

Mandla used the sleeve of his jersey to stem the flow of snot and tears. He watched warily as the policeman sat down at the table opposite him. Although the man looked cross, Mandla could tell immediately that this man was not like his uncle. There would be no blows to the head or the pinching of earlobes.

***

'Sawubona?' greeted Joseph, kindly. When they'd arrested the three poachers, Joseph had been shocked at just how young the smallest one was. He couldn't be older than fourteen. However, Joseph knew that poor nutrition was the reason many children in rural areas looked so much younger than they really were. Until they worked out his real age, Joseph couldn't, by law, ask the boy anything without a lawyer present, but then, this wasn't Durban. And he doubted that the boy would know anything of real value.

'Ungubani igama lakho?' he asked.

Mandla just about managed to whisper his name.

'What were you doing out there, mfana?' Joseph asked, unable to hide his concern. 'Those men you are with … they are bad. Very bad.'

Mandla ducked his head to avoid Joseph's gaze.

'Do you want to go to jail?' Joseph addressed him, his voice suddenly harsh. Perhaps the boy responded better to commands.

The boy's face contorted, fresh tears leaking out. 'No!' he wept.

'Shhh!' Joseph hushed him, looking over his shoulder at the closed door. 'Then talk, mfana,' he urged. 'If you don't talk, I can't keep you out of jail,' Joseph said, noting with satisfaction the effect this last statement had on the boy.

Mandla sat up straight, wiped his eyes, and cleared his sinuses loudly. 'I think,' he said, hesitantly, 'that the directions were wrong.'

'What do you mean?' Joseph demanded, excitement rising at the unexpected admission.

Mandla's eyes skittered up toward the left corner of the room, and his hand subconsciously snuck towards his lip. 'Nkosi was angry. He was shouting at Bheki. He kept saying the man must have got it wrong.'

'What man? What's his name?' Joseph urged the boy, his voice a little too loud.

Mandla began to cry. 'I don't know,' he cried. 'It sounded like *ucikicane.*'

Joseph frowned. 'Little finger?' he said, looking down at his baby finger. 'Are you sure?'

'No,' whispered the boy. 'But that's what it sounded like.' He began to pick at his lip again, a faraway look in his eyes.

Joseph stood up so quickly that the boy reared back in fright. Mandla looked down at the bloodied strip of skin pinched between two fingertips.

'*Ngiyabonga, mfana,*' Joseph thanked him with a smile, then he left Mandla alone in the room again.

10: Had them eating out of his hand
Three months prior

Jika Jika Tavern held a special place in Lucky Mhlongo's heart. It hadn't changed at all since that first day he'd arrived in Mevamhlope town. It still smelt of spilt beer, cheap perfume, and male sweat. The crack of pool balls and the thump of house music made it difficult for people to listen in, which was perfect for the kinds of conversations that Lucky shared with Samkele, his closest friend. He sat now, waiting for Samkele to arrive so that they could have such a conversation, but the man was late. Lucky was not good at waiting; there were places to go and other people to see. He tapped the bar, signalled for another beer, and then took himself outside, away from the noise and the overpowering smells. He found an empty beer crate to use as a chair under the shade of a large tree. He sat down, pulled his hat low over his eyes, and relaxed against the trunk.

He raised a lazy hand in response to a passing voice calling out a greeting. '*Unjani*, Lucky.'

He smiled; he'd not always been as fortunate as his name implied. He'd had a rough start to life, nearly killing himself and his mother when he arrived unexpectedly. She hadn't made it to Bara Hospital in time and had to pull him out of her by his feet. He'd spent his childhood in a shack in Kliptown, made from corrugated iron, cardboard boxes, and plywood. The '80s in South Africa were difficult years to grow up in, and while twenty or so years had now passed, Lucky could remember it all too clearly. The whoosh of a petrol bomb as it arced through the air, the rise and fall of protesting voices and feet, and the terrifying arrival of police Casspirs to disperse the crowds. Even now, the smell of meat cooking on the open fire behind the tavern brought back the sweet smell of the burning flesh of Baba Nyawo; the father Lucky had never had. He lived next door, watching over Lucky when Mama disappeared for days, leaving Lucky to fend for himself. It was Baba Nyawo who eventually taught Lucky to fight, after he'd come home with another bloody lip, instead of whatever he was meant to have brought back from the spaza shop.

To this day, Lucky could not understand why Baba Nyawo had not fought harder; why he'd let those men drag him out of his yard and into the street and call him a traitor. The men had kicked and punched until Baba Nyawo was on his knees. No sound came from him, even though his mouth was wide open. It was like his voice had decided to run away when his body could not. The men had placed a car tyre, soaked in petrol, around Baba Nyawo's shoulders and arms. While one of the men poured petrol all over Baba Nyawo, another lit a rag and dropped it onto the tyre. The flames danced around the ring of the tyre, then jumped onto Baba Nyawo's shirt, running up to engulf his face and fill his open mouth.

Life was not the same after that. Without Baba Nyawo looking out for him, and Mama spending her nights in the local shebeens, Lucky learnt to look after himself. If he wanted to eat, he had to provide the food. He soon learnt to use his large sad eyes and his small frame, which didn't seem to grow at the same rate as the other boys of his age, to his advantage. His eyes worked very well on large mamas, who could not leave a small crying boy alone in the street, just as night was falling. They would take him by the hand, lead him home, and place a big plate of warm *pap en sous* in front of him. And if he was very lucky, they might add a small piece of boerewors, or a spoonful of mutton curry to go with it. He easily slipped his slight body out of their bedroom windows once he'd pilfered whatever worthwhile item he could find. Of course, he soon learnt that he had to walk the length and breadth of Soweto if he were to carry off his scam successfully. Unfortunately, the mamas talked, and in time, it was he who was taught a lesson, when a large mama with a muscular arm took him home and beat his bum black and blue with a leather belt. After that experience, he was happy to put that scam to bed. Not least because he was filling out nicely from all the good home cooking, and it was no longer easy to slip in and out of tiny windows.

As the years went by, Lucky became a permanent fixture on street corners in Johannesburg, where the passing trade was regular, and no one knew his name or where he came from. From card games to shell-games, and a variety of other tricks, Lucky had them eating out of his hand. He was confident, cocky and he made the crowd believe he was whoever he chose to be that day. Even those who knew he was out to scam them enjoyed the drama of watching Lucky at play. His hands moved like lightning; no matter how hard they tried to determine how he was cheating, they simply could not.

It had been a hot, dry Saturday when Lucky met the man who would change the course of his career. Everyone knew who Joe Cele was, and more importantly, who he worked for. Pastor Ndlovu was a wealthy African healer, although Lucky believed that he did very little healing, but a good amount of thieving. Joe was Pastor Ndlovu's right-hand man, doing most of the pastor's dirty work. Lucky had been surprised, and a little worried, to see Joe standing on the outskirts of the semi-circle that had Lucky tight against the pavement wall. People usually watched for a few minutes then either moved on or placed a bet. Joe just watched; his face expressionless. He was still standing there when Lucky packed away his things, ready to spend some of his winnings on a cold beer.

'Come,' said the big man. It didn't take long for Lucky to make his decision, no one declined a command from Joe Cele. Lucky quickly shouldered his bags and trotted after Joe.

They entered a tavern and Joe headed for a table in the corner. He waited until the beers were placed in front of them, before speaking.

'How's business?' Joe asked.

'Good,' nodded Lucky, choosing to mimic Joe's sparse use of words, until he had some idea of why he was sitting across from Joe.

The big man kept his eyes on Lucky, drained his beer in one long swallow, then thumped his empty beer bottle on the table. Within seconds, a replacement was sweating in front of him.

'I been watching you. Boss's orders,' said Joe, pulling a pack of cigarettes from his shirt pocket. 'The boss needs a new salesman ... he thinks you good for the job.' He lit a cigarette but didn't offer one to

Lucky.

Lucky got the impression that Joe didn't agree with the boss, which had the immediate effect of making him want the job if only to prove Joe wrong.

'Okay,' said Lucky, with a smug grin and upward tilt of his shoulders.

'There are conditions,' Joe said, narrowing his eyes at Lucky. 'You sell only Pastor Ndlovu's products. You sell only in the places, and to the people, Pastor Ndlovu tells you to. You get a basic and 5% commission on what you sell. I do stocktake and money balancing after every trip. No balance – no money – no job. Also, you cheat Pastor Ndlovu, I break your legs, and maybe some other things. Got it?' he demanded, smacking his fist on the table.

'Got it,' Lucky said, his hand stretched out in agreement.

Those had been great days, Lucky remembered. He was nineteen, making more money than he'd ever dreamed of. He rented a clean room in a good hostel. He had a smart suit, and a travel bag filled with his boss's best 'cure' for that disease that nobody wanted, but few could seem to avoid.

Lucky had stuck to the rural communities, where HIV infections were high, and education was low. On pension and social grant days, and community meetings, Lucky made sure that he was there. Although he was told where to go and given what to sell, he could apply artistic licence to sell it to his potential customers. And selling creatively was required. Because this 'cure' was nothing more than an herbal mixture, no different to anything they could put together in their own kitchens. But they came in their hundreds, and Lucky drew on his inner actor, to convince them of exactly how powerful it was.

'Look!' he'd shout into the crowd, waving about two pieces of paper. 'This here!' he'd yell, holding up a page, 'is my first CD4 count certificate, when I was diagnosed with HIV. Thirty-six! Thirty-six! I should have been dead!' The crowd would gasp in disbelief. 'And this,' he'd exclaim, the second paper held high, 'is my last CD4 count – after taking this muthi – over one thousand! One thousand! I have been healed!'

Lucky would dance up and down the stage, knees and fists pumping to the sound of their applause. He could still see the crowds. Hear the roar of expectation, for the hope that he'd created. How he missed those crowds. They made him believe that he was a god!

'Just look at him!' they'd shout to one another. 'So healthy! So alive!'

And money would be exchanged, hand over fist, for those useless bottles of brown water. And it would work! That first week, people would genuinely feel better. But a few days after Lucky had zipped up his empty travel bags, and hopped on a taxi to take him home, he knew that the tiredness and the ill health would return.

But as Pastor Ndlovu had trained him to say: *all true healing requires faith*. If the muthi didn't work, the blame should be placed squarely on the shoulders of those with little faith.

It had been fun in the beginning, exciting and new. But soon Lucky had begun to question whether his role in the working relationship was not in fact greater than that of Pastor Ndlovu, because, without Lucky, and his ability to lure the desperate and gullible, there would be no sales and no income for Pastor Ndlovu. Lucky knew that he was one of the highest earners, selling far more than any other salesman had before him, and he wanted to be recognised for it. When he'd approached Joe Cele about an increase in his commission, the big man's eyes had glazed over, effectively removing Lucky from his sight.

'Never ask that again,' he said, dropping his cigarette butt onto the floor to squash it beneath his heel.

They'd gone their separate ways, and by the time he reached home, Lucky had a plan and he began to implement it immediately.

During the time between the city falling asleep and waking up, Lucky set about making his concoctions. It was a simple process done on his one ring stove, and by the time the birds were twittering, Lucky had his first batch of healing water, bottled and ready for the next trip. He was not so stupid as to think he could sell them alongside Pastor Ndlovu's product. He travelled to the predetermined site and spent the day selling everything belonging to the Pastor. He gave it the same amount of effort as he usually did because it was still his bread and butter. But the next day, he took himself off to another small town and plied his trade there. He left the town with money in his pocket, and a future mapped out; one that would bring him true wealth and happiness. Although he could laugh about it now, it had not been at all amusing when he figured out that Joe was on to him, and ready to follow through with his threat.

On what turned out to be Lucky's last trip, he later figured out that Joe must have planted a few actors of his own in the crowd. As Lucky worked himself up into a righteous frenzy, much like one of those fundamentalist preachers at the prosperity churches downtown, the actors began to hiss. 'Liar! Tsotsi!'

At first, Lucky pretended not to hear them, but as the jeers grew louder, and his voice began to falter, he realised that the crowd had turned. Hopeful faces became hard and murmurings became howls of 'Thief!' and 'Murderer!' Lucky knew that he had only one chance to escape the increasingly hostile crowd, so he took aim at the closest opponent, a man with a dancing *knobkerrie*. He threw the open bottle of muthi at the man's head and leapt from his beer crate. He ran as fast as he could down the dusty street, with a band of furious community members, hot on his heels. Lucky had witnessed his fair share of public retribution at kangaroo courts, and in his experience, stones were thrown first, and questions asked after. As the crowd was closing in on him, Lucky launched himself onto the back of a bakkie pulling out from the pavement, and he was saved from a certain beating.

As the bakkie picked up speed, and the crowd grew smaller, Lucky thought that he glimpsed the large figure of Joe, arms folded, watching as Lucky was ferried off into the distance. He knew without a doubt that he could not go back to his flat in Johannesburg, nor show his face in the city again for a very long time. So, he rode in that bakkie for as long as he could, and then jumped out when it passed through the town of Nelspruit. From here he considered his options. The first was to continue up towards the Kruger National Park, and make his way into Mozambique, or head down towards the coast and experience the Zulu Kingdom. Since he had a few friends in KwaZulu-Natal, he decided on the latter; hitchhiking and walking, until he came to the small town of Mevamhlope, where his friend Samkele waited.

***

Something kicked at Lucky's foot, and he pulled the hat from over his eyes. Samkele stood above him, holding out two quarts of ice-cold Black Label, a peace offering for his poor sense of timekeeping.

11: He wanted to be a boss
Two years prior

When Lucky had first arrived in Mevamhlope, he had only the clothes in his suitcase, and the money he'd collected selling his fake medicines. But he had a friend and somewhere to stay, and quite soon he was making a little bit of cash to tide him over. Samkele, who turned out to be a fellow entrepreneur, had hit on the somewhat successful business of plant 'collecting'. His grandfather, an inyanga who had moved to Durban many moons ago, would moan about the lack of access to the plants he needed for his herbal muthi. He'd have to travel back to Mevamhlope especially to collect his ingredients because he didn't trust the tsotsis down in Durban. They claimed to sell pure ginger root, when any inyanga worth his reputation, could smell it was some inferior mixed blend.

'Yoh!' laughed Samkele. 'My grandfather could moan! I thought it would stop when I agreed to help him … but yoh, he just moaned even more. I followed that man up and down those mountains looking for plants, and he moaned the whole way.'

When Lucky met up with Samkele, he had taken over from his grandfather, when arthritis made the old man's hands and fingers thick and gnarled. He had finally given in to the pain and agreed that he'd taught Samkele everything he needed to know.

Samkele's business had grown to include numerous other izinyanga, and Lucky had agreed, with relief, to Samkele's offer of a job. Lucky's knowledge of plants grew, along with his knowledge of the area and the people. Eventually, Lucky was travelling further afield, making trips in and out of Mozambique to source plants that had been over-harvested in Zululand, or didn't grow in the region.

Lucky first heard about rhino poaching late one hot and humid night. After receiving a rather healthy sum of money from Samkele, the two men went down to Jika Jika Tavern, to celebrate. A trio at the bar, wearing brightly coloured pantsula hats swathed in cigarette smoke, were also celebrating their recent windfall. Lucky couldn't help but overhear one of the men, who was entertaining the group (which included two scantily dressed women), with a story that required the waving of arms, crouching, imaginary bullet-firing, and running on the spot. The others roared with laughter, as they downed quart bottles of beer, and shoveled thick wedges of juicy meat into their gaping mouths.

Lucky nudged Samkele, with a look in their direction, 'What's up with them?' he asked, saliva glands working overtime at the smell of a *braai*, and the lip-smacking sounds that wafted his way.

'Poachers,' said Samkele, with a look of disdain. 'Must have had a good trip.'

'Poaching what?' asked Lucky, in confusion. The odd impala or nyala buck would fill a good number of stomachs but wouldn't make a man rich.

Samkele hunched low over his beer. 'Rhino horn,' he whispered.

Lucky almost spat out his beer. 'Are you serious? Rhino poachers, here, in KZN?' The revelation had an immediate effect on Lucky. Only someone with huge balls would do something so dangerous. Lucky thought for a bit; there was no way those three guys at the bar, meat juices staining their shirts, eyes bloodshot from too many quarts, had come up with this on their own. 'Who's the boss?' he asked.

Samkele beckoned his friend in again. 'I'm only telling you what I've heard. Guys like them,' he swung his head in their direction, 'talk a lot. They think they're the big boys in town now. Home to show off to their childhood friends, before they head back again. They're based up at Kruger; there's a village there that hides poachers, for a little something in return. Those three are part of a poaching ring. They say there's more rhino than fleas on a dog's back in Kruger, so who's going to miss a couple, right?'

He lifted the bottle to his mouth but found that it was empty. He wagged it in the direction of the barman, then continued. 'Two of them got recruited by some boss up in Kruger. One of them was a security guard at the park, and the other was working on a nearby farm. The security guard got his younger brother to leave his job at the petrol station in town here to join them. If you believe them, all three make more money on one successful hunt than they'd make in a year as a security guard, or filling tanks at the station.'

Lucky whistled long and low. 'Why,' he asked with urgency, 'are we playing around with plants if we could be retiring on horn?'

Samkele laughed and slapped Lucky on the back. 'Because, my friend, I'm not stupid.'

Lucky was incredulous. 'Stupid! They don't look stupid to me!'

'Lucky,' said Samkele, his face suddenly hard, and his voice serious. 'From what I hear, rhino poachers don't live for very long. And those that do survive, forget to do anything good with all the money they make.' He shot the men a look of disgust. 'Look at them ... drunk and high. Telling everyone at the bar how they got their money. They'll either get shot in the bush, or by the boss, for talking too much. If they live, eventually they'll go back to being what they always were; poor and useless.'

Lucky sat back, tapping his empty bottle on the bar counter. He didn't think he'd ever heard his friend give such a lengthy speech. He'd made some interesting points; points Lucky was certain he could exploit.

'So, no rhino poaching for us then?' Lucky said, his eyes on the men.

'No,' said Samkele, ending the conversation by thumping a fist on the bar to get the barman's attention.

Their conversation might have ended, but Lucky continued to think about it. He sat with his beer and made himself a promise. If ever he became a rhino poacher, he would make sure it would be short-lived. Because Lucky had decided that he didn't want to be a poacher, he wanted to be a boss.

When Samkele had signaled home time, Lucky decided to stay on longer. He'd been making eyes at one of the prostitutes, who kept shooting pointed looks, in his direction. He decided that Samkele would forgive him for choosing a bit of action with her, instead of walking home together. She'd been sitting near to the raucous trio, and as Samkele got up to leave, Lucky slid himself and his beer, over to her. In truth, she was of no interest to him. It was the men he wanted to get to know, so he ordered a round and within seconds, he was welcomed into their happy, drunken space, and the snake oil charmer within ensured that he bid them farewell with a strategy to secure his financial freedom.

***

A month later, Lucky wandered the crowded and musky smelling passageways of Xipamanine market in Maputo. He stocked up on plants and other items requested by the izinyanga, while seeking out the sellers of ivory trinkets and animal products. He wasn't looking to buy; he wanted a contact. Lucky knew that none of them would willingly offer up information to an inquisitive unknown asking sensitive questions about rhino horn. He also knew that asking questions drew attention to himself. So, he was pleased when, mid-morning on the second day, he felt himself lift off the floor and float momentarily until the chaos of bodies and stock in the passageways, forced his unexpected minders to alternatively drag and push him through the confusion to their destination.

The room was murky, its corners lit up by table lamps covered in gauzy pink material. It looked more like a hooker's bedroom than the headquarters of an experienced wildlife trafficker. The man was enormous, his legs stretched out from under his desk, baby blue shoes of the softest leather almost touching Lucky's quivering feet. His upper body was encased in a lemon-yellow golf shirt, and with every twitch of his chest muscles, a small green crocodile leapt, as if attempting to snatch its prey out the air. Lucky looked in fascination at the skin on the man's face. It seemed to ripple; rising and dipping as the light fell on it from various angles. The tattoos against his dark skin were just visible in the low light.

'It is the mark of my people,' said the man, at the look of undisguised interest on Lucky's face. 'My father, he was a FRELIMO fighter. A great man! He died forcing the Portuguese out of *our* country.' He picked up his crystal glass next to him and took a dainty sip.

'It took me twenty years to find *mpundi wa dinembo*, who would copy the markings of my father's face onto my own.' He lifted a hand to his face and gently rubbed a finger against his cheek.

'But,' he said, dropping his hand. 'You are not here to talk about my face.'

His long, tapered, fingers curled around a gun that lay on the table before him. Lucky, unnerved by the sudden silence, fought with himself to keep his mouth shut. The slow on-off flicker of the whites of the man's eyes, and the occasional leaping crocodile, were the only indication that something alive occupied the seat. Finally, he spoke.

'This is Bento's territory, *my* territory,' he growled, tapping a finger on his broad chest. 'It upsets me when I hear that skinny little nobodies are asking awkward questions about my work, right in the middle of my territory.'

The man see-sawed the gun so that the muzzle and the handgrip alternatively tapped against the wood of the desk. 'Why are you asking questions, when no one invited you to speak?' he asked, raising the gun to point between Lucky's eyes.

Lucky, whose throat was drier than the White Imfolozi River, gave himself a brief mental talking-to. He had one chance to sell himself, and if successful, he would probably only get one chance to prove himself. He channeled his inner salesman, toning down the charm, and focused on the facts of the deal.

'I also have a territory,' he said, licking his lips. 'And in my territory, I have a lot of what you want.'

Lucky shifted his eyes to the impossibly large head of a rhino, protruding from the wall to the right of Bento. He felt his stomach fizz with fear; he'd never seen a rhino in his life, and it was a lot larger than he'd expected. If one were to judge the size of a rhino by the size of its head, he did not want to be the one who faced it on a dark Zululand night.

Bento laughed. 'You are a cheeky little Zulu boy.' His laugh started low, like thunder in the far distance. He turned to look at the head on the wall behind him, and laughter blossomed into the room and touched the men standing behind Lucky. They too began to laugh, and in response to some invisible sign, one of them pulled the chair out from in front of Lucky and sat him down with a thud.

'What makes you think I don't already have a supplier on that side?'

Bento asked as if baffled by such a ridiculous idea.

'Of course,' said Lucky, eyes bright with anticipation. 'I have heard that you are a great businessman, one who is not afraid to take risks. So many people up by Kruger are taking advantage, but so few down in KwaZulu ... there is freedom to operate there,' he said, giving Bento his most winning smile.

Bento sat back in his chair and clicked his fingers. One of the men placed a silver tray on the boss's desk. Bento picked up the bottle of Johnny Walker Blue and poured another two fingers into his crystal glass. He tapped the glass against his chin before taking a sip.

'Go on,' he said, finally. 'I'm listening.'

By the time Lucky had made his way back over the border into South Africa, some three days later, he had his first commission. All he needed was to source a competent team, a gun and a hacksaw, a getaway vehicle, and someone on the inside who could dispense with some much-needed information. It couldn't be easier!

12: A pall of betrayal
30th November 2012

Nonhle loved Fridays at the lodge; they were always busy with activity and energy. While weekdays mostly catered to international guests, weekends saw local guests arrive for a quick break in the bush. There was nothing quite like a G&T in hand while watching the sun bow to the presence of the moon. However, today felt different. There was a sense of urgency, hushed voices, and worried looks darting between the staff. She'd been surprised to see her father in the parking lot that morning, when she arrived, rather than out on his first game drive. He was talking to a colleague, the topic of conversation, evidently upsetting to them both. Then she'd noticed that all the game vehicles were parked in their bays, not only his.

As she'd walked behind the reception desk, Sizah had grabbed her by the hand and hurried her into the staff kitchen. Sizah, who was known for her fondness for consuming copious cups of tea, given any opportunity, failed to seize the moment in the kitchen. Instead, in disbelief, tinged with excitement, she launched into a tale about the events of the night before. Three men had breached the fence line in search of a rhino, and the anti-poaching unit had intercepted them on the way out of the reserve. Although no fresh rhino horn had been found on the men, the rangers had fanned out over the reserve in search of a carcass. There was still a possibility that a rhino had been shot, and for some reason, the poachers hadn't been able to separate it from its horn. They were all anxiously waiting for more news.

'And, that's all I know,' huffed Sizah. 'They've gone all hush-hush, for 'certain ears' only. I was trying to listen in on the radio, but Mr Müller came in and took it out of the reception area. Doesn't want the guests to get upset.'

She threw up her hands in irritation. 'I mean come on! The foreign guests can't even understand anyway. It's always a mix of Afrikaans and Zulu on the radio!'

Nonhle was desperate to find her father, but she knew that he was unlikely to share any confidential information. Samson Ngubane did things by the book, and while she was mostly glad about that, it was intensely annoying on a day like today. Instead, she busied herself with sorting out the guest information sheets and room keys, as well as making sure that special requirements and requests were relayed to the relevant departments. She fielded phone calls and turned down several last-minute enquiries about whether the lodge had any available accommodation for the weekend.

At eleven a.m., feeling deserving of a break, she made her way to the restaurant where Mama would be preparing the tables for lunch.

***

A little after eleven a.m., a police van pulled up into the parking lot of The Last Outpost, its heavy wheels gouging a path through the gravel. Karel jumped out, and, not bothering to wait for Detective Joseph Dlamini, strode up to the reception desk where rows of orange juice were laid out for arriving guests. He grabbed one of the glasses and downed it in one long swallow.

With a lip-smacking, *aaaah*, he gestured to Joseph as he walked in. 'Want one? Nice and cold. *Lekker!*' He placed his glass on the desk and was greeted by the unimpressed face of the woman behind reception.

'Can I assist you, officer?' asked Sizah, coolly.

'It's *Detective* du Randt,' he corrected. 'I'm here to see Mr McKenzie. It's very important. *Shesha, manje,*' he commanded, shooing her with a flick of his hands.

She pursed her lips and gave him a withering stare. 'Which Mr McKenzie,' she asked, slowly.

Karel, reaching for a second glass of juice, met her irritation with his own. 'The boss, of course. Who do you think!'

'Unfortunately, *that* Mr McKenzie is away.'

Karel and Sizah eyeballed each other. 'Well then, get me Thomas,' he said through gritted teeth.

Sizah looked at him brightly. 'Thomas is in the reserve at present. He'll be back later this afternoon.'

Before Karel could tell her exactly what would happen if she continued to obstruct police business, Sizah smiled sweetly.

'I'll call the General Manager, Mr Müller, for you,' she said, turning her back on him to reach for the phone.

Karel stomped over to Joseph, who had chosen to remove himself from the awkward scene. Karel knew Dutch Müller well and he was relieved he'd have someone with two brain cells to rub together to deal with. Karel and Joseph watched as three rangers came in out of the blistering heat. The two younger men laughed as they strode towards the reception. Their shorts, far too short in Karel's opinion, displayed long sturdy legs in even sturdier-looking ankle boots. Slowly, bringing up the rear, was an older ranger, in his early fifties.

One of the young men bent over briefly as his shoulders jiggled with mirth. Karel moved in closer, ears straining. The man, struggling to continue with his story, finally composed himself.

'So,' he said, wiping his eyes. 'Just before my mate stopped at the old rhino bones, a guest saw some rhino skin in the grass. And …' the ranger bent over to grab his knees, as another wave of laughter hit him. 'The guy says … I didn't know that rhino shed its skin!'

His friend let out a bellow of appreciation. 'Had to be Americans!' he crowed. 'They can be so stupid!'

Behind them, the older ranger coughed subtly. A group of guests, eager for their afternoon game drive, had arrived early. They stood in an awkward huddle. The two rangers looked crestfallen, their cheeks pink with shame.

No tips for you two idiots, thought Karel, shaking his head.

The older ranger walked towards his guests and invited them to move away from the others. He was quiet and professional, greeting each guest by name, welcoming them to the afternoon drive. As he spoke, the thumb of one hand gently rubbed the little finger on his other hand. Then, his hands rose into the air as he explained an important point to the group.

Karel heard Joseph's sharp intake of breath, then felt a sharp jab to his ribs.

'*Eina!*' he shouted. 'What was that for?'

'Look at his finger,' Joseph hissed.

'Whose finger?' Karel said, through clenched teeth.

'The older man … look at the little finger on his right hand. I saw it when he started talking with his hands.'

Karel's brow furrowed as he took in the shortened finger, a bald nub where the top of the finger should have been. Comprehension quickly dawned as he made the connection between the code name, ucikicane, and the man's finger. For some reason, a partly amputated baby finger was the last thing he had expected to see. He'd assumed it might have something to do with a person's fondness for breaking or amputating fingers, if he didn't get what he wanted, immediately.

Before Karel could move towards the game ranger, Dutch appeared. 'Gentlemen,' he said, with a hopeful smile. 'I trust you have … promising news?'

Dutch Müller was a short man, with a noticeable German accent, which years of working in Africa had not managed to water down.

Karel grabbed Dutch by the arm and trotted him toward the parking lot.

'Dutch, quick man,' he said, pointing in the direction the ranger who was still addressing his group. 'How long's he been working here for?'

Dutch crossed his arms as he thought about the question. 'Samson Ngubane? Long before my time – 25 years at least. He's Mr McKenzie's number one ranger.'

'Is that so,' said Karel. The thought of such blatant disloyalty made him see red. 'Well, Mr McKenzie's going to be a bit disappointed then.'

'I don't understand,' said Dutch, concern pulling his near-white eyebrows towards each other.

Karel looked down the barrel of his sun-reddened nose at the GM. 'It looks, my friend, like your number one ranger, might not be playing on your team anymore.'

Dutch pulled his arm out of Karel's grasp, and rose to his full height, as Karel's implication hit home. Karel noticed that even when angry, the top of Dutch's head still did not reach past Karel's shoulder.

'Don't be ridiculous, Karel. The man is invaluable. Mr McKenzie would never believe that. *None of us* believe that.'

'Tough,' said Karel, ignoring such sentimental drivel. He knew the staff would be the first to turn on Samson if he was guilty. *I told you I didn't trust him!* would ring out from every quarter. 'Which one is Samson's vehicle? I want to search it.'

'Now?' demanded Dutch. 'But he's about to take our guests out!'

'Now!' Friend's be damned, Karel would not allow Dutch to delay his investigation. 'Get someone else to take his guests. Until we sort this out, he's not allowed into the reserve at all.'

Dutch nodded with resignation and walked quickly back to reception. Joseph, who'd been watching the exchange between the two men, shook his head.

'Eish, I missed it.'

'Missed what?'

'*Ngubane.* When we looked through the list of employees, I saw the surname Ngubane there. I just didn't make the connection when I heard the name ucikicane.'

'I don't get it,' said Karel, wondering which vehicle belonged to Samson. 'What the hell does the name Ngubane have to do with a finger?'

Joseph turned so that Karel had no choice but to give him his full attention. 'It's important, Karel, because many Ngubanes of Samson's age have a piece of their small finger missing. After the baby is born, part of the finger is chopped off.'

'*Sis,*' said Karel, lips revealing a grimace of disgust. 'That's barbaric man. Who would do such a thing to a child?' He shook his head and walked away. *Why were these people so cruel?*

Once Dutch had handed the guests over to another ranger, Karel, Joseph, Dutch and Samson stood looking at Samson's game vehicle. Dutch was explaining, with great apology to Samson that due to some mix-up, his vehicle needed to be searched.

He's a cheeky one, thought Karel, as Samson agreed without hesitation to the request.

'Don't bladdy apologise,' Karel huffed at Dutch. 'This guy could be the reason we're running out of rhino in this bladdy country.'

Joseph and Karel had snapped on latex gloves and were rummaging through the cubby, looking under seats and pulling up rubber floor mats. Karel had his flashlight out and was peering into every dark corner he could find.

'What are you looking for,' asked Dutch.

'Won't know until I find it,' mumbled Karel, his head stuck between the driver and the passenger seats. Actually, he had a very good idea of what he was looking for. Something small and plastic. He stuck his face as low as it could go, running the light along the tracks revealed by the seat he'd pushed back. Bingo. There she was; a SIM card. According to Mandla, the youngest poacher, Nkosi had received an SMS with the coordinates of the rhino's location, a few hours before they entered the reserve. Which meant someone on the inside had to have given the information to them. And that person was looking very much like Samson Ngubane. The man was an idiot. He should have eaten it or crushed it with a rock. Karel gently plucked the card from its resting place and raised his head. He held the card up between thumb and forefinger, waving it in the air.

'Joseph,' he said grimly, looking at Samson who had done a good job mastering an expression of utter incomprehension. 'Cuff him. We need to have a little chat.'

***

Her father, handcuffed between two policemen, was the sight that greeted Nonhle as she ran up to reception from the boma. Sizah had called the restaurant and told her to hurry, but advised her to say nothing, and leave Thuli behind. As she ran to catch up with her father, Dutch grabbed her by the arm.

'Hey!' she shouted, twisting to get out of his grasp. 'What's going on?'

Dutch pulled her towards him. 'Nonhle, please. Let him go.'

'I don't understand,' she cried. 'Why's he in handcuffs?'

Dutch, usually so brisk and professional, seemed to melt into the leather sofa behind him. She'd never see Dutch sit on the sofa, while on duty, and she felt a coldness spread through her. 'What's going on, Mr Müller?' she whispered.

'Your father, Nonhle, has been arrested ... for poaching.'

***

News had travelled quickly along the stone pathways, from the mouth of the gardener to the ear of a cleaner, who passed on the scandalous news to the chef and two waitresses. A pall of betrayal hung in the air, swirling through the aloes and the fever trees, coming to rest thickly in the reception area. Nonhle could not bring herself to look in Sizah's direction as she stalked passed the front desk, refusing to show any sign of guilt or defeat, but she caught the reflection of her friend in the mirror hanging on the wall across from the desk – her face rigid with shock.

Nonhle had fetched Mama, who seemed to have shrunk with the news. Nonhle had to support her as they walked through the lodge and into the parking lot. Nonhle's heart, beat with such severity, that she had to press her hand to her chest to relieve the pain. She surveyed the parking lot. She'd hoped that it would be empty, the engine of the staff vehicle running, ready to ferry Mama and herself out of the yard. Instead, a small crowd of game rangers was gathered in front of a row of game vehicles, their voices raised in angry discussion. They were so engrossed in their conversation that Nonhle felt hopeful of an unseen getaway. But at the sound of their footsteps, the group turned, and nudging elbows alerted the others to their presence. Her insides liquefied; a bubbling soup of panic and shame rose within her until she thought that it might burst like a dam and drench the row of khaki-clad hostility in front of her. There wasn't a face that showed a sign of disbelief in the accusations against Baba. As she turned to lead Mama to the vehicle, a phlegmy wad of spit landed at her feet.

She'd managed to get Mama into the vehicle without stumbling. The door slammed shut and took them away from the only other place that her parents considered home. The vehicle rocked and swayed its way down the dusty road, and the dense green bush formed a living wall. Nonhle and Thuli sat side by side. Their long thin fingers intertwined in a complicated knot of mutual devastation. They had to halt at the main gate while the guard signed in another vehicle: a Land Cruiser. As it passed by, she saw Senzo Mdletshe, his face grim.

***

That evening, back at the police station, Karel sat with his head in his hands. He was exhausted, frustrated, and furious after what had turned out to be a completely uninformative questioning session with Samson Ngubane. Karel had given the man plenty of time to sweat it out in the airless room, before marching in and slamming the door behind him. Before Karel had begun questioning Samson, he'd done a bit of research on the ranger, looking into his background at The Last Outpost, as well as his character. If he turned out to be innocent, there was no doubt in Karel's mind that the man would be sainted upon his death. From William McKenzie, the lodge owner, down to the gardener, not one person had anything bad to say about him. Yes, some of the other game rangers had been aggressive in the parking lot, all talk and bravado, but that had been an immediate reaction to something far too close to home.

Once the testosterone and anger had died down, a truer account of Samson had emerged. Karel would need hard evidence to tie the man to the case because a dubious character reference was not forthcoming. They hadn't bothered sending the SIM for fingerprint analysis because there weren't any on it. Joseph had gone to the local stores to check whether Samson was owing anything on layby, or if he had a loan out with one of the local loan sharks. The ranger had come up clean there too, and Karel knew that a foreign benefactor was paying Nonhle's university fees. Samson wasn't in debt, and according to friends and colleagues, he was the last person on earth likely to be involved in poaching of any kind.

But Karel knew that even the nicest of people could be pushed to do something out of character. *What*, he wondered, *had pushed Samson Ngubane to this point?*

13: What's dead, is dead
Three months prior

Once Mthunzi was confident that he'd sent Zodwa Shezi lumbering back down the mountain, certain in the knowledge that he had a plan for her desire for revenge, he could barely contain himself. Her timing could not have been more perfect. He was so pleased that he decided a visit to his old friend, her uncle, was in order. It was unwise of him, but the visit would help him to prepare better for the plan he was laying, for Zodwa to fulfil.

Mthunzi took his time dressing up in his finest traditional attire; he wanted to make a grand entrance when he arrived at the man's home. He had not seen his old friend in many years, and he wished to show him how well he'd done – despite the man's great betrayal. Mthunzi looked down at his belly, which had changed shape markedly over the years. He was proud of the way the fabric of his shirt strained against the roundness of his belly. Now that he no longer had to go in search of plants for muthi himself, Mthunzi's lean body had turned to fat. He walked the last hundred metres towards his destination, having made the hired driver drop him around the bend.

At the sound of heavy breathing and dragging feet, Mthunzi stopped, turning to glare at the figure behind him. 'MaNoxolo, I said you could stay at home, or better yet, take the shape of a bird. You could be flying right now, instead of huffing and puffing your way in this heat.'

'Mthunzi, if you do not hold your tongue, I will turn you into a snake. Then you can slither all the way there on your belly,' she retorted, in a fit of rare annoyance. 'You will not look so regal with red dust running like a road down the front of your body.'

Mthunzi was rendered speechless at her outburst; it was so unlike MaNoxolo. With the rebuke ringing in his ears, Mthunzi continued walking. He could see the houses ahead of him. His hand automatically patted his bag of bones, and he did a quick mental visualisation of what the bag on his back contained. Apart from wanting to see his friend and commit to memory the happy home life, which would shortly be a distant memory, his main intention was to portray himself as a forgiving friend, and healer of the seemingly unfixable. For what true healer could ignore the visions of the ancestors and fail to warn his childhood friend of his impending downfall. And if the man was so inclined, Mthunzi would be honoured to determine, and then revoke, the terrible curse that had been placed upon the man and his wife. Mthunzi chuckled with glee at the thought of the self-righteous so-and-so trembling with awe and gratitude.

As Mthunzi walked through the gates, the spectacular sunset suffused the sky in liquid rose gold, and the smell of cooking made his stomach grumble. As he passed the various dwellings, a few curious faces poked out of doorways, no doubt wondering why someone nearby might need the services of a traditional healer.

Finally, he reached the correct household. He looked through the kitchen window, just as the familiar face looked out. He held up a hand to wave, but she disappeared before she could see it. Then, she was back and Mthunzi felt his heart contract as Samson Ngubane, his once dearest friend, peered out at him. He felt his confidence leave him as Samson registered his presence. His old friend did not look happy to see him. But then, the door opened and the man, who had caused him so much pain and inconvenience, stood strong and at ease in the doorway of his home.

Mthunzi was shocked at how quickly those feelings of betrayal overwhelmed him. He felt both vulnerable and powerless, like a small boy who'd just been caught red-handed. He did his best to control his emotions, continuing up the path until he came to stand at the foot of the stairs. The scene briefly threw Mthunzi; this was not at all what he had envisioned. Although only a few stairs led up into the kitchen, Samson was standing above him, so Mthunzi's much imagined grand entrance fell somewhat flat. Samson looked down at him, and Mthunzi felt rather like a servant meeting his master.

An awkward silence filled the small kitchen as the three humans – and the unseen guests – stood around looking at one another. Words seemed to elude them all until Samson coughed gently, and Thuli – as if awoken from slumber – offered Mthunzi a cup of tea. Kitchen chairs were pulled out, and once the tea tray was placed on the table, Thuli left the room to give the two men some privacy. Mthunzi was disappointed; he'd hoped to spend time in Thuli's presence, excited to determine how much both would be affected in the coming weeks. MaNoxolo and Mzamo chose to remain with Mthunzi in the kitchen, while Zenzile followed Thuli; her small frame drifted out the kitchen door and down the stairs. She came to rest at Thuli's side as a light gust of wind, causing Thuli's skirt to dance a small jig of surprise before it settled against her legs.

Back in the kitchen, Mthunzi placed his large hands around the mug of tea and stared into its depths. 'I know you are surprised to see me, my friend, but I have something that I must share with you.' He sighed deeply before continuing. 'Not even the great betrayal could stop me from doing so.'

Samson laughed softly with a shake of his head. 'The great betrayal? Mthunzi, come now. Do you still believe you were right in your actions?'

It took all Mthunzi's willpower not to defend himself against Samson's righteousness. Instead, he smiled boyishly. 'Let us not dwell on days gone by. I thought perhaps we could forget the past, as it cannot change. *Isilo asithintwa.*'

'No, it cannot – what's dead, is dead,' said Samson with meaning.

'Indeed,' Mthunzi countered, with determination. 'I am willing to put aside our differences, more so because the ancestors have called on me. I am here on their mission.'

'The ancestors?' said Samson; his clasped hands opening briefly, inviting an answer.

'Come now, brother,' Mthunzi responded, his brow knitting at Samson's strange tone. 'The ancestors have spoken, they assured me that it is my duty to help you, to save you, despite …' he said, shrugging because words were surely not necessary.

Samson leant back in his chair, the tension on his face replaced by something akin to ... Mthunzi struggled to place it. Was it peace?

'Mthunzi,' Samson said, firmly. 'I was saved a long time ago. I do not need your ancestors to do it for me now.'

Mthunzi frowned. *Your* ancestors? *Your?* Then it dawned on him, and Mthunzi felt a cold wind travel the length of his spine. Surely, by now, Samson had given up on that nonsense. He watched MaNoxolo and Mzamo touch briefly in a rare moment of solidarity, then part as they recalled their differences. Mthunzi knew very few Zulu men, especially from rural areas, who had converted to Christianity and turned their backs completely on their culture. Women, yes; he had personal experience of that, but not men. Everyone knew it was wise to keep your options open. A white god was good for some things. But what could a white god possibly know of things related to Zulu culture?

Mthunzi – desperate to regain control of the conversation – sat up in his chair; an air of authority settling over him. He chose to ignore Samson's revelation and continued with his tale. He moved his head a little, causing the beads at the end of each braid to rattle slightly, and closed his eyes.

'Two nights ago, the ancestors showed me your future. I had a vision of this house, and of all who have lived in it. Over the house hovered a rain cloud, so full of water it sat black and heavy, touching the roof in some places. But when it rained, the cloud released the feathers of a black chicken, which fell to the ground. They landed in great circles around the house. The feathers rose and fell, rose and fell, with the earth's breathing.' Mthunzi opened one eye a fraction and peeked at Samson; to his consternation, not a line of concern marred the man's face. Mthunzi lowered his eyelid quickly and cleared his throat.

'I felt that there was a familiar yet foreign presence around the house. I could feel it but could not see it. I knew immediately that it was someone you knew, but no longer had a relationship with. Once the dream left me, I threw the bones, and the truth lay in front of me.' Mthunzi paused for effect, hands clasped as if in urgent prayer. His eyes sprung open and locked with Samson's. 'My friend!' he cried. 'Someone has bewitched you. They are out to destroy you.'

Mthunzi reached across the expanse of wood between them. 'That is why I am here. To help you; to undo what is yet to be done, because the umthakathi walks close by and will not stop until you are done.'

If she had been in the room, Mthunzi knew that his smallest ancestor would have clapped at his theatrics. Mthunzi was a fantastic actor, a skill he'd perfected in his early years when working with particularly uninteresting clients, who demanded a show for undeserving personal problems.

Finally! Mthunzi felt delighted at the surprise that registered on Samson's face. This was a good sign. He knew in his heart that Samson had not fully turned away from his culture.

'I think,' said Samson, slowly, 'that my wife should be here.' He rose from the table and went to join Thuli outside.

Mthunzi sat on his hands, unable to tame the feeling of glee exhibiting itself across his entire being. He would take a private walk around the property to determine where the umthakathi had hidden muthi on the property. Of course, he would find the numerous offending items he'd brought with him; items that would truly strike fear into the very foundation of the Ngubane household. He didn't care what god Samson served; signs of witchcraft had the same effect on everyone.

Soon Mthunzi began to fidget. They were taking an overly long time. He stood up from the table to go and investigate, poking his head out the kitchen door. His body connected with Zenzile, who came flying up the stairs, and dove straight through him. The thunderous look on her wizened little face made Mthunzi's chest constrict with anxiety.

Then, Samson and Thuli stood hand-in-hand before him. Thuli's free hand rose to curl around a small crucifix on a chain hanging from her neck. Samson cleared his throat and gestured towards his wife.

'We've discussed it, Mthunzi. Thank you for your offer, but we must decline. If there's a curse on us, our God will remove it.'

Mthunzi, in the process of swallowing the excess saliva that his nerves were producing, almost choked on his spit. A fit of coughing followed as he struggled to pull himself together. The last part of this visit needed to take place – his plan depended on it!

'Please,' he said, hurrying around the table to grasp Samson's elbow. 'Please, then let me help you bring your god's attention to the problem.

Let me find the items that have been cursed. Then you can put them before him when you pray for protection.'

By this point, Zenzile and Mzamo had moved to stand behind Samson and Thuli. Mthunzi breathed out as he saw them nod their heads in agreement, pleased with Mthunzi's quick thinking. To Mthunzi's great relief, Samson and Thuli shared a look, then Samson tilted his head towards Mthunzi.

While the Ngubanes waited inside, Mthunzi marched around the yard, poking his head under bushes and into crevices, lifting breezeblocks and dislodging a pile of stacked wood. At every potential hiding place, he'd quickly glance over his shoulder to check that the Ngubanes were not looking, then pretend to retrieve a hidden item. Under a red brick, near the front door, he 'discovered' a coin. He carried it, along with the other items in his bag, into the house. It was an inconspicuous coin resting on a fold of fabric. He reminded them of the practice known as *umbhulelo*. The umthakathi had rubbed the coin in bad muthi, which would either kill or make the person who picked it up, very sick.

With each item that Mthunzi revealed to the Ngubanes, Samson would murmur. 'Do not worry, *Unkulunkulu uzokusiza*. Jesus will make it right.'

Mthunzi frowned but ploughed on. 'You must be careful,' he implored. He told them he couldn't yet be sure which family member the witch was trying to target, but Mthunzi kept his eyes firmly on Thuli as each item came to light. Then, with great ceremony, he placed a small doll-like figure on the kitchen table. It was crudely made from black fabric, and a string of pink plastic beads was wrapped around the figurine, like a chain. A silver acacia thorn lodged deep into the doll's body, at the exact location a human heart would beat.

'Yoh, yoh, yoh,' Mthunzi said, worry etching deep lines into his forehead as he gently rotated the doll. He looked up at Thuli, sadness turning his eyes glassy.

'Eish, Mama,' he said. 'This is not good. It is a symbol of a girl child, one who has lived under your roof but has left to pursue another life.'

Mthunzi had no doubt over which of the girl children Thuli's heart would contract in fear. For, after meeting her, Mthunzi knew that very few hearts would even consider the wellbeing of his granite-faced client, Zodwa Shezi.

14: He is here, only for himself
Three months prior

The driver, who hadn't seen Mthunzi approach the car, let out an unmanly squeal when the isangoma almost ripped the handle clean off the door. With Mthunzi's furious face up against the window, the driver leant over and unlocked it. Mthunzi threw himself in, muttering darkly as he arranged himself and his attire, on the seat. He felt betrayed all over again. And, once again, Samson appeared to be completely unaware of the damage he had caused with his words and actions. Samson's words swooped and dove, like swallows in his mind, and Mthunzi felt himself grow dizzy with fear and insecurity.

The noise in his head was overwhelming, and the chatter in the backseat was too much for him to bear. '*Thula!* Shut up!' he yelled, spit flying in their direction as he levelled the ancestors with a feverish glare. 'Be quiet! I must think.'

He slumped back into his seat, and an unhappy silence filled the car. The driver turned slowly to look at the empty backseat, then quickly faced the windscreen, and sank lower into his seat.

The car bumped along rutted roads; giant ilala palms threw sharp shadows that slashed across the driver's face. While the silence became heavy with resentment, Mthunzi focused on his breathing and his next steps. He was angry with the ancestors; why had they not anticipated Samson's conversion? He was even angrier at Samson, who once again had managed to undermine Mthunzi and the work he had been called to do!

He let out a deep shuddering breath, then berated himself. *I'm blaming Samson for thinking I have no powers when I'm not using the very powers he claims do not even exist! I am going to show him that his god has as much strength as an ant trying to pull an aardvark away from the ant's nest.* With renewed confidence, he turned to look at the stony expressions of Zenzile and Mzamo but chose to ignore the unhappiness evident on MaNoxolo's plump face.

'Forgive me,' he said. 'I should not have shouted. I was upset. Why didn't we foresee Samson's defection?' Mthunzi checked himself; his voice was rising again. 'No, no,' he said, shaking his head to control his temper. 'Let us keep focused on this problem. We are going to do things very differently from now on, and I need you. We need to work together. It will never be said that the power and might of Mthunzi Mnguni, was overshadowed by the power of a white god.' He nodded encouragingly at them and felt relieved that two of the three faces had appeared to have forgiven him.

By the time the car had ascended the mountain, Mthunzi felt his body relax. Hunched shoulders softened; clenched fists became open palms. He would begin again, and to his delight, just the person to help him was seated on an upturned drum outside Mthunzi's home. Lucky Mhlongo sat in a pool of light cast by a lantern swinging gently from the roof above him. Mthunzi felt his pulse quicken at the thought of the small pouch that Lucky was sure to have brought. How he had come to rely on the contents of that pouch. He was glad to have met Lucky, although it had taken some time for him to feel this way. So much had changed because of Lucky, and those changes hadn't always sat well with him.

***

Mthunzi first met Lucky during a worryingly quiet period in his practice. Few clients were knocking at his door, and Mthunzi's anxiety had grown out of control. He began to question his calling, rather than considering the out-of-the-way location of his home, and the rise in transport costs. His home was so far up in the hills of Intaba Yemikhovu that only a trickle of clients came his way. He had thought that perhaps he should open some rooms nearer to town, but MaNoxolo reminded him that if that were necessary, the ancestors would direct him. Until then, he should be content that the ancestors would send those who most needed his help, regardless of the distance.

So, when a young man did arrive – hot and sweaty from the long climb up to Mthunzi's house – Mthunzi assumed, with relief, that he was a client. The young man sat down and slowly peeled back the folds of his coat. To Mthunzi's dismay, from within the folds, the man withdrew a bundle containing withered vulture heads. Their strong beaks looking lethal, even in death.

'Haaaah,' breathed Mthunzi, standing up in shock. 'Why have you brought those things here?' he demanded. There were izangoma who used the vulture brains to improve intelligence and help the user to see into the future. Mthunzi tsked in irritation; those izangoma were wrong to use such methods. There were other ways; correct ways to practice the art of healing. Mostly, they were simply fooling the client, taking money, and then blaming the client when things did not turn out as hoped. If the ancestors wanted your horse to win the race, or for you to win the Lottery, they would make it happen. The only time when Mthunzi would use certain parts of an animal for muthi was if the ancestors specifically required it for healing to take place or to appease the ancestors during a ceremony. Mthunzi had visited many izangoma whose rooms looked like the local pharmacy, but between the bottles of pills and tonics, were scales and snakeskins, bones, and beaks. Mthunzi had been friends with Samson long enough to know that it was illegal to keep such things. His friend would talk on and on about such matters and the price for breaking the law.

He made to push the young man towards the door. 'You take those things somewhere else! They are not wanted here!' he shouted.

'Makhosi,' the young man pleaded, surprised at Mthunzi's aggressive response. 'I see you are not that type of isangoma, but please I have other things I can show you.' He quickly pulled out other small packages of dried plants, some of which Mthunzi recognised as being difficult to source locally. Mthunzi took in the spread before him and glanced happily at MaNoxolo; it would be good to have a supplier nearby. It would save him the cost of the transport, over the border to Mozambique, where he bought his supplies. MaNoxolo stared back at him, her hands clasped at her chest, her face pinched with concern.

Lucky smiled. 'Good, I see some of this is to your liking!' He took out a small pouch from one of the coat pockets. He opened the pouch, took a long sniff, and invited Mthunzi to do the same. Mthunzi leant forward and as he inhaled the fragrant contents of the bag, he felt himself grow calmer. He nodded to Lucky, who set about rolling a joint for them to share.

Mthunzi took the proffered joint and signalled for the young man to continue.

'How is your business doing, Makhosi? I have visited many izangoma now, up in these parts, and they are struggling, with all the young men leaving for the city to look for work.' Lucky shook his head, with sadness. 'It's tough out there, no work, no money. What must they do?' said Lucky, with a shrug of his shoulders.

Mthunzi nodded; he knew such young men. They used to come to see him, desperate for muthi to change the course of their lives. Mthunzi had tried to reason with them. Moving to Durban or Johannesburg did not guarantee a job. So many of them returned eventually, sick in body and spirit, at the hardships faced in the big city. Mthunzi thought of the youth all over the country who arrived in the sprawling cities, based on lies told by fellow youth, who'd made the same trip before them; of the many mothers, desperate for their children, who had come knocking on his door to plead for divine intervention.

He sighed. He felt he had failed them. He could prepare them as best he could by asking for the blessing and the direction of their ancestors, but when they came asking for muthi other than what the ancestors dictated, he turned them away.

'You know,' said Lucky, intruding on Mthunzi's internal reflection. 'There are some izangoma who are doing very well, very well, despite the poor economy.' As he spoke, Lucky picked up one of the vulture heads, cradling it tenderly in his hand. 'Yes, I was in Joburg, not so long ago. The izangoma there, yoh!' he exclaimed with a bright smile. 'They are doing well. All those youth who leave our towns, they are going up there, and those izangoma are getting rich! They are finding those boys' jobs, and rich girlfriends, and those boys are visiting their isangomas again and again. Business is good!'

Lucky shrugged again. 'But it is not always good for the boys. How do you think they get the money to pay for the izangoma? Sometimes, they must do bad things to get that money. But,' he said, 'if you were showing them a good direction to take before they left, it would be better for them, and for you.'

At Lucky's words, Mthunzi felt a rising sense of discomfort. *Was Lucky right?* he wondered. *Had he, Mthunzi, contributed towards their failure? Certainly, his calling was to do good for those who sought his service. Had he been doing them a disservice instead?* He shot MaNoxolo a look of uncertainty. *Had Ma been misleading him?* For it was she who had directed his works; and now, he was suffering financially. Perhaps, Mthunzi thought, he would let the young man continue. There was no harm in listening to what Lucky had to say. Mthunzi could always send him away if he objected to what was being offered to him.

Mthunzi nodded to Lucky, who carried on as if he were party to the worries that circled in Mthunzi's mind.

'Makhosi,' he said quietly. 'I must also tell you about what I am hearing from the other izangoma around here.' Lucky let out a long, nervous breath. 'It is difficult to repeat such things to your face, but I think it is important for you to know.'

'Heh! What are they saying?' Mthunzi demanded as an immediate flood of shame ran through him.

With a grimace, Lucky shot Mthunzi a look of apology. 'They are wondering what has happened to the great Makhosi of Intaba Yemikhovu. They say you have weakened, and that perhaps your ancestors are not happy with you.'

Mthunzi almost leapt out of his skin at the sound, of what he realised was MaNoxolo's voice, filling the room.

'Mthunzi! You know very well that it is not you who is powerful, but the ancestors. Do not be fooled by this tsotsi. He is here only for himself.'

Mthunzi had never seen or heard MaNoxolo like this. Her voice boomed; her body vibrated with anger. Mthunzi was torn; he looked between MaNoxolo and Lucky. Despite his more frequent bouts of self-doubt, he was a proud man, and it did not sit well with him that people thought he was useless. He enjoyed the respect that his position afforded him. But MaNoxolo was right. His position in society existed solely because they had chosen him. But maybe …

Mthunzi's eyes closed to the vision growing in his mind of a better life for himself. It was hard up here on the mountain, alone, but for the quiet presence of MaNoxolo. He would like a car, and someone to drive him around, so he could get out more. He would like a bigger house, and maybe a new velvet lounge suite. The fake leather couch he currently sat on was splitting; the fabric scratchy and worn with use.

Mthunzi's reverie was interrupted when he felt the weight of a vulture's head pressed into one of his open palms.

Lucky smiled. 'You take this one, Makhosi. It's on me. I will leave my number, and you call me if you change your mind.'

The young man gathered his things and made his exit, whistling as he went. It was only after Mthunzi and MaNoxolo had come to an impasse in their argument, for and against the benefit of having a steady supply of animal parts, that Mthunzi noticed that Lucky had left the small pouch on the table. He picked it up and inhaled deeply, then, with relish he began rolling himself a fresh joint.

***

When the car came to a stop before him, Lucky laughed softly at Mthunzi's dramatic exit; obviously, his visit to Samson had not gone well. The isangoma stomped over to where Lucky sat, and Lucky knew that he was not alone. It had taken Lucky many visits to understand that the muttered conversations Mthunzi seemed to have frequently, with thin air, were with his ancestors. At first, it appeared that there was a particular ancestor that Mthunzi spoke with; Mthunzi referred to her as MaNoxolo. But as time went on, Lucky came to understand that others seemed to have arrived, and with them had come frequent arguments and unhappiness.

Lucky followed Mthunzi into the house, and while Mthunzi ranted about what had happened at Samson's home, Lucky's quick fingers got to work.

Mthunzi took the offered joint greedily. 'No more, Lucky. No more will I be Mthunzi Mnguni, forgiver of betrayals,' he declared, drawing deeply. 'I will make sure that they regret the day they ever turned their backs on the ancestors!' he shouted. He gave the joint back to Lucky and began discarding his attire, piece by piece. 'They think they serve a powerful god. They will see.'

Lucky laughed. How many nights had he sat in this house listening to Mthunzi whine and moan about the great betrayal of Samson Ngubane? By the time the moon had risen over the house on the hill, and the joint passed back and forth between them, Mthunzi was in full flow. Lucky had heard it all before, so he listened with one ear while considering his own problem.

It had recently come to Lucky's attention that one of his poachers, a young man whom he trusted, who he'd brought out of poverty, was eating from Lucky's right hand while stealing from his left. And that made Lucky very unhappy. Now that he knew that the two-faced tsotsi had been ripping him off, while pretending to be a loyal employee, something would have to be done. Lucky had sat on the problem for a week. He'd ensured that the poacher was not included in any new excursion, while he decided how best to deal with him. He'd never been faced with this situation before. No other poacher had been so bold – to steal from the boss right underneath his nose! Of course, there had been other incidents, but Lucky only had to make mention of the terrifying curse that he'd have an isangoma place upon the poacher, and all wrongdoing would come to an immediate end. Although Lucky – having grown up in an urban and distinctly non-traditional environment – was dismissive towards the supernatural, he appreciated that out here, in rural Zululand, it could be as powerful as a gunshot to the head.

Most of Lucky's poachers had little or no education, and no other forms of income. They looked, at best, a month into the future, but lived for the moment. Money made from a successful hunting trip lasted until the next successful trip. Their lifespan as a poacher came to an end either when they died out in the veld on a hunt, or more likely, in a tavern brawl. Or on dark rural roads at night, their drunken selves weaving from one side of the road to the other, until a taxi flung their limp bodies up and over the vehicle and into a grave of brittle vegetation.

Lucky sighed. This could not be said of Nkosi Zungu. The young man reminded Lucky too much of himself; a man on a mission, ready to launch himself up the ladder of entrepreneurial success; which was why Lucky had not dispatched him yet. However, as much as he admired those characteristics in himself, they were problematic when displayed by one of his staff. Nkosi had his sights set on some greater outcome for his life, and although he had yet to display any of Lucky's darker qualities, Lucky got the feeling that at some point, he'd been standing in Nkosi's way. Lucky's slowness to act was also rooted in his belief that Nkosi could be tamed and his enthusiasm and skillset be used to benefit Lucky's business.

Lucky's thoughts were interrupted by the sudden presence of a red-eyed, and foul-smelling Mthunzi at his side.

'Samson!' Mthunzi slurred. 'Samson must be taught a lesson! He thinks he's better than me? Me! The great Mthunzi Mnguni!' And with that final declaration, Mthunzi rolled over onto the couch and began to snore loudly.

Lucky stubbed what was left of the joint out on the table and flicked it across the room. He needed some fresh air to help him apply his mind to Mthunzi's problem. He was sick to death of hearing about Samson Ngubane, and he had to admit that the issue of Samson seemed to rear its head far more when Mthunzi had one too many of the joints that Lucky rolled. Mthunzi thought that they shared those joints equally, but Lucky was careful. He'd have a puff or two but then hand it back to Mthunzi, who didn't seem to notice that he managed to finish them on his own. It was serious stuff that Lucky got from the markets in Mozambique; mixed with dagga, it had a powerful effect on Mthunzi's sensitive spirit.

Mthunzi's problem was that although he said he hated Samson, Lucky knew the hatred was not strong enough for Mthunzi to truly teach his old friend a lesson. If it had been, Mthunzi would have done something by now; something to make Samson suffer for the shame, and the loss of income, he'd inflicted on Mthunzi. If Mthunzi would only listen to Lucky, this problem would have been handled properly long ago. Mthunzi would have moved on and focused his energies on becoming the isangoma that Lucky needed him to be.

Lucky stopped pacing. That was it. He needed to treat the two problems as if they were one. Samson's betrayal of Mthunzi was a betrayal of friendship. Nkosi's betrayal of Lucky was one of principle. Both were a betrayal of loyalty. And both could be dealt with in a way that returned those betrayals with devastating consequences.

15: May the good Lord deliver us
Three months prior

By the time Nonhle put the phone down, having convinced Mama that all was well down in Durban, she felt unsettled. She was shaken by the very real fear she heard in her mother's voice. Her mother had assured her that she still believed that they were covered by the blood of Jesus, but the sight of that evil doll meant to represent Nonhle had placed a crushing weight upon her heart.

As Nonhle lay in bed, her bedside light casting a soft glow across her room, she ran through the details of Mthunzi's visit. At the thought of someone … something … creeping around their yard, planting muthi meant to harm them, Nonhle gripped the sheets under her chin in a weak attempt at protection. She scolded herself; she was being ridiculous. With that final admonishment, she reached an arm out from under the covers and turned out the light. Through the open window, the night was impossibly still. Not even the muted conversation of students coming home could be heard. Then, the unexpected eerie call of a fiery-necked nightjar punctuated the air; Nonhle almost levitated off the bed. She sat up and fumbled for the light switch. The spill of light across her bed did little to ease her thumping heart.

Nonhle had never heard a nightjar on campus before. Its repetitive whistle transported her back to the less complicated years of her childhood. Back then, when she heard its call carried on the wind, she would run to her parent's room and slide in between the two of them. No nightjar could find her, sandwiched between their warm bodies. There she was safe from its blood-sucking antics. This dreaded fear of such a harmless looking bird was Mama's fault. And perhaps her own. She really shouldn't have been listening to the conversation between her parents as they sat at the kitchen table after Mama's evening shift.

All those nights ago, out on the deck of the restaurant that overlooked the veld, the nightjar had started its lament. The table of diners had stopped mid-conversation and an English guest accompanied the bird with the haunting refrain.

'May the good Lord deliver us.'

An enthusiastic discussion amongst the birders had followed, regarding the various types of nightjars that could be found both in South Africa and in other parts of the world.

'You know, Samson,' Mama had said, with a laugh, 'you could have told them a few stories!'

Mama, who had been listening to the group with one ear (her other ear tuned to the table behind her), had become fully engrossed in a story about a bloodsucker. The Englishman had shared a bizarre tale of how the nightjar had mistakenly become known as a bloodsucker – feasting on the blood of goats in the twilight hours – until the animals went blind. How this association between the bird and the goats had come about was not quite certain. It might have had something to do with how the birds flew low across the fields, swerving around the goats, who dawdled on their way back to the farmyard.

The conversation had then turned to other fairy-tale creatures that sucked blood. Which is how Nonhle had come to hear about El Chupacabra, a creature that haunted her dreams and made visiting the bathroom in the night-time, a terrifying ordeal. Mama had stumbled over the name when she tried to recall, in exquisite detail, the lizard-like body and favoured technique of El Chupacabra to inflict injury and death. Nonhle could contain herself no longer. She let out a long wail of distress and hurtled into the kitchen as if El Chupacabra himself was at her heels. She flung herself onto Baba's lap, tears streaming at the thought of the monster, that was sure to visit her that night.

But that had been a long time ago, and El Chupacabra had eventually given up his hiding place beneath her bed, slinking off to torment some other poor child in another household. In fact, up until now, Nonhle had very little to fear of things that went bump in the night. This could be directly attributed to her parents who had, quite unexpectedly, become reborn Christians when Nonhle had turned fifteen. Like all the families who lived on the compound, Nonhle's parents had practised their cultural Zulu beliefs, in perfect harmony with their low-key Christian beliefs. Although they did not often go to church because both Mama and Baba worked on most Sundays, every night she was made to kneel next to her bed, and petition God for protection and blessings. Equally, ceremonial rituals were taken very seriously, and only the best animals were chosen for slaughter, to please the ancestors. Nonhle remembered very well her *umhlonyane* ceremony. It was when she had finally become a young woman. The finest goat had been selected, to offer as a sacrifice, and Nonhle had felt like a queen for the entire day.

***

The life-changing event had occurred one Sunday when Nonhle was home for the holidays, and her parents were on leave. Baba had heard that a family of American missionaries, who had come to South Africa to preach the good news, had arrived in Mevamhlope. As the Ngubanes sat in the community hall, the oppressive heat of summer made worse by the bodies packed closely together, the message had affected Baba deeply. The missionary, a large man with a kind face, was earnestly imploring the congregation to understand that every person can, and should, commune directly with God.

'We do not require the intervention of a saint, an ancestor or a man of the cloth, to ensure that prayers are heard and answered,' the missionary had beseeched the shocked congregation.

The message was spoken with such intensity, that it was impossible not to feel affected. But Baba had been physically overcome; his eyes welled with tears, and his hands shook as he grasped one of their hands in each of his. Nonhle had winced in pain as her father gripped her hand as if he were using it as an anchor to keep himself rooted to the chair. When the service came to an end, Baba had gone off in search of the missionary, leaving Mama and Nonhle standing awkwardly in the crowd. When Baba had returned, his anxious face was wreathed in a smile. Unlike many other visiting pastors who chose to stay in the hotel in town, the missionaries were residing with a local pastor, and they were happy to set up a few private meetings over the weeks of their stay. Baba wanted to hear more about this line of thinking and how he too could have direct access to God.

On that first meeting, Baba had insisted that Nonhle and Mama join him under the tree with the pastor. They sat with two Bibles (one in English and one in isiZulu) open on their laps, and the missionary led them through the fundamentals of what it truly meant to follow Christ. Baba suddenly understood that over the years, in local churches led by prominent men, the word of God had not been taught as per the Bible in front of him. Bibles were an unnecessary expense, and many people could not read in isiZulu, let alone in English, so only the priest had a copy of the book. Being the holy man of God, the congregation simply believed in what was being preached, and Baba now understood that they had been lied to. And often they had been made to part with hard-earned money to receive the blessings of God – which frequently did not manifest. If they were to question this state of affairs, it was their unbelief that made God disinclined to answer their prayers. Mama had been concerned about turning their backs on the ancestors; surely it would be wise to have both God and the ancestors looking out for them.

By the time the Americans were on their way to the airport in Durban, the Ngubanes had been baptised in water. The baptisms took place in a plastic paddling pool in the back garden, as there wasn't enough water in the river to fully submerge the new converts. They renounced all their former ways, ancestral worship included, although it took Mama some time to make peace with this new belief. Nonhle still felt the shame they had been made to feel by friends and family alike. Once wind of their defection had reached the extended family, a full-blown intervention was launched, and the elders descended on the Ngubane household with fury. Unable to change Baba's mind, the elders had left, muttering at the cost of the ceremonial sacrifice that would have to take place to appease the ancestors and apologise for Baba's loss of fear, respect, and ultimately, sanity.

Some even brought up the family's first dereliction of duty, when Baba had refused to chop off a third of Nonhle's little finger. Every Ngubane child went through this tradition, Baba included, and the elders had known the ancestors were not at all happy that the tiny fingertip was not buried in the family kraal in Baba's village, along with all the other fingertips. Samson, when he'd held his small girl for the first time, knew that he could never inflict such pain on her tiny body, regardless of what the ancestors and his family thought. Nonhle looked down at her little finger, pleased that the tip was still attached to it.

The months following their decision to follow Christ alone had been riddled with hardship. At times, the three of them questioned whether they had made a terrible decision, and were being punished by their ancestors. For God had seemed to have abandoned them completely. They were treated warily by some of their neighbours … for surely only the truly evil needed to be saved? And then, one day, three months after the Americans had left, Samson received a call from the missionary. He seemed to know exactly what the family was going through; encouraging them with specific scriptures related to their hardships. He recounted the experiences of families living across Africa, who had had to grapple with similar challenges. He talked of a new battle being fought in the heavens – a battle between good and evil that was being waged on their behalf – to keep the enemy from pulling them back into their former ways. Satan was angry, and he would stop at nothing to discourage them, that was why life seemed so difficult at present. The call had renewed Samson's faith, and the family continued to march against the beat of their cultural drum.

***

And now, in the unusually still night, the call of the nightjar made the hair on her arms ripple with alarm. Nonhle could think of nothing but the ancestors and what they might do to punish the family. Because, while her parent's faith had grown with the passing years, her time spent in boarding school, then away from home in Durban, had done little to further her faith journey. She believed, of course she did, but things were not as clear to her as they were to Baba.

Her mind conjured up an image of the umthakathi that Mthunzi believed had spent many a night roaming their garden, circling their home. She saw the figure of a small shrunken woman, wrapped in black, placing small packages in strategic places, and spells, woven like webs, covered the grass. When the woman turned towards the house to place the coin under the brick, Nonhle – to her shame – saw the face of Zodwa peering out from beneath the hood of the cloak.

Where did that come from, she thought, with a nervous laugh.

She slipped back under the covers but decided that the light could stay on. As she talked herself into falling asleep, the image of the horrid little doll, wrapped in bright pink beads, an acacia thorn protruding like a knife, was vivid. No amount of praying to God could remove the image from her mind, nor dislodge the fear, glowing like a lump of coal, in her chest.

16: The great betrayal
Three months prior

Mthunzi stumbled out of his front door with an aching head and a curse on his lips. It was always the same after Lucky's visit. For some reason, he always woke up feeling like he'd been buried for a hundred years. He stretched his arms over his head and yawned with enthusiasm. His arms fell to his sides, and he turned in circles, nose on full alert.

What was that foul smell? And where was it coming from?

He slowly raised an arm, then hiccupped with laughter as he took a tentative sniff. He rubbed his tummy and walked a few metres to take in the view of the Lubombo mountains. Mthunzi never tired of the great expanse of land that strode out to meet the sea in the far distance. His eyes caught a slight movement to his right, and there – under the only tree – sat the large frame of MaNoxolo. He sighed deeply. He hated that he was such a disappointment to her, but honestly, she disappointed him too! He knew exactly what she was doing over there. Thinking. Thinking about how Mthunzi, who for most of his life had lived according to an ancient code of ethics and values, had turned his back on everything he stood for. He knew this because she raised the point … often. She really could be unbearable.

In his opinion, he hadn't turned his back entirely. He knew that he could be much worse. It was only because she chose to stand by him, reminding him of the good that lay somewhere within him, that he managed to keep himself from doing things that would bring him more wealth and more status. She was his conscience. He had walked a long road with MaNoxolo, and sometimes he longed for those simpler times, even if it meant a life of loneliness and poverty. But only sometimes. He sighed again, a great big frustrated exhalation of air, then set off towards the tree. He lowered himself down next to her, and together, they thought about how he'd come to this place in his life.

Mthunzi was a traditional healer; an inyanga – one who healed using plants, and an isangoma – one who healed through divination. And although he wasn't much of a healer these days, people still referred to him as isangoma. As a young boy, he had grown up in the house of his father, Baba Mnguni, a well-known herbalist. During his childhood, there was a constant flow of people looking for physical healing from Baba Mnguni. As a small boy, he'd follow his father into the wide-open veld, along the banks of the Mkuze River, and up into the steep inclines of Intaba Yemikhovu, in search of plants that would be used in the art of healing. Later, when a teenager, his father would send him off to wander alone, testing his abilities to return with the right specimens for a certain cure. After the long years of training, he could identify every plant and shrub, tree and grass, indigenous to the Zululand region.

Then, when Mthunzi turned fourteen, he began to suffer from blinding headaches. Without warning, an intense pressure would traverse his spine and wrap itself around the base of his neck; sharp incisors gripping him in an iron headlock. It would move up and over his scalp, and two sharp claws would dig into his eye-sockets, the soft tissue of his eyes mashing into the bone. Overcome with nausea and pain, he'd hunch over in agony for hours at a time. His father sat in his *ndumba* day after day, mixing muthi to cure his boy. When the concoctions had little effect on the headaches, his mother insisted that he be taken to the local hospital. Much money in transport, and many hours waiting in queues, were spent trying to determine the source of the headaches, but even the doctors were baffled.

Mthunzi grew up in a household that straddled two spiritual worlds. While his father followed traditional African beliefs, his mother had become a Christian in her early twenties. Like Samson, she had turned her back on her ancestors and became a devoted follower of Christ. Mthunzi didn't remember it as a child, but later he understood that her defection had resulted in the strained years within the household, as both his parents attempted to practise their respective beliefs alongside each other. For Baba Mnguni, it was not so difficult. He welcomed

Jesus into his home; the prophet was accorded the same respect as other holy men, but not revered like the ancestors. Mthunzi's father had been a mischievous man, and it had become obvious to Mthunzi that his father enjoyed watching his wife attempt to be a good and dutiful wife while trying to serve another god. Mthunzi wondered if his father knew that his mother would wait along the path for patients leaving the ndumba, so that she could share the word of God with them.

After the many unsuccessful visits to the hospital, Mthunzi's father insisted that Mthunzi be taken to the isangoma to determine the true cause of the headaches. The isangoma read the bones, once for himself, and then a second time at the insistence of Baba Mnguni. The results were the same; Mthunzi was being called by the ancestors. He was to become an isangoma. The calling was strong and should not be ignored. Mthunzi remembered that long walk home like it was yesterday. He felt terrified. He didn't want to be an isangoma. Truthfully, he didn't want to be an inyanga, either. He'd hoped that if he did well enough in school, he could be a policeman. Or maybe a pilot. Imagine the world that existed up there above the clouds! His father had taken his hand and told him not to worry; he was still young. They had a few years in which they could respectfully ignore the calling. The path took them up and over a small hill, their homestead visible on the rise. They could see his mother in the doorway, her body rigid, her hands clasped to her chest, awaiting the verdict.

Mthunzi had been amazed at her response. Instead of falling about weeping, she'd set about gathering women from her church to pray for her son. She looked Mthunzi's father square in the eye, and she told him that she was not about to lose her only son to a lifetime of slavery to the ancestors and their bidding. It was the first time that Mthunzi had seen his father beat his mother, and their mostly peaceful home had turned into a battlefield. She continued her prayer meetings in the homes of other women. Mthunzi had been pulled into the middle of these prayer sessions, hands laid on his head and his body as the women prayed for God's forgiveness, love, and healing to fill him. Eventually, the headaches subsided, becoming less frequent and intense, and in time they stopped altogether.

Then eight years later, the headaches returned, and with them came terrifying dreams and bouts of madness. After an intense night of feverish sweats and incoherent babbling, his father told him that it was time; avoiding his calling would kill him in the end. So, at the age of 22, he had become an initiate undergoing training with the same isangoma who had revealed Mthunzi's calling.

Mthunzi felt MaNoxolo shift beside him, her voice soft against the wind, and his days of training faded away.

'Do you remember,' she said, 'those days we used to go out at the full moon and pick clivia?' She looked so sad it almost took Mthunzi's breath away. 'You sang so beautifully, Mthunzi.'

'Yes, Ma,' he said, patting her arm. 'I do remember those days.'

They'd spent long sun-soaked afternoons and cool evenings in the hills collecting the right ingredients for his muthi. He was careful to harvest only what he needed, leaving the rest to grow freely so that there would be enough on his return trips. It had been just himself and MaNoxolo in those days. The other two ancestors, Mzamo and Zenzile, had not yet arrived. In truth, he could not say that he regretted their presence. Yes, they were mischievous, and often unkind, and certainly very selfish. They considered themselves before anyone else, but they were happy to side with Mthunzi when his ideas and actions led him astray. And they eased the loneliness of living up here on the mountain, with only MaNoxolo to help pass the time.

After his initiation and his resettlement on Intaba Yemikhovu, he saw little of anyone, apart from his family. He found that friends were less inclined to visit him, but they were happy to chat on the occasions they crossed paths in town. The only friend who had not alienated him, was Samson, his most precious childhood friend. Mthunzi felt a pang of regret at the loss of that friendship. As young boys, they'd spent every day together, walking the long distances to and from school, and the holidays exploring the hills and valleys. They had competed daily, trying to outdo each other over who was more knowledgeable. Samson, obsessed with all living creatures, while Mthunzi retorted with facts about plants and trees.

He felt MaNoxolo's gaze upon his face. 'You are thinking about him,' she said, her eyes wet at the corners.

'Yes,' he said, with feeling. 'I am always thinking about him.'

The great betrayal had occurred a year after Lucky had paid his first visit to Mthunzi. It had taken him more than six months to test out

Lucky's theory on repositioning his business, and once it started, he couldn't seem to hold the stream of clients back. His once uncluttered room began to fill up with all manner of interesting things that had either lived, or adorned the body, of a once-living creature.

He had not been expecting Samson that day. In fact, he hadn't seen his old friend in well over 18 months. Samson worked full time at a game lodge, and his time off was spent at home with Thuli, or out visiting his cattle on his family land. Samson had not come up to Mthunzi's home in years; it was more convenient to meet in town. So, when he heard a car inching up the mountain, he assumed that it was Lucky. He almost leapt out of his skin when the deep voice of Samson Ngubane called out a greeting.

'Hayi!' Mthunzi shouted. He panicked and shut the door, locking Samson out. He scurried about to try and cover up some of the buckets containing the worst of the evidence. But he could not; there were more buckets than blankets.

A knock at the door forced him to open the door a crack, only his head poking out.

'Sawubona, *umngani wami!*' he shouted, a little manically. He slid through the crack with difficulty and took the hand that Samson offered. 'You are here?' he said, unable to hide his dismay.

Samson looked contrite. 'I am sorry, Mthunzi. I took a chance. I could not reach you on your phone.'

'No,' said Mthunzi, their hands still clasped together in greeting, 'the reception is still bad.'

'I had to visit someone nearby, so thought I would see if you were here. It has been too long!' he said, with a big smile, and gave Mthunzi's hand another good shake.

'Come, come,' gestured Mthunzi, trying to lead Samson towards two chairs placed under the tree. 'Let us sit there.'

He pulled Samson by the hand but felt resistance. Then Mthunzi's hand swung free at his side. He looked back and saw Samson kneeling on the floor. There, between his fingers was a pangolin scale. Mthunzi would never forget the look on Samson's face. Before he could stop him, Samson pushed open the door, allowing a rectangle of sunshine to illuminate the horrifying contents of Mthunzi's home.

Mthunzi skulked in the doorway and watched Samson take stock of the contents of Mthunzi's home. When his friend finally turned to look at him, Samson's eyes very clearly said, *I no longer know who you are,* and the thought pierced the soft centre of Mthunzi's heart. Surrounded by the primal smell of animal pelts, Samson could not see Mthunzi's point of view that without this type of muthi, he'd be passed over by his clients for another healer; a healer who would happily give them what they needed.

Samson simply could not find it in his heart to accept that this should be done at the expense of endangered creatures. The two men argued bitterly, but no compromise could be reached. Samson flew down the mountain and Mthunzi believed that he would never hear from his friend again. Lucky had warned him to hide whatever he could, especially the rare specimens, and he was glad he had. A few days later, a vehicle arrived, just as the sun began to burn the dew from the grass. He went to investigate the unexpected guests; it was the local anti-poaching unit, there to fetch his muthi and present him with a fine for a first offence. They were disappointed to find that most of the muthi had disappeared, but they would be watching him, they said. The fine hurt him only mildly; he'd stashed away a sizeable amount since he'd started his new trade. It was the threat of surveillance that caused him the most pain. For months, he'd kept a low profile, and bought nothing from Lucky to replenish his stocks.

It was Lucky who helped Mthunzi through this time, and he sought the advice of the ancestors, Mzamo and Zenzile, more than MaNoxolo. Even though he chose to largely ignore her, MaNoxolo remained, devoted to her task of steering him in the right direction. And something within Mthunzi would not get rid of her. The others had addressed him countless times on how easy it would be to dispatch her, but he could not. He was not sure why, but in the rare times when his head felt clearer, he felt comforted by her presence.

The wind whipping through the leaves above alerted him to the coming presence of Mzamo and Zenzile. Then, they stood before him, positioning themselves so that MaNoxolo was excluded from the group. He gave her arm a squeeze, then got up and followed the ancestors back into the house.

17: You people!
1st December 2012

The day after her father's arrest, Nonhle woke from a bad night's sleep. She'd eventually succumbed to exhaustion, wrapped around the weeping form of her mother. She had a crick in her neck and a tight band of worry around her chest. She disentangled herself from Mama, then sat at the pine table, with a pen and paper. She jotted down a few notes for the day ahead, feeling better once a plan of action had been decided upon. She stole out to the ablution block and gave herself a quick wash with a facecloth and cold water.

When she returned, Mama sat at the table, the page in front of her covered with her neat script. She looked up at Nonhle and passed the note over for Nonhle to take.

'Here,' she said, gesturing for Nonhle to hold out her other hand. Nonhle looked at the folded wad of hundred Rand notes Mama pressed into her hand.

'Mama,' pleaded Nonhle, 'I have money, let me get them.'

'No, my child,' said Mama, sitting up straight, her voice a little stronger. 'Let me do this while I can, we will be depending on you if this does not go as we hope.'

Nonhle took the money and leant down to kiss her. She closed the door quietly behind her, leaving her mother at the kitchen table, hands clasped in prayer.

As the taxi entered Mevamhlope town, Nonhle took in the waves of humanity that lined the streets. It was a small town that served a big geographic area, and everyone seemed to have descended on it, for their Saturday shop. Nonhle eyed out the familiar landmarks as they drove down the main street that split the town in two: the Catholic church, the butcher, the Boxer Superstore, and a new Chinese mall with towering piles of cheap plastic junk outside its front door. Now and then, her eye would be drawn to a riot of green, purple, and pink flowering bougainvillea that seemed out of place next to date palms and candelabra cactus. The main street ran for about five hundred metres and was lined with flat-topped acacia trees: their sharp white thorns giving the town its name.

The taxi pulled up to a petrol station, and Nonhle got off with the rest of the passengers; a process made painfully slow by the wobbly exit of the three elderly women in the front row. A large tourist bus, which would head on to one of the game lodges, perhaps even The Last Outpost, was refuelling. Pale-faced tourists peered out of the large windows. While some smiled down at the group of small boys, whose skinny arms were outstretched in the hopes of sweets or money, others looked around nervously, waiting for partners or friends to return safely from the garage shop. Nonhle was by now familiar with both types of tourists: those that savoured every moment, and those that were overcome with fear at this strange place, and even stranger people. She took one last look at the tourists, wishing that she could trade places. With a sigh, she headed back up the main street, towards the police station.

Because she was nervous about what lay ahead, Nonhle walked slowly. She took in the wide assortment of goods for sale on the cracked and greasy pavements. Her eyes wandered over zips, batteries, baby diapers, and washing-up liquid. A cow's head, its glassy eyes staring at her balefully, sat next to large balls of white *umcako* and red *ibomvu*; the face of a vendor covered by ibomvu's mineral substance, to ward off the harsh rays of the sun. As she passed a bottle store, the thumping beats of *kwaito* spilled out to greet her, then made way for the plunking guitar strings of a maskandi musician leaning casually against a wall. The streets were littered with rubbish, and a woman in the gaudy orange jumpsuit of the municipality, lazily swept the debris as she bellowed across the road that separated her from her friends. Nonhle's stomach leapt at the smell of *shisa nyama*; large slabs of meat roasting over a charcoal fire had enticed a group of humans, and dogs alike, with its delicious smell. While customers waited for the main course, they bit into boiled mielies, cheeks and chins plastered with bits of the white chewy kernels.

When Nonhle reached her destination, she stood looking at it from behind the concrete palisade fence. The yard was filled with police vehicles and a line of people requiring assistance of some kind. Nonhle braced herself, adjusted her weave, and marched with purpose past the line. The cool of the concrete interior greeted her as she made her way inside, and she scanned the long wooden desk for a familiar face. She eventually located his thatch of red hair behind a glass window and headed in his direction.

'Hey, sisi!' A large policeman grabbed her by the arm as she tried to move past him. '*Uyaphi?*'

Nonhle set her face in a way she hoped gave her an officious air. 'I need to speak to that man,' she said, gesturing towards the man she'd seen leading Baba away.

The policeman pointed to the line of people waiting to be served. 'You can wait, like everyone else.'

'It's urgent. I have an appointment,' she said, coughing in embarrassment at her blatant lie.

'*Haibo!* I'm not stupid. There're no *appointments* here!' he shouted.

When the policeman began to push her towards the door, Nonhle dug in her heels, her voice loud enough to entertain the line of people he'd directed her towards.

'Don't you *dare* touch me!'

The more the officer pushed, the louder she got, until eventually, Karel came striding out.

'What the bladdy hell is wrong with you people?' he shouted furiously at the officers ignoring the scene before them. 'Do I have to do everything myself? You!' he pointed to the officer who still had his hand on Nonhle's back. 'What the hell is going on?'

'Detective,' said Nonhle quickly, inserting herself in front of the policeman. 'I'm Nonhle Ngubane. I'm here to see my father, Samson.'

'Oh! You are, are you? And would you like a cup of tea while you wait for him in the visitors' lounge?' He smiled and gestured towards the back section of the station. The officer next to her began to laugh as Nonhle looked eagerly in the direction of Karel's pointing finger. She felt the heat suffuse her cheeks; he was mocking her.

'Come with me,' he said, and led her by the elbow towards the entrance, out into the yard.

'Why are we going outside,' she cried, looking back over her shoulder. The curious onlookers continued to gawp at the spectacle she was making of herself.

Karel turned her so she was facing him. His big face, covered in red bristles, was uncomfortably close, and his finger punctuated the space between them.

'Your father is in big trouble, my girl. Big trouble!'

Nonhle took a step back, shaking her elbow loose from his grip.

'Surely he has rights. Why can't I speak to him? What about a lawyer?'

'A lawyer,' Karel brayed. 'This is obviously not the first rhino he's poached if you people can afford a lawyer!'

Nonhle crossed her arms firmly across her chest. *Who did this man think he was?* 'You've got it all wrong,' she said, her voice vibrating with anger. 'There's no way...'

To her astonishment, Karel brought his hands together in a resounding clap. 'Listen, you're a smart girl, or so I've heard. Let us do our job. If your father's innocent, we'll figure it out. Now please, go away,' he said, steering her towards the pedestrian gate.

When she didn't move, he again took her by the elbow and escorted her out of the yard, leaving her to stand miserably like a discarded box as human traffic navigated around her. It was only when a young man, with a gold tooth and a wink, sidled up to her that she joined the crowd moving in the direction of the Boxer store.

She walked quickly, dodging small children and goats munching on weeds and plastic bags on the pavement edge. She tucked the list of questions she'd hoped to ask her father, and Karel, into her bag, and retrieved Mama's list of groceries. Right now, something practical was required to stop the overwhelming sense of anxiety that was making her feel utterly hopeless.

Outside the store, a queue had formed. Pay day weekend meant triple the shoppers, and there weren't enough trolleys to go around. She sighed in annoyance; her list was short, and she'd hoped to be done in half an hour or so. She stood facing the road, her eyes scanning up and down the length of it as she waited her turn. It was filled with cars, people, and stalls shrouded in smoke rising off the shisa nyama fires. Her eyes came to rest on a khaki Land Cruiser, and her heart thumped as she noted the sticker plastered to the door; it belonged to the company Senzo worked for. And then, approaching the vehicle, was Senzo Mdletshe himself, cell phone clamped to his ear. Nonhle did a small dance of indecision as she tried to decide whether she should speak to him. The sight of him pocketing his phone, and moving away from her, forced her to give up her position in the queue.

'Hey,' she called as she ran up behind him. She had to pluck at his shirt to get him to stop moving.

Nonhle felt herself deflate as he turned to face her. He looked just as irritated now as he had on the day he'd dropped her at home.

'*Ngingakusiza*, sisi?' he said, with a frown. 'Oh, it's you.'

'Yes, hi …' she replied, wringing her hands. 'I could do with some help, please.'

He lifted his hands as if to separate himself from her. 'Look, if this is about yesterday, I can't talk to you. Detective du Randt is handling the case. If you have anything that might help the case, you need to speak to the police.' He gave her a tight smile and then started to turn away.

Nonhle grabbed his arm. 'Wait!' she pleaded. 'I already tried to speak to him. But he's not interested in what I have to say.'

'Well, he must have had a reason then. He's a good detective. Maybe he'd already heard it? Now, if you'll excuse me,' he said, looking pointedly at her hand on his arm.

'Senzo,' she said, realising that he thought she was just one of the employees at the lodge. 'Samson Ngubane is my father.'

His frown made way for an expression devoid of emotion. 'We have nothing further to talk about,' he said, brushing past her and moved quickly to his vehicle.

'Please, Senzo,' she cried, rushing after him. 'I don't know who else to turn to!'

He spun around, his aggression causing her to stumble backward. 'You're talking to the wrong person! There's a special place in hell for people like your father.'

Before she could argue, he was back in his vehicle, slamming the door. He turned the key, and drove off, leaving her coughing in a haze of diesel fumes. Nonhle watched the Cruiser bounce over potholes and swerve around people walking in the street. She turned and walked numbly back to the store. Several people had filled the space she'd left during her outburst. She couldn't return home empty-handed, so she joined the back of the queue, and waited her turn.

She managed to stand still for about two minutes, then she launched herself back into the street. It was a small town; his office must be nearby. So far, he was possibly the most mean-spirited person she'd ever had the misfortune to meet, but he was all she had. She power-walked up the main road until she came to a stop outside the police station. She looked around nervously, until she saw two policewomen outside, walking towards her. She got to them before they entered the gates to the station, and they pointed her in the right direction. She took the few minutes' walk to compose herself before she reached the modest Umkhombe Anti-Poaching Unit offices.

She turned the door handle with a sweaty hand and cautiously peered inside. Her plan would unravel quickly if Senzo was standing in the reception area, but a quick sweep revealed one large bottom on display, its owner bent over a small plant.

'Sawubona, Ma,' she greeted the bottom.

The woman jumped, her hand to her chest. 'Haibo, sisi! You gave me a fright!'

'Sorry, Ma. You were so busy there.'

'Yes, I am trying to keep this one alive. I'm not very good at remembering to water them,' she laughed. 'What can I do for you?'

Nonhle gave the woman the best smile she could muster. 'Ma, I am looking for Senzo, I just have a quick message to give him.'

The woman gave Nonhle an approving once-over. 'Good luck,' she said, pointing to an office.

Through the window running the length of the office, Nonhle could see Senzo standing in front of a large map of what she presumed was the Zululand area. He was pushing pins into strategic points on the map, his phone pressed to his ear again. She took a deep breath and knocked on the door.

***

He was still talking when she pushed the door open. Concentration quickly turned to disbelief when he saw her walk into his office. Unable to shout at her, he motioned with his free hand as if flicking away a bothersome fly. She ignored him and sat down. He scowled, said a few words to end the conversation, then dropped the call.

'What part of 'we can't talk', didn't you understand?' he said, moving over to her chair. 'If you don't get up, I'm more than happy to help.'

As he leant down towards her, and she let out a squeak of fear, and then did the one thing she swore she wouldn't do; burst into big, noisy, tears. Once she started, she couldn't seem to stop. She looked around frantically for something to wipe away the tears and stem the flow from her nose. She heard Senzo stomp out of the office and down the corridor. On his return, he pushed a roll of toilet paper, into her hands.

'Thank you,' she managed as she gave a hearty blow. The action had a calming effect. After one last blow, she looked up at Senzo,   who leaned against his desk. 'Sorry,' she mumbled. 'It's just been a very upsetting time.'

'Look,' he said, his voice somewhat softer. 'I'm sorry. I know this is difficult for you. But I really can't speak with you. I —'

Before he could finish, the receptionist bustled in with a tray laden with mismatched mugs, an open sugar bowl, and a pot of tea.

'No, *Ma*,' he said, in exasperation. 'She can't stay —'

'Hawu, rubbish!' the woman scowled at Senzo. 'What would your mother say?' She gave Nonhle a quick wink before departing.

Senzo pushed himself away from the desk and flung himself into his chair.

'Please, Senzo,' Nonhle begged softly. He wouldn't look her in the eye, instead, he busied himself with making two mugs of tea. She waited until he finally looked up. 'My name's Nonhle, by the way.'

Senzo gave a quick nod of acknowledgement and pushed the better looking of the two mugs in her direction.

She took the gesture as a sign to continue. 'Can you at least tell me why you think he's involved?' she asked, picking up her mug.

'Evidence,' he said, and took a big slurp of tea.

'Evidence?' She exhaled the word, and her hands shook, tea slopped over the lip of her mug, and onto her skirt. 'You can't be serious! What did you find?'

'I can't discuss that with you, Nonhle. It's an ongoing investigation. For all I know, you might be involved!' he said, eyeing her suspiciously. Nonhle felt a wave of shock run through her. Was he serious? *No, surely, if they'd suspected her, she would have been arrested already.*

She rallied and gave him a withering stare. '*That* is a ridiculous statement to make. This is serious, Senzo,' she said, placing the mug firmly on the desk. 'Without their jobs, my parents have nothing. There's no plan B for them.'

Senzo turned to look at the wall on his left; photographic evidence of countless killings made in the name of greed and corruption. He got up and stood in front of the map, tracing his finger between the various pins scattered across it.

'You're right, it is serious,' he said, over his shoulder. 'Let me show you.'

He turned back to the map and pointed at a blue pin with a marker. Before he could utter a word, the sound of raised voices was heard, coming from reception. The door flew open, and from the dark curls sticking out from behind the door, Nonhle was dismayed to realise that it was Thomas McKenzie. They hadn't spoken since that day out in the veld when they'd argued about poaching for the pot. And now, no doubt, he was here to ensure that her father was found guilty, along with the rest of them.

'What are you doing here?' Senzo said, throwing the marker onto the desk.

'My father is away, so I'm afraid you have to deal with me until he's back,' replied Thomas, apologetically.

Nonhle sat up. Something was going on here. She could feel the dislike between the two men like a psychical presence.

'Well,' said Senzo, gesturing to Nonhle, 'as you can see, I'm busy. You'll just have to wait.'

Thomas opened the door fully, his eyes coming to rest on her, and to her confusion, he gave her a sad smile.

'Actually, I'm glad Nonhle is here,' said Thomas. 'I'm sure we're here for the same reason.' He turned back to Nonhle. 'You don't believe that your father is guilty, and neither do I.'

18: A hypocrite in all of us
1st December 2012

The atmosphere in the office was tense. The hostility between Senzo and Thomas was undeniable, and Nonhle briefly forgot her woes as she watched the men with interest. Senzo stood behind his desk, legs wide, arms crossed over his chest as if to ward off his two intruders.

Senzo stared at Thomas for longer than was necessary. 'And I suppose you have evidence to support this claim?' Nonhle winced at the mocking notes in Senzo's voice, but she found herself looking up at Thomas, hopefully.

He pulled up a chair beside her. 'Not quite,' he said, 'but I have a feeling —'

Senzo snorted dismissively. 'I don't work with 'feelings', Thomas. We work with evidence, so unless you can show me something —'

'Senzo, I've known Samson since I was a small boy,' Thomas said, his voice rising in exasperation. 'As you know, everything I know about the bush, birds, animals … you name it, is because of Samson. He's been our longest standing game ranger – never been sick a day in his life, and not one act of misconduct. If you told me I had to choose between Samson or any other ranger at The Last Outpost, I'm telling you right now, I'd choose him over the lot. He's that loyal.'

'Loyalty,' said Senzo, his lip curling into a sneer. 'We both know that's not something to be trusted.'

Thomas sighed. 'Not now, Senzo. This isn't the time.'

Definitely something going on here, Nonhle thought. When they continued to glare at each other, she cleared her throat, to remind them that she was still in the room and that it was her meeting.

The noise had the desired effect. 'Well, that's all very touching, Thomas. But, childhood memories, and tears,' Senzo said, nodding in Nonhle's direction, 'won't cut it in court.'

He picked up the marker and focused on Nonhle. 'Before the interruption, I was about to tell you about the seriousness of the situation.'

He stood in front of the map again, sweeping one hand across it. 'All of these little pins mark the spot where an animal has been poached. I've categorised them in two ways.' He pointed to a row of coloured push pins and below it, a row of pins with strips of paper attached, a number written on each one.

'The coloured pins represent animals, and the pins with numbers, represent the poaching method. For example, red for rhino, blue for elephant, one for snares, two for guns, three for tools, such as axes and pangas, and so on. As you can see, there's a lot of pins, which means a lot of dead or wounded animals.' He cast a grim expression Nonhle's way. 'Most wounded so badly, that we put them down where we find them. In KwaZulu-Natal, we've lost about 60 rhino this year: in South Africa, it's around 600. For every poacher that gets shot or arrested, ten more are lining up to take their place.'

He said it so matter-of-factly, that Nonhle realised that it must be the only way to deal with the reality of the situation. Feeling like she was in a lecture theatre, raised a hand. 'If it's so dangerous, why do they do it?' she asked. It made no sense if the odds were that poor.

Senzo nodded. 'Good question. Poverty, greed, traditional beliefs – all of it drives poaching in these rural areas.' He looked away from her and asked, 'Do you think your father is the first game ranger that's been arrested for poaching an animal he's meant to protect? I've personally known —'

Nonhle smacked her hand on the desk in frustration. 'My father's not like that —'

'Nonhle,' he responded with equal passion. 'Not everyone is as they seem, even those we think we know well.' Nonhle caught Senzo's eyes slide towards Thomas, then quickly return to hers. 'There's a hypocrite in all of us, if the reward is big enough.'

'Other people, maybe, but not my father.' She knew that she was a long way from convincing him, so she asked her next question, instead. 'Why is it so hard to catch them?'

'Because it's big business. People are involved who you'd never imagine; politicians, the police, vets, game rangers ... it's a complex network overseen by a wildlife mafia. Added to that, it's no longer as simple as a couple of locals jumping over a fence, hoping for the best with their homemade rifles. We're dealing with money and expertise. Poachers have night vision goggles and high calibre rifles. They've got drones and helicopters. Mostly, up our way, we get the guys who are old school. They don't have any fancy equipment, but their knowledge is excellent. They know what they're looking for and exactly where to find it. Everyone thinks that shooting a poacher dead is the answer. It's not. We have to get to the top.'

He uncapped his marker, cleaned a space on the whiteboard next to the map with the eraser, and began to draw.

'This is a simple version of a complex network of people involved. Let's start with the horn and the poacher,' he said, drawing a horn with two stick figures next to it. 'The poacher is either local or part of an organised syndicate. The local guy is taking his chances, hoping to find a buyer for the horn. He's generally disorganised and lacks resources, but they can still get away with it. It's the poacher linked to a syndicate that's the bigger problem.'

He then drew a line connecting the poachers to another stick figure. 'The kingpin takes the horn from the poacher to the smuggler. The smuggler is the guy who must get the horn out of the country – by road, by air or by rail. Now, we have a railway line running right along the N2 that connects with a harbour in Richards Bay. That line also bisects or runs past many game farms in the area. And, we're right near the Mozambican border; there's a harbour in Maputo. So that's two exit points right there.'

'So, a perfect escape plan,' she said.

'A smuggler has a network of people at the harbour, the railway stations, and the airport. From the luggage guys to the top department supervisors. He's got them in his pocket. The smuggler hands the horn over to a wholesaler who then finds a buyer. The buyer could be a medicine manufacturer in China or Vietnam, who sells on to doctors, pharmacists, and traditional healers. Or it could be to a manufacturer of knife handles, made from rhino horn, called *jambiya*.'

By now the board was filled with emaciated figures and pointing arrows. 'This is just the simple version of how the horn gets from here to there,' he said, moving to a map of the world, and making an arc with his finger between South Africa, China, and Vietnam.

'Okay, so how does the poacher know who to sell the horn to?' she asked, her mind looking to make the connections between all the role players.

'Kingpins,' said Senzo. 'We're closest to Mozambique. Up there is a town called Massingir. Seems like many of the poachers going into Kruger National Park come from there. Massingir, like the rest of Mozambique, is poor. There are few jobs and people are hungry, desperate. So, when one of the kingpins has a poaching job, he's literally got hundreds of men to choose from. He simply puts out the word, and he's got new recruits within hours. In a country with virtually no employment, these guys are offering the unimaginable. The same goes for some communities around reserves in South Africa.'

Nonhle knew that people were desperate, but to go out in the dead of night into a reserve with wild animals, armed with a torch and a gun, seemed insane.

'How much does a poacher get paid?'

'Well, that depends on who they are in the hierarchy. They usually work in teams of three. There's the shooter; he carries the rifle.' Senzo began extending a finger at a time as he continued with his list. 'The navigator; someone has to know how to get around in the dark and find the rhino, and then there's the guy who hauls the weapons and equipment, and whatever they'll need for the time they're out there. Depending on the size of the reserve, they can be out there for up to five days. Each person gets paid according to their level of skill.'

When Senzo named an unbelievable figure that covered all three poachers, Nonhle was stunned. At the higher end of the spectrum, that was more money than both her parents, combined, made in a year. A few jobs like that and Mama and Baba would be able to build their own home on retirement, with an inside bathroom, and add to Baba's herd of dappled Nguni cattle. He would be a changed man, a contented man.

A sense of discomfort began to rise within her. *Was it possible that he'd finally given in to the visions of a different future for himself and his family?*

Thomas, who'd until now sat listening, painted a bleaker picture. 'To make matters worse, Nonhle, as Senzo already mentioned, those that are supposed to be protecting our animals, are in on it too. Syndicates target guys in key positions, like the police, offering them money they can't refuse. Poachers get arrested and documented, but then the dockets go missing. You can't prosecute a poacher when there's no docket. You have to let them go. That's an inside job.'

'He's right, Nonhle,' agreed Senzo. 'We're facing one of the greatest conservation battles of our time right now. And every time we think we have the answer, they prove we're ten steps behind. You know why they want the horn, right?' he asked her.

Finally, something she did know the answer to. 'Yes. I did a small section on Chinese traditional medicine in my medical anthropology course,' she explained. 'We were exploring various types of traditional medicines around the world. Like us Zulus, the Chinese also practice non-Western medicine. They use the horn to cure cancer and fevers, and other ... issues,' she said, trailing off.

'That's right,' Thomas agreed. 'But it's gone beyond health and healing and moved into something far more dangerous. The poor still get tricked into believing that buying rhino horn will cure cancer, but those people can only afford a small amount. It's the ones looking for higher status in society that are the most dangerous. They've got the money to spend, and friends and potential business partners, to impress. 'And now,' he added, 'we've got an even bigger problem – the Vietnamese. The Chinese have cornered the market for years, but in recent years the Vietnamese have wanted in on it too; for them, it's all about status and business. A businessman who offers rhino horn at a party is at the top of his game. They use it to show off.'

'And to cure hangovers,' added Senzo.

'So, what you're saying is that this is not as simple as telling people it's only hair, and to stop wasting their money?' said Nonhle.

'Exactly,' replied Senzo, tossing the marker back onto the desk. 'Just like you can't convince some of us,' he said, looking at Nonhle, 'that burning monkey fur will chase away bad dreams.'

Nonhle frowned at the thought, feeling anxiety well up within her.

Senzo was effectively telling her that her father, if he was involved, had become tangled up in something far more dangerous than she'd ever considered. Truthfully, she'd thought that this was a simple misunderstanding that could be sorted out within the week. She'd thought that if she could prove how dedicated he was to protecting, and conserving wildlife, they'd see how ridiculous the idea was that he could have played any part in what had taken place at the Last Outpost. Instead, there was a possibility he might be involved in the same complicated ring as kingpins, spotters and poachers, politicians, vets, and conservationists; all corrupt, all driven by greed.

No, she thought, shaking her head. *There was absolutely no way that her father would be involved.* She needed a break from the conversation; she couldn't take in any more information. 'Could I have a glass of water, please?' she asked Senzo.

While Senzo organised the water, Nonhle purposefully ignored Thomas, who seemed to understand her need for quiet. Instead, she let her eyes journey around the room. One wall was given over to mug shots of men she imagined must be poachers. While some looked dazedly into the camera, a few stared out defiantly, challenging whoever was on the other side of the lens. There were photographs of various houses, vehicles, and buildings, one of which Nonhle recognised as Jika Jika Tavern, which was not far from town, on her route home. The other wall was covered in photographs of what appeared to be poaching crime scenes. Bloated carcasses, some so disfigured she couldn't work out quite what she was looking at. There were crocodiles and snakes, raw and pink, their skin peeled off, and the partially severed leg still attached to a snarling leopard. Nonhle managed to raise a hand to her mouth before a small burp escaped.

'Horrible, isn't it?' said Thomas, who picked up the glass of water Senzo had placed on the desk and handed it to her. She took it gratefully and swallowed half of it in one long gulp, hoping that it would distract her gag reflex. Then, an idea struck her.

'Can you do something to the horn? If it's just hair ... could you poison it? Not so that it kills the person who eats it, of course,' she backtracked quickly. 'But enough to make them really sick. Surely that would put people off if they knew there was a chance that it could put them in hospital?'

Senzo gave her a look that told her he'd been down this line of inquiry before. 'It's definitely been considered, but it's hugely expensive. Firstly, you'd have to dart the rhino and sedate it before you can inject the horn. Imagine trying to capture and dart thousands of rhino – it would be a costly operation.'

'And to be honest,' said Thomas, 'it's unethical. You'd be surprised at how many people don't actually know how the rhino horn came to be ground up in a little vial. To them, it's just a powder that has the potential to cure cancer.'

Nonhle felt exasperated. One minute they were keen to hang anyone associated with poaching, and the next they were worried about hurting the same people who benefited from the horn of a slaughtered rhino.

'Well, what about the people who do know – like the Vietnamese, you just mentioned. They know exactly where it comes from.'

'Okay, let's make this personal,' said Thomas. 'You know exactly where meat comes from. A cow is herded into an abattoir, terrified and stressed, and then they shoot a bolt through its head, or cut its throat, hang it upside down and drain it. You know that's how it died, but you still buy it off the shelf and happily consume it.'

Nonhle, who'd never seen Thomas turn down a piece of meat at a staff meal, raised her eyebrows at him.

'Exactly,' he smiled, reading her mind. '*I* know all of this, but you still can't hold me back from a rump steak. My point, Nonhle, is that we can't expect others to play by the rules when we don't. Humans like to idolise some animals while treating others as a commodity. You can't eat a dog, but you can eat a cow?'

'And it's really not as simple as poisoning the horn,' said Senzo, looping back to Nonhle's original question.

'Remember the kingpin? He's only concerned about his money. What happens after that, isn't his problem. There's been some talk about dyeing the horn pink, so that it acts as a visual deterrent, letting the poacher know that the horn is poisoned. Even when they grind it up into powder, a scanner, like at the airport, will pick up the colour of the dye, alerting them. But the fact is, it's not certain whether every rhino would even survive that process.'

As the conversation continued, Nonhle felt conflicted as issues of poverty and unemployment, greed and excess, and centuries of cultural and traditional beliefs were raised. As an inexperienced anthropologist, she had become somewhat righteous in the belief that every culture should be left to their own devices, and that a Eurocentric worldview had damaged much of the world's indigenous cultures. Living in a country like South Africa was proof enough of what happened when one culture imposed itself upon another. But now … now she was faced with the reality that because of these beliefs, her own country, and its natural resources, were being plundered; but equally, the poverty experienced by so many South Africans, particularly in the large tracts of isolated rural land that surrounded the parks and reserves, forced people into a life of crime that added to the decimation.

The lull in conversation gave Senzo an opportunity to look down at his watch. 'Guys, I have to go,' he said, grabbing a note pad and pen off the table.

Both Nonhle and Thomas stood up quickly, Thomas moving to block the door.

'Hang on, Senzo. Where do we go from here?' he asked, placing a hand on Senzo's shoulder. Nonhle watched him withdraw his hand quickly, in response to Senzo's mutinous stare.

'No idea,' Senzo said, with a shrug. 'I don't mean to be harsh, but it's actually out of my hands. It's up to the police now. My job was to coordinate the ground team for an arrest. Now I have things to do. So, if you'll excuse me,' he said, pushing past Thomas.

19: To float in her orbit
1st December 2012

The rumble of the truck's diesel engine, and the racket encouraged by the corrugated road beneath them, meant that they didn't have to say much to each other. They sat in silence, each contemplating what lay ahead. As the truck chewed up the kilometres, Thomas stole an occasional look in her direction, but since Nonhle had an uncanny knack of turning to look at him at precisely the same moment, he gave up. Instead, he allowed the weight of her disappointment to weigh heavily on his mind. He felt as certain as she did that Samson was innocent, but all he had to go on was the strength of their friendship, over 15 years earlier.

When he thought about it, he knew very little about Samson Ngubane and his family. Before now, he hadn't ever really given Nonhle any thought. Back then, he'd probably spent more time with Samson during the day, than the man had spent with his own daughter. As a young boy, it had never even crossed his mind to ask the older man about himself. He was so caught up in his misery and loneliness, that his only concern was ensuring that the attention Samson paid him, continued. Thomas had spent hours peppering Samson with endless questions about birds and animals, and other things. Inane questions, most of them, but Samson answered each with patience and care. Thomas had not once asked the man about his home, his wife, or his children. Quite frankly, it didn't even occur to him that Samson might be a father or a husband. Back then, Samson was Samson; game ranger, black man, and employee. Thomas cringed inwardly at the thought.

Thomas had lost touch with Samson during his teenage years. He'd gone off to boarding school in the Midlands, returning home for the holidays every few months. On his return, he no longer sought Samson out, choosing instead to spend his time with the guests of his age. They formed holiday gangs, moving between the cool waters of the pool, the shaded games room with the foosball table, and back to the sun loungers to watch the setting sun. The teenage Thomas soon learnt that his position as the owner's son bought him a certain prestige; children his age and older wanted to be around him. They admired the smooth caramel of his skin, his endless knowledge of anything that moved, and the isiZulu that tripped off his tongue when talking to black staff around the property.

And if Thomas were truthful, he knew he'd been a privileged brat as a teenager. He'd shown off in front of his new friends, parading about like a young chief, demanding drinks, and returning food that was not quite to his satisfaction. His reign had come to a humiliating end, when his father had witnessed him reduce a young waitress to tears, in front of a group of boys. Like a stealthy leopard, William had stalked his son, then pounced on his prey. He'd pinched Thomas's ear between his thumb and forefinger and dragged him about on his tiptoes. William had made him apologise publicly to every single member of staff on duty at the restaurant that day. William had been keeping tabs on Thomas, and his false sense of entitlement. William even made Thomas apologise to the boy who washed the dishes. Thomas still blushed at the memory.

As they neared the four-way stop that would take them to the compound, a shrill whistle pierced the air. Thomas turned left towards the lodge, but the boom at the level crossing came down before he could cross over. He hit the steering wheel half-heartedly with the palm of his hand, then turned off the engine. They'd be waiting for some time. The train, which had stopped a few hundred metres down the track, would inch its way towards them, slowly. The sudden quiet amplified every sound. The cooling engine ticked and popped, and the vibrating screech of cicada beetles engulfed them.

Thomas felt Nonhle staring at him. Then she cleared her throat and asked, 'What's the deal between you and Senzo?'

Thomas looked at her out of the corner of his eye. 'How'd you mean?'

'Well,' she said, carefully, 'he's not the friendliest guy, but I got the impression that he doesn't like you ... at all.'

Thomas looked away. 'Ja,' he muttered to himself. 'He's got every reason not to.'

Thinking about it brought all sorts of uncomfortable feelings floating to the surface. If he'd had any idea that this past week was going to force him to take a long hard look at himself, his beliefs, and his past, he might have taken the leave that was owed him. He'd done quite a few things over his thirty years of existence that still had the power to colour his cheeks; but how he'd behaved as a teenager had merely been a rehearsal for the way he'd treated Senzo. It was nearly eight years ago, but he had the same visceral reaction whenever he thought about it.

They'd met at university, in the Afrikaans speaking city, of Pretoria. Thomas had attended an expensive boarding school, with only one career path on his mind. He had every intention of returning to The Last Outpost and making considerable changes. Until he had a degree under his belt, and some experience on another farm, his father would continue to treat him like an idiot. Like Thomas, Senzo also had his heart set on only one field of study, but his options were limited. Senzo had needed a scholarship to afford the fees to study wildlife management, otherwise, he'd have to find a way to fund it himself.

Both entered university in the same year, but it wasn't until one Friday in mid-July, both desperate to escape the freezing halls of academia, that they'd ended up on a long weekend trip to KwaZulu-Natal with a group of avid birders. While the rest of the group went in search of the elusive African Broadbill, Thomas and Senzo had cemented their friendship, and their return to their home province, over an ice-cold beer at 11 a.m. For the next three years, they were inseparable. Both fluent in isiZulu, they took great delight in speaking it together; an act of defiance against those Afrikaans students who refused to speak in English. In December, they travelled back to KwaZulu-Natal for the holidays. At first, Senzo would stay in Durban, and Thomas continued to the game farm, but in time their holidays merged, and Senzo became a regular visitor at the lodge.

It was in his final year that Thomas fell in love, not the boyhood lust pretending to be love, but rather a life-altering, ideology-shifting, type of love. Khethiwe was unlike any woman Thomas had ever met, and he would have walked to the very ends of the earth if it meant he could float in her orbit. And although he seemed blind to them, there were, in fact, two truths he could not avoid: she was Senzo's girlfriend, and her skin was as bronze as a hamerkop's feathers. Four years of friendship were laid to waste the moment Senzo caught them intertwined, like the aerial roots of a ficus tree searching for purchase. If it had not been for the contrast of their skin in the low light, Senzo would have found it difficult to distinguish the contours that divided Thomas from the girl beneath him.

At the time, Thomas hadn't the words to adequately express either his shame at deceiving his friend, or the all-consuming fire he felt for the woman with the high, wide forehead and throaty laugh. Both acts, love, and deception, had not come naturally to Thomas. He'd been raised by a father who'd never recovered from the loss of his wife. Thomas had no example of the intricate dance of falling and staying in love. Thomas knew that one day love would be inevitable, but he had never once, growing up, imagined that he would fall in love with a woman of another race. The only mixed-race couples he'd ever encountered were the foreign guests at the lodge. He'd gone to a private, multi-racial high school, and had black classmates, but none had joined him at the game farm during the holidays. Only once did he ask his father if a black friend could come home, but William had declined.

'Give the country a few more years to settle in,' he'd said.

Thomas hadn't given much thought to it, and he hadn't asked again until he met Senzo, and by then he didn't feel that he had to ask permission. Rather he simply informed his father that he was bringing a friend home.

When he realised that he couldn't stop thinking about Khethiwe, it had come as a complete shock. He found himself cataloguing their differences, as a way of talking himself out of it. But, when they finally leaned towards each other, his relief that her mouth and tongue were as warm and inviting as any girl before her, was met by her relief, and he roared with laughter when she opened her eyes and said in wonder, *'You don't taste like garlic, at all!'*

Back then, it was not only thoughts of Senzo finding out about the affair that kept him awake at night, but also the thought of his father's reaction if he were to find out about his relationship with Khethiwe. Although his father now considered himself a 'liberal', content that the shackles of apartheid had been broken, his liberal notions did not quite extend to his son crossing the colour bar. Thomas knew this because his father had tut-tutted over his coffee one morning when Thomas had cautiously brought up the topic of the few cross-cultural relationships he'd seen at the university. He'd asked, rather crossly, what William's issue with it was, and then felt a wave of panic threaten when his father had replied with genuine concern. *'No one thinks of the children. They'd have a leg in both worlds, but who would they really be?'*

At the time, all Thomas could think about was making a life with Khethiwe, and any coffee-coloured babies they produced. Thomas had tried to point out the various pros of mixed-race relationships, such as forging ahead in a new and progressive South Africa, and the obvious need for races to accept each other as equal; what better way than to share a home and a life? But William, who had looked at his son sharply, had brought the conversation to an end. He stood up from the table and placed a hand on Thomas' unruly mane. 'Son,' he'd said gently, *'for all their similarities, not even black and white rhino mate.'*

But that doesn't mean they can't, thought Thomas as he watched his father leave the room.

Thomas and Khethiwe had managed to live a somewhat satisfying parallel life for their final year at varsity. Thomas learnt to live with the intense guilt he felt, which only reared its head when he spied Senzo across the lecture halls and the campus grounds. They mostly kept to themselves once Thomas concluded that, in general, people shared his father's sentiments and could not seem to keep their opinions to themselves. Both were worried that one of their families would find out and force them to give up what they felt was a love that would never be replicated in their lifetimes. But in the end, it was Khethiwe who began to tentatively unwind the strands that bound them together. It was clear that Thomas was heading back to the game farm, and she could not imagine herself living out her days in some small rural town in Zululand. She'd done everything in her power to change his mind, but Thomas had his life mapped out, and he wanted the soundtrack to feature the clatter of the acacia pods in the wind, and the screech of the francolin at dusk.

After completing his studies and working at a game farm in the Eastern Cape, he returned to Mevamhlope. He hadn't seen Senzo since graduation and he was under the impression that their paths were unlikely to cross again. Then, about a year ago, while on an errand in town, Thomas caught a glimpse of a man who could have been Senzo's twin, getting out of an Umkhombe APU vehicle. Thomas found himself fast-walking towards the vehicle, then hid behind a delivery truck, his heart pounding. When he came out from behind it, the man had disappeared into one of the shops, but a quick phone call confirmed his suspicion. They managed to keep out of each other's way, for the most part, only crossing paths when it was unavoidable.

But Thomas told none of that to Nonhle. He simply closed his eyes at the conjured vision of Khethiwe's wide, smooth forehead, and dancing smile. 'He's like that with everyone,' he said, instead, with a wan smile. 'They're all like that. It's a stressful job; they've forgotten what normal is.'

She stared at him dubiously, but when he didn't offer anything further, she flopped back into her seat in defeat.

'Back there, at the office,' she said, then stopped, catching a fingernail between her teeth. She caught herself and dropped her hand back into her lap.

'Before you came in. Senzo mentioned some evidence they'd found that made him certain that my dad is guilty. Do you know what he's talking about?'

She wouldn't look at him. Instead, she turned her head towards the open window. A flock of starlings, resting on a powerline, scattered into the sky at the blast from the train as it readied itself to move.

'Okay,' he said, his fingers tapping gently on the doorframe. 'Technically, I shouldn't be telling you this, but if it were my dad, I'd want to know. Senzo's right. It doesn't look good for Samson.' He was silent for a few moments, then he continued. 'Yesterday, the police found a SIM card under the front seat of Samson's car. It had been hidden between the runners of his seat.'

Nonhle turned slowly to look at him; she looked so miserable that Thomas reached over and rested his hand lightly on her shoulder. 'The number of the SIM card is the same number used to send the poachers the SMS with the coordinates of where to find the rhino.'

Before Thomas could react, Nonhle swung the passenger door open, just managing to get to the verge before throwing up into the bushes. She stood with her hands on her knees, spitting into the dirt, then she slipped slowly back into her seat.

Thomas, who'd frantically searched the vehicle for a cloth of some sort, handed it to her. 'Sorry,' he said, 'it's all I've got. It's just windscreen dirt.'

She sat back against the leather; her forehead beaded with sweat. 'Why,' she said quietly, 'did you even come to the office if you knew that? Surely you believe he's guilty?' Her voice rose in agony, and she began to cry. 'I mean, I would!'

'But you don't, Nonhle,' said Thomas, softly. 'And neither do I.'

'That's great, Thomas,' she said, wiping her nose with the rag. 'But remember what Senzo said. Memories and good feelings mean nothing. We need evidence.' Suddenly, she reached for his hand and gripped it tightly, her face hopeful. 'You have a plan, don't you? You just didn't want to say it back there.'

'Not yet,' he said, with a wince. 'But I'm working on it ... I promise.'

In the chaos of the day, Thomas hadn't had a chance to properly talk with Dutch Müller about what had happened yesterday. Annoyingly, the man had gone to bed early and his lights switched off, by the time Thomas had finished working with the security team out in the reserve. Thomas had spent the rest of the evening on the phone with his father, who was in Johannesburg. What Thomas knew about Samson; he'd learnt from Detective Karel du Randt.

As they crossed the tracks, Thomas knew that he had his work cut out for him. There were enough reasons why Samson might have done it, starting with money. Game rangers didn't earn a fortune; they relied on substantial tips from foreign guests. For various reasons, occupancy had been much lower over the past six months, and everyone had been taking a bit of strain.

20: It's all up to you now
1st December 2012

She stood outside the Musgrave Shopping Centre in Durban, at the drop-off point, which was clogged with cars double-parked on the road. The blare of angry horns, and the high-pitched shrieking of birds in the solitary baobab tree, assaulted her ears. She watched a man emerge from the dark blue Range Rover he'd parked under a large marula tree. It was her primary school principal, and she followed him with her eyes as he walked past her, into her childhood school. The room he entered, once her Grade 2 classroom, was now a bottle store. He bought a crate of quarts and a young boy in school uniform carried them back to the principal's car. The man flicked a coin into the air, out of reach of the boy, who dropped to his knees, scrambling about in the dirt for the silver treasure.

Nonhle averted her gaze, embarrassed by the change in this formerly kind man. Instead, she focused on the concrete on which she stood, the sun warming her legs through her skirt. The sunlight had cast itself around the many pillars, creating alternating blocks of light and dark. The lines of her block were perfectly straight, until one became distorted, by a probing shadow. The shadow slowly entered the block and appeared to be dragging a reluctant tortoise behind it. Nonhle felt thrilled at the unexpectedness of the small, shy creature heading towards her. It stopped just short of her feet, its head bobbing slowly from left to right, before retreating into its shell.

She held her breath, until the tip of its beak finally reappeared, followed cautiously by its head and wrinkly neck. Moist black eyes tracked around the block of light, and when it was satisfied with what it saw, or didn't see, it continued to extract itself from its hard, helmet-shaped home. Nonhle's delight turned to horror as the dark, leathery limbs attached to a pale, soft torso were exposed to the harsh sunlight. The de-shelled tortoise made its way across the corridor, eventually slithering through the grate and into the gutter. Its shell, once glossy and covered in textured whorls, had become sun-bleached and smooth. It had somehow aged a hundred years in less than a few seconds. She reached down to pick it up; it was light as a feather. She turned it gently to look at its underside, and an exodus of tiny tortoises, like thousands of baby spiders, flooded out of every opening and onto the floor. Nonhle jumped into a star position, her feet planted wide, to avoid crushing the babies.

Suddenly, the feet of shoppers on the outside of her perfect block of light encroached at its edges. She watched as two policewomen, large feet shod in police issue boots, stepped back towards the streams of tiny reptiles that were trying to escape the light.

'Hey!' she yelled, trying to warn them as her arms shot out, forming a shield of protection.

The women were oblivious, braying like donkeys at a joke Nonhle hadn't heard. She swung her handbag in an arc, catching one of the women on her arm. The woman swivelled round, hand on the gun at her hip.

'Please,' Nonhle implored, pushing them back with her hands. 'You're going to kill them! Watch where you step.'

The woman laughed, her accent rolling thickly off her tongue. '*Agh*, please *meisie*,' she said, looking down at the moving mass at their feet. 'There's plenty more where they came from.' She smirked at Nonhle, raised her foot, and brought it swiftly down on the baby tortoises, severing the line in two.

Nonhle cried out and gave the woman a hard shove to free the squirming tortoises trapped underneath her shoe. 'Please,' she yelled, to the other policewoman. 'Please, you can still help them!'

She looked at Nonhle scornfully. '*Ag*, child,' she said. 'It's too late. No one can help you. It's all up to you now.'

Nonhle woke with a start. Her head thick with a headache, and her eyes gummy with the blending of tears and sleep. Her light was on, and she was still dressed in yesterday's clothing. She reached for her phone, sitting up she saw it was the same day – she'd slept right through dinner. She heard the clink of dishes being washed and made her way into the kitchen.

'Why didn't you wake me, Ma,' she said.

Her mother, who was at the kitchen sink, turned to face her with a slow, sad smile. 'You looked like you needed it, my child.'

She placed a bowl of food on the table, gesturing for Nonhle to sit. Nonhle lowered herself onto the chair and inhaled the familiar, comforting scent of curried cabbage and pap, swimming in a juicy tomato and onion sauce. Thuli watched Nonhle taste her first spoonful, before turning back to the sink, where she submerged her hands in the soapy water. She hesitated for a while, then said in a quiet voice, 'I saw Thomas McKenzie drop you off. Did he see you walking on the road?'

Nonhle's spoon hovered in mid-air. When she'd come in, Thuli had been lying on her bed, eyes closed. She assumed that her mother was asleep and had crept into her own room. She'd been relieved. On the drive back, she'd wondered how she would tell Thuli the news of the SIM card. There was no doubt in her mind that the small-town grapevine would be vibrating with the news, which would reach Thuli, sooner than Nonhle was ready for.

She put her spoon down and held out her hand. 'Sit down, Mama.'

By the time Nonhle had put her mother to bed, a cup of rooibos tea, and a sleeping tablet on her bedside table, she was close to exhaustion. Mama had simply nodded her head at the news of the incriminating find, but she'd looked at Nonhle, lips tight and jaw set. She would not even consider the possibility that Baba was involved in the poaching of a rhino. The SIM belonged to someone else. Someone had planted it in Baba's vehicle. Nothing could convince her that the man she'd spent much of her life with, was guilty. They might not have much, but they had enough. More than many.

Nonhle sat at the pine table as she went over the day's events. Not seeing her father at the station had left her feeling that she had failed him. Neither Mama nor herself had been able to talk to Baba at all since his arrest. She'd simply wanted to hold his hand and tell him that they believed in him ... were here for him. She knew her father would know that, without a shadow of a doubt, but she wanted the chance to say it to him. For him to hear the words said out loud in a place where guilt was assumed. She should have left a note for him – surely, they would have allowed that?

The time spent with Senzo and Thomas had been eye-opening, but ultimately, depressing. Now she understood what one of her lecturers had meant when she'd once said that knowledge had the power to mobilise or paralyse. Listening to the why behind the growing desire for horn, and so many other animals in Africa, was overwhelming. Would they ever win this war? Would it be possible to educate so many people in the short space of time left? Was it already a lost cause? Should they focus on other things? Senzo clearly believed that it was worth trying. But she could see that it had come at great cost to him. Not only was he impatient and rude, but his skin was showing faint lines, like the map documenting the extent of poaching across two provinces. He was aggressive and mean, and she wondered who would put up with that in a partner. Was it easier to excuse that type of behaviour in someone who had such a clear call on their lives? Could you forgive them because of what they saw and dealt with day after day?

Senzo's decision to work in such a meaningful profession, at great risk to himself, made her question her own career choice. Her parents had been bewildered when she'd come home declaring that she was going to major in anthropology.

'But what do you do with it?' they'd asked. She'd been stumped by that question.

She wasn't entirely sure; all the anthropologists she knew lectured at the university. As it turned out, that had been the right answer. A daughter lecturing at a university. *What more could parents ask for?*

Over her years of study, she had felt strongly about certain topics, but then some new information came to light, and her heart moved on quickly. Up until a week ago, she was still waiting for something to ignite the passion within her. Something that would light up her path in a clear direction.

The green whirr of a praying mantis flew in through the window, landing on the table, a few centimetres from her hand. It turned its slow gaze upon her, extending a tentative limb in front of its face. The shadow it cast onto the table released Nonhle's dream from the holding pattern of dreams waiting to be remembered. It wasn't the vision of thousands of baby tortoises being crushed that mobilised her, but the parting words of the policewoman: *'It's all up to you now.'*

21: Eh-eh, sisi
1st December 2012

The distorted vibration of the bass travelled out the door of Jika Jika Tavern, crossed the sandy yard, and entered the tree she was leaning against. The song came to a sudden end, and the sounds of laughter and clicking pool balls, floated out to meet her. Two patrons, quart bottles in hand, stumbled out of the tavern and found a place to relieve themselves against the peeling tavern wall.

Although the night was humid, Nonhle stood shivering in the short skirt and skimpy satin top she'd managed to put together. Finding the right outfit to impress a man had not been an easy feat. Even in Durban, away from her parents, she didn't wear skirts that ventured above her knees or necklines that plunged south. She had a stretchy pencil skirt that she folded at the waistband until the soft curves of her thighs were just visible. The top was a negligée she'd bought in a fit of madness, being the only person for the foreseeable future who would view it. But she had been unable to resist the soft slide of material against her skin. The black patent leather of her work high heels reflected the coloured lights that flickered across the doorway.

The dream had settled for Nonhle that, if Samson was going to be found innocent, it was up to her to prove it. It was blatantly clear that she would get no help from Senzo or the police, and there was no doubt in her mind that Thomas would have vetoed this ridiculous idea. It was the photo on Senzo's wall that had led her here. The photos of soulless men had terrified her as much as those of the butchered animals, but amidst the carnage and death was a bright patch of red and white.

A place where answers might be found on the lips of drunk men. If Samson was involved, for whatever unimaginable reason, then perhaps someone inside would know something and be willing to toss her even the tiniest nugget of truth. No one would speak to her if she went in with a notebook and pen. She had to blend in.

The music started up again, and she wondered – not for the first time – if she was in any way prepared for what could unfold in the dark corners of the tavern. She hefted her backpack crammed with the pumps, dress, and jacket she'd worn over her outfit, into the crook of the tree, and slipped a fifty Rand note into her bra. She took a few deep breaths, curving her lips into what she hoped was a seductive smile. She walked the short distance from the tree to the open door of the tavern and attempted to sashay into the room.

Surveying the confines of the tavern, the sour smell of spilt beer and dagga assaulted her nostrils. She'd never been inside before, only ever having viewed it as a passenger in a passing taxi. In the daylight, with Jika Jika painted across the lintel in thick white lettering on its faded red walls, the tavern had an air of abandonment. On those days, she might see an elderly man sitting on an upturned paint drum outside, or the occasional chicken scratching in the dirt for an unsuspecting grub. But in general, it did not appear to be the centre of social engagement that it was when darkness fell. The bar was lined with men on stools, tipping back quarts of Black Label, rolling cigarettes, and thumping each other heartily on the back as stories passed between them. An argument started at the pool table where two men were fighting over whose two rand coin had been next in line. A pool cue was wrenched back and forth between them, in an unfriendly game of tug of war.

Two women wove like cats between the motley crew propping up the bar. At the sight of Nonhle standing in the doorway, young thighs on display, the women all but hissed. They rounded on her in a flash, pushing her towards an open door, and spat her out like a rotten piece of meat. Nonhle stumbled, almost twisting an ankle to avoid the spare car parts that littered the yard. She turned and took in their thunderous faces. Before she could open her mouth, the first prostitute jutted a hip to the left and stuck a fishnet-clad leg out at an extreme angle. She waved a crimson tipped finger in Nonhle's face.

'Eh-eh, sisi,' she said, her head swivelling in time with her wagging finger.

The second prostitute, lips pursed in irritation, crossed her arms over her ample bosom as if trying to prevent their escape.

'Is there a problem?' stuttered Nonhle, the last of her confidence draining rapidly away.

'The problem, sisi,' said the first, jabbing Nonhle's left breast with a razor-sharp claw, 'is you.'

'*Yebo,*' said the other. 'Is this place called Jika Jika Jika? No! It is not! It is called Jika Jika. This place is not big enough for the three of us.'

'Oh! No!' Nonhle sputtered as the woman's meaning dawned on her. 'I'm not here for … you know. I'm just here to look for someone specific —'

'We're all looking for someone, sweetie,' said the second woman. 'But you need at least three Mr. Someones if you want to keep looking like this.' She swept her hands up and down her body, then patted her weave.

'No, really,' stressed Nonhle. 'I don't need a man for *that!*'

The prostitutes shared a look and an incredulous laugh. 'We don't understand, sisi,' said the first, suddenly serious. 'What else would you need a man for?'

Nonhle felt close to slapping these two single-minded women. She felt overwhelmed by the turn of events. 'I'm looking for information, that's all,' she said with resignation. 'I need to talk to someone who knows something about rhino poaching.'

The two women looked at each other sharply, an eyebrow on each face curved high over wide eyes. They each grabbed an arm and propelled Nonhle further away from the tavern.

'Are you crazy?' said the first, eyes swinging around her like the beam of a torch. 'You can't just walk in here asking about these things. Are you trying to get killed!'

Nonhle's skin pimpled despite the heat; their fear suddenly thick around her. 'Please,' she pleaded, prying the woman's hand from her arm. 'This is really important. I'm not trying to make trouble.'

'No,' whispered the second, harshly. 'No one can help you here! You are a stupid, stupid girl. You need to leave.' She shoved Nonhle in the direction of the road.

Nonhle shoved back, resignation turning to anger. 'I'm not leaving!

Just point me in the right direction, that's all I'm asking.'

'You are mad!' the woman spat. 'Do you know what happens to people who talk?'

The second prostitute pulled a finger across her throat, the whites of her eyes round with fear. 'You think because you're young and pretty they won't do anything to you?' The overwhelming ripening of the woman's cheap perfume confirmed how upset the conversation was making her.

Nonhle grabbed her by her shoulders, her breath hot on the woman's face. 'My father is in jail! They say he's involved in rhino poaching. I know he didn't do it. I just need to prove it. Someone must know something. I'm not leaving until I find that person.'

Before the woman could respond, a large SUV pulled into the parking lot, its headlights catching the entangled trio in a shaft of yellow light. For a moment, the three were frozen in place, then just as quickly the light moved on, releasing them into the darkness. Nonhle ran in the direction of the tree to grab her bag, and the prostitutes tottered back into the tavern, ready to fight over their favourite customer.

***

He walked towards the bar, an unfamiliar feeling welling up inside him. For the first time in years, he felt guilty. Yes, that was it … he felt a sense of personal responsibility for what he'd just seen. He'd seen the three women bunched together, but only one face took him by surprise as it stared blindly in his direction. But then, he thought, while he sat at the bar – only a few days had passed since her father's arrest. Surely, things were not so financially dire that she felt she had to resort to prostitution. Surely there were other ways for such a clever girl to make money. She could head back to Durban, or even Richards Bay; plenty of positions for a girl with her qualifications there. Before he could think any further about Nonhle, a cold quart was placed in front of him. He pulled a cigarette from his pack, flicking his worn and beaten silver lighter into life. The sudden display of light had his favourite prostitute appear next to him. She wafted the plume of smoke away with a delicate wave and gave him a beguiling smile.

'Hello, Dutchy,' she giggled and kissed his neck. 'Ready when you are.'

Dutch laughed, giving her bottom a gentle squeeze, 'How many times do I have to tell you, Toks? First a drink, then a game of pool, and then you.'

Toks pouted, 'Uh-uh, Dutch! It's never one drink. Then I have to work extra hard to make things *work*.'

Dutch let out a whoop of laughter, knowing she would forgive him. He was the only one who treated the prostitutes with kindness. The other men often dispensed a backhand or two the drunker they got. There'd been a few occasions where Dutch had broken up a fight between the ladies and their clients. There might be a punch or two thrown in Dutch's direction, but usually, it was nothing a cold beer couldn't sort out between the men.

When Dutch tipped his head back to take a long drink, Toks made to leave in search of another client. He wrapped a hand around her wrist and pulled her back to his side. 'Hang on, Toks. What was going on out there,' he said, gesturing with a quick nod of his head towards the front door.

The prostitute bit her lip; Dutch watched her closely as she figured out how best to respond. Finally, she turned and gave him a bright smile.

'Oh,' she said, waving her hand dismissively. 'That silly girl; shame. Her father was arrested and is in jail. He didn't do it. *Obviously*,' she laughed, with a roll of her eyes. 'She thinks someone here knows something about rhino poaching and can help her.'

Dutch had the strangest feeling that he was floating. He saw the look of concern on Tok's face, and he watched her mouth the words, 'I told her she's crazy, of course.'

He brought himself back by squeezing her wrist hard. 'What else did she say?'

'Ow, Dutch,' she whimpered.

'Quickly, Toks,' he urged, his fingers squeezing the delicate bones.

Toks began to cry softly. 'Nothing Dutch, I promise. Hlengi and I told her she was a stupid little girl. That she was looking for trouble. We were trying to make her leave. When we saw you come in, we left her out there.'

Dutch released her wrist and stood up. He gave her a quick hug and kissed her head. 'Sorry, *liebling*, I didn't mean to hurt you. You did the right thing.'

He left her standing at the bar, rubbing her bruised wrist, while he hurried outside to see if Nonhle was still around. The yard was dark, she could be hiding anywhere. He ran to the toilet block, holding his breath as he checked inside. Out on the road, there was no sign of her. He got into his car for some privacy and pulled out his phone.

His palm beat the steering wheel while a wretched tune played instead of a ring tone. It was his absolute worst irritation with the staff at the lodge; ridiculous, tinny songs that grated on your nerves as you waited for the caller to answer. *No, I do not want to pay R5 for this ringtone!*

'We have a problem,' he said, by way of introduction. 'I'm at Jika. The daughter of Samson Ngubane was just here, dressed as a prostitute; I thought she was trying to make some extra cash.'

'Shut up, Lucky!' Dutch felt his face colour at Lucky's lewd jibe. 'She was asking questions before I got here; trying to find someone who might know something about Samson.'

'No, she's gone now. I've looked everywhere. Someone needs to find her, and stop her from poking around.'

That poor girl, he thought, dropping the phone onto the passenger seat. *She doesn't stand a chance.* He flicked a cigarette butt into the darkness, then headed back inside.

22: What would old Mavis do?
1st December 2012

The phone call with Lucky had left Dutch anxious; he felt as if a moth had made its way down his oesophagus and taken up residence in his chest cavity. He hated to admit it, but he had a feeling that he was going soft. Even the positive energy of the tavern, and the heady scent of Toks, couldn't lift his spirits. He sat at the bar, his quart long past the stage of sweating merrily. It stood in a pool of water, warm to the touch. He pushed it aside, signalling for another. If he was honest with himself, he had to admit that this entire situation didn't sit well with him.

He'd known the Ngubane family for two years now; and although he could be as cold as the next guy, setting Samson up for the fall had disturbed him. He liked the man. When Dutch had first arrived, Samson had been the ranger to acquaint him with the lay of the land. He'd learnt more about game and birds, in one game drive with Samson, than he had in his entire time in Africa. However, Dutch had a strong sense of self-preservation. Which had only grown stronger over the years of working with Bento – the Mozambican – and now Lucky. Dutch was under no illusions about Lucky. Once Dutch proved unnecessary to Lucky's plans, he was sure Lucky would find a way to rid himself of Dutch.

He downed half the contents of his beer. The moth in his chest sent a warning back up his oesophagus to slow down. There was only so much space for beer and anxiety to share. The same stifling sense of claustrophobia that he'd experienced back in Tanzania, years earlier, enveloped him. Back then it had choked him like a strangler vine does a tree, and he realised now that the vine had never actually withered and died. It was as if his body had retained the memory of it all and was reproducing it verbatim; different location, same physical response.

Back in Tanzania, when the noose had begun to tighten, and the air in his luxury apartment had turned fetid with fear, he swore he'd never get involved with poaching again.

If only he could get out of the country unscathed, he thought.

For two glorious years he'd enjoyed a position of privilege; a white man who'd been taken in as one of the country's own, making his way up the ranks, befriending politicians and high-status foreigners and providing a key service that was remunerated financially. Oh, the life he had lived. It hadn't been the life he'd planned for himself, but it had certainly turned out to be one he could bear.

He smiled now as he thought of the early days before his newfound career in the indirect trade of animal parts. He'd worked as General Manager in one of the best hotels in Dar-es-Salaam. Westerners had such an archaic view of Africa; if it hadn't been for a friend who'd worked in the country before him, he'd have imagined the only buildings were beachside shacks and worker compounds. Instead, his days had been filled with white linen, silverware, and endless blue skies; his nights with gorgeous women, international friends, and just enough drugs to ensure that he didn't ruin his perfect life.

It was on one of these nights, after popping two pills, that he'd met Bento. They'd locked eyes as Dutch had taken in the sight of the six-foot four-inch giant, who sat at the bar beside him. The pattern of raised lines and triangles in dark ink on the man's face seemed to pulsate with energy. Dutch tentatively reached out to touch them, then quickly withdrew his hand.

'A wise decision,' said Bento, his voice a low growl.

Dutch looked down at his right hand; short stubby fingers, which matched his short compact frame. He stretched both hands out in front of his face – turning them this way, and that. The sight of them amused him greatly, and his body shook like a bobblehead doll on a bumpy road. The vision of a hysterical, miniature, blonde German, made Bento roar with laughter, right along with Dutch. By the next morning, when the effects had worn off, and strong black coffee replaced liquor, Bento and

Dutch had their first real conversation, one that would change Dutch's life forever.

They were seated in a discreet alcove at a neighbouring hotel. Dutch sat in a puffy leather armchair and felt comforted by its embrace. A waitress served coffee and tiny petit fours on a silver tray.

'I've heard good things about you,' said Bento.

His heavy accent elongated his words. Everything about Bento, from his voice to the cut of his clothes, spoke of power and confidence. Bento stirred three heaped spoons of sugar into his coffee, popping one of the ridiculous sized treats into his mouth. He leant back and stared out to sea, his eyes tracking the small wooden skiffs searching for fish. In the light of day, the fierceness of the Mozambican's face had softened. The pulsating triangles and lines had become lethargic with the dawn. He wore an expensive Rolex, a Lacoste shirt in pale blue, and white linen pants. His feet were encased in fine leather, the colour of which perfectly matched his shirt. Arms, neck, and chest, built like a street fighter. And, although Bento appeared perfectly relaxed, sitting on the veranda with the cool breeze blowing in from the ocean, Dutch got the impression he'd be struck in the throat with snakelike speed, if he even breathed in a way that offended the man.

Bento continued his scrutiny of the horizon. 'I'm looking for someone with your level of discretion. Someone with intelligence and the ability to operate under the radar; someone who wants to make a very good living but doesn't feel the need to tell everyone how he goes about doing it.' Bento picked up his cup of coffee and took a dainty sip to test the quality of the brew, before taking a long pull. He lowered the cup, positioned the teaspoon just so, and looked over at Dutch. 'Do you understand what I'm saying?'

Dutch licked his lips, clearing his throat with a dry cough. Of course, he wanted to make more money, who didn't? But the energy pulsating off Bento was so unsettling that Dutch was afraid – afraid to say yes, but even more afraid to say no.

He knew exactly what Bento meant about discretion. It was the nature of his job. Dutch's clientele featured politicians and local celebrities, all of whom seemed to live a double life, and expected Dutch to take care of any potential misunderstandings. Just yesterday, Dutch had prevented an ugly scene between a politician, his mistress, and his fiancée. The local politician had turned up with his mistress, just as his fiancée had emerged from the ladies' room in the lobby. The man had already been through one messy divorce, losing a considerable portion of his wealth, in the process. Dutch was in time to signal to one of his staff to steer the fiancée towards the bar, with a promise of a complimentary glass of champagne on the house, while he ushered his guest to the elevator. He was so used to these scenes that he hadn't even broken into a sweat.

Dutch managed to collect himself, his eyes finally meeting those of Bento. 'What would it entail?' he asked.

The Mozambican laughed, then drained his cup. 'How strongly do you feel about wildlife and the export business?'

That had been a few years ago. His first two years working with Bento had been exciting; he got to do what he did best. He continued in his role as GM at the hotel, and used his excellent skills at orchestrating events, and overhearing crucial information, which he passed on to Bento. The adage, loose lips sink ships, certainly applied. Dutch's information ensured that Bento was generally ahead of the pack and could swing his negotiations in a fortuitous direction.

When Dutch's ears began to overhear information that led him to believe that his cover was very likely on the verge of being blown, it was Bento who had organised Dutch a new position in a new country. Dutch had always wanted to visit South Africa. It was just that he'd imagined that the blonde sands of Clifton Beach would coat his feet, not the red, dry earth of Mevamhlope. The beautiful expanse of ocean in Dar replaced by the veld and acacia trees, and the incessant cacophony of birdlife.

Dutch was under no illusion that Bento cared for him on a personal level. A new line of business had sprung up unexpectedly a few months previously, and it suited Bento to move Dutch to his new supplier destination.

Why now? Dutch had asked Bento. Bento certainly hadn't jumped at the opportunity to join in on the action when it started to heat up down south in the Kruger National Park. Things were going well in Tanzania. Bento was receiving more than enough ivory and horn; thanks to the information he was receiving from Dutch. But then an unlikely individual from over the border had appeared, looking for a buyer of the horn he planned to poach. *Planned*, being the operative word. Dutch had been incredulous when Bento had told him about Lucky Mhlongo. Dutch was sure the man hadn't poached anything more dangerous than a branch from the sweet thorn tree, before the meeting. But there was a vitality around him that led Bento to believe that he might be able to pull it off, and, Bento had nothing to lose himself. He'd sent the young man back over the border with a proviso; if Lucky organised the entire mission under his own steam, and presented Bento with a horn, a partnership would be considered.

Dutch had to swallow his words when Bento's instincts had proved correct. Bento had called him; with an almost imperceptible rise in octave, alerting Dutch to his boss's excitement. Lucky and his team had somehow managed to detach the horns from a full-grown white rhino, without injury to themselves, or detection. Bento revealed that Lucky had not been part of the excursion; the trio of poachers had politely told him that he would be of no use to them. It was likely that Lucky would get them killed or caught, so his job was to drive the getaway vehicle; and, because he had no capital to pay any of them, one of the men had stuck to Lucky like a limpet on a rock, until the payment had been received. Bento had arranged for one of his transporters to meet with Lucky to fetch the horn, and to educate Lucky on the intricacies of getting horns from South Africa to Mozambique, in the future.

After the third package of horn had reached Bento in Mozambique, he decided that it was time to diversify his supplier base. He orchestrated a position for Dutch at The Last Outpost Lodge, for the simple reason that one of his cousins worked there. She was a cleaner and with a little financial encouragement, had accused the current GM of trying to coerce her, and a few others, into providing sexual favours. The confused man had been suspended while the investigation took place, but the family humiliation had proved too great in the small town, and he left.

Dutch took to his new role with renewed vigour. Although the lodge offered absolutely no highlife, politicians, and celebrities being few and far between in the bushveld, he felt safe there. He enjoyed the lack of pomp and ceremony, and constant kowtowing to their strange whims and fancies. His role was to become good friends with the men in town; those in law enforcement, and conservation, and to keep abreast of the growing concerns that rhino poaching would eventually spillover from the Kruger Park, into the less well-monitored KwaZulu-Natal province.

Dutch relied on his chameleon-like qualities to fit in. He found he could hold his own on a rugby field; what he lacked in height, he made up for in swiftness. He could prop up a bar with the game rangers or flirt with the cleaning ladies in the laundry room. Down at Jika Jika Tavern, the patrons knew him as the foreigner with the fondness for black women, and Black Label. He played pool, winning enough games to pose a challenge, and losing enough to be challenged repeatedly. He was free with his smokes and happy to drink alone or with company. All the while he kept his ears open for conversations that might give him an inside lead on the competition, or alert his team to any unwanted third-party knowledge of upcoming excursions.

Because Bento was innately suspicious, Dutch also kept an eye on Lucky. Lucky had been openly hostile when Dutch had arranged to meet with him for the first time. Lucky had done just fine transporting his horn over the border to Bento. What possible role could Dutch play, other than get in the way, and take a share of the profit? As far as Lucky was concerned, the fewer people between himself and Bento, the better. Dutch was quick to assure him of the practicality of his involvement. Integrating himself into the lives of people Lucky was unlikely to have access to, such as Karel and the anti-poaching unit, was bound to reveal vital information.

'People just don't realise, Lucky,' he said, his voice thick with persuasion. 'They get complacent. They assume everyone's on the same side. They forget who's listening. They ignore the cleaning lady; failing to ask themselves, *what would old Mavis do with this information?* But old Mavis has a son, a son who wants his two boys to go to a nice school, so they can get a good education; and like old Mavis, the men also forget to limit their conversation around the braai, when I'm around. You know what it's like. When the beer flows, men … they like to brag, to show off.'

When Lucky had come to him, handing over an envelope with the SIM card inside, Dutch had laughed in disbelief.

'Have you gone insane? Why would you bring the police to our door?' Dutch watched with annoyance as Lucky nonchalantly removed the matchstick from his mouth and inspected its masticated end.

'I've been thinking,' Lucky said, popping the match back between his teeth. 'They're going to get suspicious – how come no one has tried to poach the rhino at The Last Outpost? Nearly every lodge has had some attempt, except this one. This way, we all win. I get to teach Nkosi a lesson for stealing my horn, Mthunzi gets his revenge on Samson, and you,' he said, one eyebrow raised at Dutch, 'you won't look suspicious. It's not just us blacks involved in poaching. I hear there's lots of *abelungu* in positions just like yours, up by Kruger, getting involved.'

Dutch hated to admit it, but there was a small part of him that feared Lucky. There was something about the man that had changed in the years since they'd met. A hardness had crept in.

Now, sitting at the bar, Dutch knew for certain that he was an expendable pawn in Lucky Mhlongo's game. He should have acted earlier. He had known that Lucky was only interested in himself. Anyone who got in the way would be despatched, one way, or another; and he'd use anyone to get his way.

Just look at Samson Ngubane, he thought. *What had the man ever done to Lucky to deserve such a fate?*

Dutch sighed heavily. He should have been devising a parallel strategy to ensure his security; had he learnt nothing from his Tanzanian experience? Dutch knew exactly where the problem lay. He had only himself to blame. He was perfectly happy to ride on the coattails of others – benefiting from their daring exploits – as long as his bank account was more than healthy, and he didn't have to risk life or limb in the process.

Although he was certain no one had seen him plant that SIM in Samson's vehicle, he had a worrying feeling that his involvement, might come out before he was ready.

23: Wild leaps of logic
2nd December 2012

Thomas's mouth curved upwards as he watched the antics of an egret struggling to keep its balance on a particularly grumpy buffalo bull. A large herd was making its way across the dirt road and into the bush. His amusement subsided as he thought about the conversation ahead. He started his vehicle and wove his way to the workers' compound. The events of the night before had been completely unexpected, and he was surprised at how anxious he had felt driving to fetch Nonhle near Jika Jika Tavern.

It was after 11 p.m., and he'd been in bed rereading one of Ian Player's books when he'd received her call. Initially, his brain was unable to compute what she was saying. He thought maybe she was drunk – perhaps she'd gone to Jika to unwind – to forget about the day's events. He didn't know her well enough to say whether drinking was her way of coping with stressful situations but choosing to drink at Jika would indicate another level of stress. But then she managed to convey, in a fierce whisper, that she was currently hiding in a bush and needed a lift, for him to understand she'd done something incredibly stupid and dangerous.

He'd done a slow drive by the tavern, looking for a small backpack on the side of the road. When he'd pulled over, she'd streaked out of the bush and into his car.

'What the hell —' he began.

'Don't say anything,' she'd pleaded.

He'd wanted to grab her by the shoulders and make her tell him exactly what she thought she was playing at, but her face, rigid with shock, and the way she hugged her bag to her chest, stopped him. When they reached the compound, she'd tried to exit the car without any further discussion, but Thomas caught her hand.

'Tomorrow, Nonhle,' he'd said. 'We will talk about this, tomorrow.'

***

The compound was quiet by the time he entered through the gate; most of the inhabitants having left early for work with the staff vehicle. As he made his way to her house, he remembered that the last time he'd walked through the staff accommodation of the cleaners, restaurant staff, and security, had been over two years ago. One of the employees had been spotted walking through the thick bush behind the compound, carrying an impala carcass on his back. A search of his room revealed a stack of pelts, ready for sale.

Thomas vaguely remembered the shabby feel of the place. But now, as he drove through the compound, he allowed his eyes to travel properly over the area. He saw long rows of hostel-style rooms for the single people and a few two-bedroom houses for the married couples. From this vantage point, he could see the broken windows, the frailty of the doors where white ants had eaten through the wood.

He saw the shared ablution blocks, with the peeling paint and the puddles of water created by leaking taps. Washing draped over large juicy aloe leaves because the washing lines were broken, their long-frayed ropes swinging in the wind. Irritation rose within him; why hadn't they fixed things? Why hadn't they tried? How hard was it to fix a tap, mend a washing line? He felt himself becoming annoyed at the laziness that was so evident.

It was the mentality of *It's not mine, so why should I fix it?* Then, an image of the old house he'd rented with fellow students in Pretoria came to mind. Hadn't the four of them driven the landlord demented with their constant calls to fix things that had broken? The landlord could not understand how the young men, capable of fixing run-down Land Rovers with seemingly only a piece of string and kind words, could not fix a broken cistern. No, their time and their money had been precious back then; and frankly, it wasn't their responsibility to fix it.

He made his way over to the Ngubane household with a growing sense of rising discomfort. He had always considered himself to be very aware of the circumstances of many in South Africa, circumstances that he knew others in his position did not, or would not, consider to be true. He knew that he had it better than most, much better. And he tried to be mindful of that, but perhaps he had judged himself too generously. If the state of the compound was anything to go by, he'd simply been turning a blind eye.

It wasn't that the accommodation was completely uninhabitable. The walls were concrete, the roofs were intact, there was electricity, and communal water taps. But if he were honest, he knew that if they tried to house a white game ranger, or an upper-level staff member, in this environment, they would never stand for it. They would speak up for themselves. Human Resources would get an earful about their rights to decent accommodation. Only last week he'd heard one of the rangers complaining about the malfunctioning air con unit in his room; Thomas was certain that there wasn't one ceiling fan in the compound.

Nonhle's home was situated a little further away from the rows of single rooms. They had a small garden, most of which was given over to limp vegetables in need of a good soaking. The door opened, and a drawn and tired face peeked out to greet him.

'Mama's still asleep,' Nonhle said, quietly. 'She's not doing very well. It's like her spirit left her body when they took Baba away.'

He nodded and felt a deep sense of sorrow at how the situation was affecting them all. 'Let's talk outside then.'

Nonhle stuck her head out the doorway and looked around. 'Do you think that's a good idea? People might talk.'

'Let them,' he said, drawing her away from the house.

She took the lead, ducking under the rusted razor-wire fence that separated the compound from the road. He watched as she jogged over the road to the verge, stopping at a fallen marula tree. The trunk offered them a place to sit and gaze onto the open land of The Last Outpost.

Nonhle pulled at a long blade of dry grass, its parched roots easily releasing the plant into her care. She gave Thomas a nervous smile as he sat down next to her.

'So,' he said. 'Want to tell me about last night.'

The sound of a quad bike coming along the fence line gave her a short reprieve. The bike came into view and the rider came to a stop when he saw them.

'It's okay, Jabs,' Thomas said, waving the man on. The man nodded his head and set off to continue his check of the fence.

Thomas gave her a pointed look, encouraging her to continue.

'I know,' she admitted, sheepishly. 'It was stupid of me. But I didn't know what else to do! Everyone's taking too long ... it's been too long!'

She brushed a hand across her cheek, wiping away a tear before it fell. Thomas couldn't bring himself to berate her any further.

'Did you at least learn anything last night?'

She was silent for a while, then she glanced sideways at him.

'Well, I did see Dutch Müller ... I don't think he saw me, but I saw him when I was trying to find a hiding place. He got in his car, made a call, then went back in.' He nodded. Dutch hanging out at Jika wasn't news to him. Nonhle frowned at him. 'Doesn't that concern you?'

'In what way? It's not a crime to drink at a tavern,' he shrugged.

'Well, I mean, he's the GM of the lodge, and he hangs out in the same tavern that's in a photo stuck on Senzo's wall. That must mean they're worried about what goes on there, or who goes there. And if they're worried, shouldn't you be, knowing your GM drinks at a bar where something to do with poaching happens?'

'Woah,' he said. 'You're making wild leaps of logic there!' He dropped a hand and grabbed at the thin stalk of grass that was tickling his leg. 'To be honest, we've always kind of viewed it as an opportunity to gather information ourselves. Dutch is incredibly well-integrated for a foreigner. He doesn't care what anybody thinks of him, he just acts as if he belongs, and he doesn't seem to see colour, or even class. So, he's accepted in places that I probably wouldn't be because he's seen as one of them. He likes their beer, he likes their women, he speaks passable Zulu, and he's generous. He also knows who some of the community informants are, so he keeps his eyes and ears open.'

'But it's possible,' she pressed, 'that he could be involved, and you just don't know about it?'

Now it was Thomas's turn to frown. 'Of course,' he said, slowly. 'There's always that possibility. But to be honest, I just don't believe that Dutch could be capable of something like this.'

Nonhle gave a hollow laugh. 'And yet you're okay with believing there's a small chance that Samson is?'

'Hey!' he said, hurt by the implication of her words. 'That's not fair! I'm doing everything I can to prove Samson's innocence.'

Nonhle crossed her arms, her eyes focused on his. 'Really? Like what, exactly. Because as far as I can tell, no one has done anything to bring us closer to the truth.'

'I …' Thomas looked away. 'Okay,' he agreed. 'It's not looking good. We did try and locate the CCTV footage of the game vehicle parking bays for Thursday night. I was told a technician had been called out a few days before to work on a faulty wire. He got it working, and then the wire shorted again around 5 p.m. on Thursday. The technician could only come back out mid-morning the next day but by that time … well, you know the story.'

'Are you serious!' she cried, leaping up from the trunk.

'Shh, Nonhle. Come on.' Thomas pulled her down and turned to see if anyone over the road paid them any attention.

'Don't you think,' she said, her voice vibrating with anger, 'that it's just a bit of a coincidence that the CCTV camera isn't working on the very same night!'

'Of course, it is,' he agreed. 'But it doesn't tell us who messed with it.'

'But do you agree it could have been Dutch?' she countered.

'Perhaps,' he said. 'But it could also have been any number of other people … including your father.'

Nonhle's head dropped into her hands. 'Did you at least let Detective du Randt know?' she mumbled through her fingers.

'Of course, we did it at their request. The police were there. There's also one other interesting thing I found out,' he said, shifting uncomfortably.

'What's that?' She lifted her head warily.

'The poachers revealed the code name that the police used to identify your father.'

'Code name?'

'Ucikicane,' he said, struggling a little with the pronunciation.

'Little finger?' she said. 'But …' she turned to him with such hope on her face that Thomas felt his heart lurch. 'Thomas! That would mean it had to be someone who knew Samson well. Knew him well enough to know that that name would lead the police to him. Someone like Dutch!'

Thomas gave a short bark of laughter. 'Nonhle, as integrated at Dutch is, I seriously doubt that he would know some obscure Zulu custom that not every Ngubane practises anymore.'

His words seemed to have little effect on her excitement. 'Well, maybe Dutch is working with someone. Someone else on the staff who would know that kind of information.'

Thomas held up his hands to stop her from going any further. 'I get it, Nonhle. And I promise we're not just looking at Samson.'

The truth was, she could be right. He wasn't so naïve as to imagine that it couldn't be someone on staff. He could name at least three people who might fit the bill; and all three of them were on final warnings.

'Listen,' he said. 'I think that if you're right about this, the police will figure it out. Karel might not have the best personality, but he is good at his job. Between himself and Detective Dlamini, they'll find the person responsible. They've got a big network of community informants – someone will speak up, especially if money is on the table.'

***

He left her sitting on the log, gazing blindly into the reserve. He pulled away from the compound, and once again, he found himself thinking about the lives of those who lived there. If this were his life, would he do it? Would he take an offer he couldn't refuse? A few months' salary, maybe more, to pass on some information about a rhino, to turn a blind eye. What other chance was there to move up the ladder? For their children to move out of this place, and on to somewhere better, something better?

24: Not her fault, at all
2nd December 2012

Despite the ban on selling beers on a Sunday, some taverns still did a roaring trade. A taxi, its side door pulled wide, vibrated to the music blaring from oversized speakers. Young men shouted to each other about the evening's plans, and if the length of the queue in the bottle store was anything to go by, those plans included large amounts of Black Label flowing down thirsty throats. Crates of the dark brew were being ferried out by young boys into the back of the taxis. Zodwa finally reached the till, paid her money, and hefted the bags off the counter.

Her fingers burned with a fiery intensity under the weight of the four plastic bags she carried. Each contained four quarts of beer. Lunga, her long-time partner and useless father of her children, had dispatched her to the nearest store to buy them, while he sat under the tree with his equally useless friends. She remembered that years ago, when they'd been young and in love, he would have tucked the money into her bra with a cheeky wink. But those days were long gone. Now the money was slapped into her open palm with muttered instructions as he turned to resume his position as chief entertainer.

The bags kept banging against her legs, and with every thud, she cursed him enthusiastically and creatively. She didn't come into town often, but Lunga was playing in the local soccer league that weekend with all his friends. She'd decided to go with him, to meet up with a cousin, who was keen to find herself a new boyfriend amongst Lunga's pathetic circle. The soccer pitch was a patch of land that the goats and the cattle kept mowed, with makeshift goal posts made from creosote poles at either end. Lunga generally didn't like her to come along, as she usually ended up insulting one or two of his friends. Back in her youth, the men had loved her. She knew that watching her cross the veld in the afternoon sun was enough to send them falling all over each other as they tried to get her attention.

The wind would pick up her skirt, revealing a hint of thigh, and the soft light would dance across her Vaselined skin. Of course, back then she'd played her part well; she'd look at them from under her lashes, and giggle behind her hand. They'd all been very disappointed when Lunga had won her over. But not these days. They were vocal about their lucky escape and kept their distance. It was true; she was no longer pretty and fun. But that was Lunga's fault. And Thuli's. And now she could add Samson to that list. Yes. It was not her fault at all.

As she made her way back to Lunga and his friends, she thought about Samson sitting in a jail cell in town. The news had come as a shock. As much as she hated the Ngubane family, she could not imagine her uncle being involved in any form of poaching. He was always so self-righteous in this regard. She scowled. It was just another way that Samson Ngubane had tried to prove that he was better than the rest of them. But then, later that day, she had received a very short SMS from the isangoma.

'*It is done,*' it said, mysteriously. It had taken a long moment of staring blankly at the message before its content made sense.

Yoh, she'd breathed. *Yoh, yoh, yoh! This would break Thuli's heart!*

Perhaps she should pay him a little visit; see how he was doing in jail. She chuckled. The thought of him in an overcrowded cell, on a Sunday no less, made her very happy. She turned to look in the direction of town, then down at the rapidly cooling beers. A thought struck her; being arrested was one thing. Being convicted and sent to jail was another. A feeling of concern for someone other than herself overcame her, but then disappeared as quickly as it had arrived.

How would Mthunzi guarantee that Samson would go to jail? She stuck a hand down her shirt and dredged out her old Nokia, which she kept hidden between her substantial breasts.

She frowned when she saw that her phone was on silent; Lunga would be furious. But, she noted with alarm, it wasn't Lunga who had left twelve missed calls. It was Mthunzi. The first at 7 a.m. and the last three minutes ago.

***

That afternoon, according to Mthunzi's plan of action, Zodwa found herself hiding behind an ilala palm, on the road near Samson's house. Her challenge was not that Nonhle would not be at home, but rather, that her cousin might not be inclined to do what Zodwa asked. She'd wanted to meet Nonhle in town, but her cousin hadn't answered her numerous calls. Zodwa really couldn't blame Nonhle; there was no love lost between them. They hadn't spoken in years.

The day Zodwa stormed out of the house for the last time, she'd banged the door so hard, a screw had popped out of the wooden doorframe. The event that had led to her eventual departure was the announcement that she was leaving school and was pregnant. Zodwa was thrilled! Finally, she had an excuse to leave the agony of schoolwork behind her, and an opportunity to get out of chores. She intended for the pregnancy to leave her weak and unable to help with the most menial of tasks but, by the end of the third month, she'd lost the baby; and Zodwa was convinced that Thuli had poisoned her meal with muthi, to induce a miscarriage.

The atmosphere at home became truly unbearable. She went out of her way to pick fights, particularly with Nonhle, whenever she came home from that fancy school. By seventeen, when she fell pregnant again, Samson allowed Thuli to convince him to choose his family over Zodwa, practically pushing her out the door. Samson didn't even demand that the father of the baby pay *inhlawulo*, the damages fee, for having a baby out of wedlock.

Earlier, when she spoke to Mthunzi, he told her to wait in town that afternoon; a red Citi Golf would come to fetch her. Zodwa had expected Mthunzi to be driving, but when the car had pulled up, there was a stranger behind the wheel. The man wore a denim pantsula hat pulled low, the collar of his jacket high against his neck. He looked exactly like a tsotsi, and Zodwa was not in a rush to get in. The man, impatient at her hesitation, had leant across and flung open the door.

'Hurry up, *wena*,' he'd hissed, with a click of his tongue.

She had peered into the back seat to see if perhaps Mthunzi had lain down, tired after a long day of listening to people's problems and concocting muthi. He was not, she noted with dissatisfaction. However, she got in and the man handed her a cell phone.

'Press the green button,' he'd said, and peeled the car away from the curb.

Zodwa had peered at the phone uncertainly, then she gingerly pressed the button. She held the phone scrunched between her ear and shoulder, then almost dropped it into her lap when the deep gravel voice of Mthunzi boomed through the speaker.

'Ndodakazi, there's been a change in plan,' he'd said, by way of introduction. 'The ancestors have spoken, and we must obey.'

The changing of plans had not suited Zodwa at all, regardless of whether the ancestors had spoken or not. Her nerves were tattered, and she'd felt insecure in this stranger's car.

She'd struggled to keep the irritation out of her voice, 'Makhosi?'

***

She huffed as she forced herself to leave the relative safety of the palm, and head towards the path that led to the Ngubane household. The timing was not perfect; it was still light, and it was not often that Zodwa Shezi called on her former home. She was aware that if anyone with nothing particular to do saw her at that moment, they would be surprised. But then they would work out that she'd gotten wind of Samson's arrest. No one would think she was there to commiserate. It just wasn't in her nature.

She peeked in through the kitchen window hoping to see her cousin, but only a clean pine table and empty chairs greeted her. It was too early to start dinner preparations, and the sound of the TV could not be heard. She nonchalantly walked around the corner of the house and stopped at Nonhle's bedroom window, noting the height. She looked around for something to use and saw a breezeblock lying not far off. It would provide the necessary height for her to see inside. She dragged the block over and cautiously stepped up. With a wobble, she pulled aside the net curtain through the burglar guard and saw Nonhle on the bed. Her cousin was stretched out, her phone next to her, earphones embedded in her ears. Zodwa leaned forward and angled her face so that her lips and nose protruded through the bars.

'Nonhle,' she called softly. *'Pssst.'*

Her calls went unanswered, her cousin completely deaf to Zodwa's attempts to attract her attention. Zodwa had no intention of crossing paths with Thuli, so had kept her voice low. She waved her arm through the window, but not even the frantic movement seemed to have any effect on Nonhle. She looked down at the breezeblock, scanning the ground around it. Hopping off the block, she located a cluster of small stones.

The first stone hit Nonhle on her arm. She ripped out the earphones, and the immediate all-consuming fear of an intruder at her window played out across her face.

'Nonhle,' Zodwa called, her fingers wiggling through the bars as she squashed her face between the metal.

'What are you doing?' Nonhle yelled, leaping off the bed. 'There's a front door, for a reason!'

'Nonhle,' whispered Zodwa, pleading for her cousin to lower her voice. 'I need to talk to you. Please.' Zodwa teetered on her unstable block. 'It's about Baba,' she cajoled.

Nonhle stood with her hands on her hips, an all too familiar pose for Zodwa. 'What about him?' she demanded.

'Please, Nonhle,' she said, Nonhle's mutinous face causing her to panic. 'Can you come outside and talk. I've got news. But I'm going to kill myself standing on this block.'

Zodwa could see Nonhle's indecision; her cousin dropped her arms and looked at the door.

'Hang on,' Nonhle said, finally. 'I'm going to check if Thuli's asleep. If she is, I'll let you in.'

'No!' Zodwa slapped a hand over her mouth, casting her eyes to the doorway behind Nonhle. 'Please,' she begged. 'Come outside and I'll explain everything.'

Zodwa allowed herself a small jiggle of glee as her cousin gave her a final look, nodded, and left her bedroom. Zodwa let out a small shriek as the block wobbled, and she found herself in a heap, on the sandy bed.

25: Worked like a charm
2nd December 2012

In a small conference room at the local hotel in town, a group of men sat slumped around the boardroom table. The mood was sombre. The usual friendly banter of men who'd known each other for years absent as each processed the events of the last few days. Only a few hours after Thomas had climbed back into bed, after dropping Nonhle home from Jika Jika Tavern the night before, a band of poachers had breached the fence line at Jabulani Private Game Reserve. Two rhino had been felled with precision, their horns severed from their heads, and left to die in agony.

After Thomas had left Nonhle sitting at the fence line, he drove into town to meet a friend for a late lunch at the hotel, then joined the meeting. The last shaft of afternoon sun cut the room in half as it stole through a slit in the curtain. Karel had called the men from the scene of the crime, calling an emergency meeting. It had been a long morning. The attack had been completely unexpected; not least because The Last Outpost had only recently been hit.

'Okay, gentlemen,' said Karel, rubbing his face roughly with both large hands. He was seated at the head of the table, a laptop open in front of him. 'December 15th is just around the corner, and with the tradesman's holiday, every bladdy worker will be coming home. Then we've got Christmas and New Year's.' He cast a watchful eye around the table. 'I don't need to tell any of you how vigilant we have to be.'

The door burst open to admit the apologetic figure of Dutch Müller. Karel waved him in while giving the German a once-over. '*Yirre*, Dutch.

Bad night?'

Thomas took in the rumpled clothes and bleary eyes of his usually immaculately turned out GM. By the looks of it, Dutch hadn't slept a wink. Thomas shot him an inquiring look. Dutch raised his eyebrows and dipped his head by way of response, then cut eye contact by giving Karel his full attention.

'Not sure how much everyone knows,' said Karel. 'So, I'll just start from the beginning. I don't need to reiterate that this is classified information. I'm sharing it with you because we all have a vested interest here. I'm not going to lie,' he huffed in embarrassment. 'I don't have a lot of confidence in some of my colleagues, so the more like-minded people I can pull in to assist, the better. 'Oh,' he said, to clear any misapprehension, 'Joseph Dlamini is still at Jabulani, which is why he's not here.'

Karel fiddled with his computer until a projected image of the crime scene appeared on the screen at the front of the room. 'Sorry about this, Mervynne,' he murmured in the direction of the owner of Jabulani.

Thomas shifted his gaze to the devastated face of Mervynne van Heerden. The man's eyes glistened as he gazed at the carcasses of his two prized rhino. Thomas felt an overwhelming sense of helplessness engulf him. Listening to Karel unpack the details of the crime made him feel that the battle would probably never be won. They simply didn't have the resources to take the fight to the next level. Poaching had been on the increase in the province since 2010, and while he knew that improvements had been made in the anti-poaching presence in private and state reserves, it came at huge expense. Requiring extra security, better fencing, the hiring of air patrol aircraft, the list of expenses went on and on; and while they tried to raise the money, rhino continued to die on their watch.

'Was this last night?' asked Dutch. 'I don't understand,' he stammered. 'It's so soon after The Last Outpost?'

'Ja,' nodded Karel, wearily. 'You'll notice ...' said the detective, his expression grim as he clicked through the images until he came to a scene of a fence that had been cut and rolled back, '... that there are a number of small plastic bottles tied to the fence at irregular intervals. A quick investigation of their contents revealed buttons, pieces of hair – human, we think – beads, and other small biological items like animal teeth and nails.'

'Didn't you just put in that serious surveillance equipment to monitor activity at the fence line, Mervynne?' asked Thomas.

'Ja,' he said. 'Cost me a bloody fortune. The bastards cut the fence right there, right under the central unit.'

'So, you've got no visual evidence of how those bottles got there, or the poachers cutting through the fence?' said Thomas, in disbelief. Those units came with a hefty price tag attached. 'And it didn't send out an alert?'

'No,' said Mervynne, uncomfortably, then looked down at his hands. 'The equipment hadn't been touched. Nothing registered on the system to show there was a breach. It was working perfectly this morning when the guys went out to check the fence line.'

'We found these tied to the unit.' Karel flipped to the next image, and they all grimaced at the two sightless eyes that stared up at them. 'Animal,' he said, to everyone's relief.

Mervynne coughed. 'Some of my black staff think they're the reason why the unit didn't work. Like it went blind, just like the eyes.'

One of the other owners, a big man with a bushy beard and nicotine-stained fingers, raised his voice. 'What's the big interest in the superstitious stuff, Karel? It's not like criminals haven't been using muthi to protect themselves for ages. Man,' he laughed, 'even old Hennie Labuschagne brought a sangoma in to bless his farm. His staff told him the only way to stop the tsotsis stealing his cattle was to get a sangoma to walk the land casting spells. Worked like a charm, man. No cattle went missing after that. The blacks round here have always believed this kind of superstitious nonsense … no offense, Senzo,' he said, nodding briefly at the APU team leader.

'Well,' said Karel. 'I'm wondering if there is a connection. There was muthi involved in The Last Outpost job, and now this.'

'It's unlikely,' said Senzo, joining the conversation for the first time. 'The muthi aspect of the cases are nothing alike. In the first case,' he continued, tipping his head in Thomas's direction, 'there was a bottle of muthi found in the car. 'But this,' he said, gesturing at the screen, 'this is on another level. It looks like the work of one of those powerful isangoma up in the Nongoma area.'

'Sorry,' said Thomas. 'I'm confused. Do you think that the poaching rings are being controlled by a local sangoma?'

Karel took a deep breath and then gave an affirmative nod. 'It's a possibility, yes,' he said. 'Or, one of the kingpins has a sangoma doing some of his dirty work for him.'

A chair groaned at the other end of the table, as Dutch leant forward. 'But,' he said, 'you have no concrete leads yet?'

Karel glared at everyone around the table. 'Again, this is strictly confidential. Those bladdy poachers sitting at the station, won't admit it,' he seethed. 'But we think this is the work of a guy called Lucky Mhlongo. The sangoma might just be supplying the muthi, or he might play a bigger role. Either way, we've got nothing to connect Lucky directly to any of the cases. So, I'm casting my net wider.'

'You all right, Dutch?' asked Thomas.

His GM had grown even paler than when he'd come in. The purple smudges under his eyes, now dark charcoal.

'Ja ... ja,' said Dutch, giving Thomas a wan smile. 'It's been tiring. I've never dealt with anything like this, you know. In Germany ...' he said, with a shrug, and gestured to that far-off place, with his hand. As Thomas's eyes left Dutch's face, they came to rest on Senzo's, and Thomas could not help but notice the look of undisguised interest in Senzo's eyes. Suddenly, Senzo looked at him – a silent message, just like the old days – reaching him loud and clear.

'Karel,' Dutch said, breaking the moment between the two former friends. 'What about Samson? I ... everyone back at the lodge ... would like to know if there's been any progress there?'

Karel gave a loud and uncomfortable cough, his fingers tapping his notebook.

'Well, has he said anything?' Dutch pushed.

Karel gave a hollow laugh. 'Of course! He's innocent, just like the other two.'

'What about the CCTV footage?' said Thomas, addressing Dutch.

Dutch let out a long sigh. 'Ja, that was unfortunate. What terrible timing,' he said, going on to explain to the others about the coincidental break in connection. 'I have been wondering,' Dutch added, cautiously, 'could Samson have planned it ...?'

'It could just as easily have been anyone,' Thomas interjected, glaring coldly at Dutch, 'who had access to that camera.'

Karel slapped his hands on the table. 'Gentlemen. Please.' He turned to Thomas. 'While that might be true, only one person had a physical trait that could be linked to the code name ...' he said, raising his little finger. 'And that same person had the SIM card hidden in his vehicle. 'Thomas,' the detective said, with a kindness that surprised Thomas. 'I know that you don't want it to be true, but we must trust the evidence. Right!' said he said, rising from his seat. 'Let's take a quick break before we talk about plans for the next few weeks.'

Thomas slouched in his chair, feeling like a sulky teenager. His eyes followed Dutch as the GM left the room, while Dutch's eyes were glued to the phone in his hand, worry written all over his face.

Thomas took the opportunity to reach down and grab his phone from his bag. During the meeting, he'd felt the vibration through the sole of his shoe but ignored it. He frowned now as he saw he'd missed a call from Nonhle. He accessed his voice mail and felt the blood leave his face as he listened to her message.

'Karel,' Thomas called out, intercepting the detective who was heading out the door. 'You need to listen to this.' The concern in Thomas's voice drew Senzo to his side. Thomas pressed speakerphone and watched Karel's skin tone begin to bloom as he listened to the voice mail. 'That's not all,' Thomas said before Karel could say anything. 'Nonhle was at Jika Jika Tavern last night ... doing a bit of investigating on her own.'

The detective's face went a startling shade of magenta. 'For *foks* sake!' he yelled, spittle flecking Thomas's face. 'That bladdy girl will ruin this entire investigation with her meddling!'

'And ...' continued Thomas, glancing at Senzo and gesturing for him to close the door next to him. The three men instinctively came together in a huddle.

'Dutch Müller was there,' said Thomas.

'So,' said Karel, fixing Thomas with a hard stare. 'Dutch is often there.'

'And that doesn't bother you?' Thomas asked, aware that he was putting Karel in the same position Nonhle had put him, last night.

'It bothers me for other reasons,' sniffed Karel, looking away.

Thomas turned to Senzo. 'What do you think?'

'We've been watching the place, watching Dutch,' Senzo admitted.

'But so far, nothing.'

'Of course, nothing,' shouted Karel. He looked quickly at the door, then continued, his voice low. 'I might not agree with his ... lifestyle, but the man's a friend. He goes to my church ... when he's able. He donates to my wife's charity!'

'So,' said Senzo, folding his arms across his chest. 'He's in and out of your house? Comes for dinner, an afternoon braai?'

'Yes,' said Karel, warily. 'What's your point?'

'How often do you speak about work? About poaching; about what's going on out there?' he demanded, the air between them growing thick.

'How dare you!' hissed Karel, who moved threateningly towards Senzo, then changed his mind.

'Guys!' said Thomas, placing a hand on each man. 'Please. Nonhle could be in real trouble. Can we focus!' Karel stepped back, but his eyes remained fixed on Senzo. 'Let's look at the facts,' Thomas said quickly. 'Dutch works at the lodge; has access to the cameras; has access to the vehicles; hangs out at Jika and may have seen Nonhle last night. And now Nonhle's going off to talk with a sangoma who allegedly knows something about her father and his involvement in the case. Nonhle got into an altercation with two prostitutes. How do we know that they didn't tell Dutch what she was doing there?' They remained silent, so he forged on. 'We all saw him come in earlier. The man's a wreck. Dutch is always in control. Always!' He looked at each man, in turn, willing them to agree.

To his relief, Senzo nodded. 'It makes sense,' he said. 'When you connect all those points, there's a strong possibility that Dutch and Samson have been working together. They would make the perfect team.'

All the air that Thomas hadn't registered he'd been holding in, came out in one long exhalation of dismay. 'Are you kidding?' he exploded.

'Thomas, Samson has access to the camera; knows where the rhino are at any given time; speaks with Dutch daily; the SIM was found in his car,' he said. 'And ...' he finished the sentence by waggling his little finger.

Thomas fought to control his emotions. He needed them on his side to find Nonhle, so fighting over Samson was pointless.

'Okay,' he said, closing his eyes on a deep breath. 'Can we at least agree that something needs to be done?' He opened his eyes and saw each man nod in agreement.

'Great! Karel,' Thomas said, suddenly rejuvenated by the promise of action. 'You want to find the sangoma you believe is behind the poaching. I think Nonhle is on her way to see him, right now. Surely one of the poachers can be persuaded to give up a name?'

Karel laughed scornfully. 'We've asked them already,' he said, drawing a pinched thumb and forefinger across his lips. 'But Samson, well, if he knows that his daughter has run off to meet his connection, maybe he'll feel differently about sharing.'

'Excellent!' Thomas turned to Senzo.

'I'll follow Dutch,' said Senzo, raising his eyes when Karel's stance became defensive again. 'He left here in a hurry, fixated on his phone. No harm in checking up on him.'

'Good thinking,' said Thomas, relieved that all possibilities would be covered. 'And Senzo,' he said. 'That definitely wasn't one of our work phones.'

26: A jealous, spiteful man
2nd December 2012

It was the suffocating scent of burning imphepho that woke Nonhle from her inflicted slumber. The faint liqorice smell failed to mask the stench of death and decay around her. Her eyes stung; vision blurred against the throbbing of her head. She felt drunk or drugged. Her tongue thick in her mouth. A low humming, and the sound of dry palm fronds scraping against the floor, emanated from somewhere to her left.

She opened her eyes, mere slits, just enough to survey the scene and locate herself in this strange place. A swaying form emerged; a large, bare belly, a wig festooned with red and white beads, and an arm sweeping back and forth, clearing the air with a wildebeest's tail. Behind the isangoma, Nonhle's gaze came to rest on a crouched figure. Its hair wild about its face; a terrible slash for a grin made her stomach lurch in fear.

Was that ... a tokoloshe? No. She didn't believe in such things. She blinked rapidly to make it go away, but the figure remained, its head swaying like a snake ready to strike.

Behind her, something moved. She stifled a scream as it rolled against her body, but then her hand was squeezed gently. Zodwa. Relief washed over her that she was not alone, but then, small snatches of the hours preceding came back to her, and fear gripped her by the throat. Her cousin had brought her here; knowingly had brought her to this place.

A low keening erupted into a shrill warble. It seemed to emit an electric charge that altered the energy of the room. The tokoloshe came to life, leaping from its frozen position, arms, and legs akimbo. The women screamed, as the creature grabbed each by their hair, and tried to haul them into a kneeling position before the isangoma. Nonhle could not sit up; she felt disconnected from her body, her limbs refusing to respond. Zodwa, on coming face-to-face with the tokoloshe, let out an almighty shriek then fell to the mat in a dead faint. The tokoloshe threw back its head and cackled, dancing around the women on its long skinny legs.

It's too tall, she thought, *irrationally. The tokoloshe is too tall.*

Her eyes then focused on the mat in front of them. On it lay two items: a knife and an old-fashioned wooden Zulu headrest. The long blade of the knife, after its loving contact with a whetstone, caught the low light of gas lamps dotted about the room. Next to it stood the squat headrest on two stubby legs. It's wooden surface smooth and bald from centuries of slumbering heads. Beside her, Nonhle could feel Zodwa stirring, then hysteria rose in her cousin's laboured breathing. Zodwa's fingers sought hers, looking for reassurance.

The isangoma stood before them, the whites of his glassy eyes stained a hideous pink. They seemed to rest only on Nonhle.

'I'm so glad you are finally here,' he said, with a naughty giggle. 'It has been so long ... too long.'

Nonhle looked down at her cousin, imploring her to say something, do something. *Why had she brought them here?*

He flicked the wildebeest tail at her. 'She can't help you, Nonhle,' he laughed, leaning his sweaty face into hers. She flinched at his rank breath. 'She's the reason you are here.' Nonhle turned to look at her cousin. Zodwa stared at her, eyes wide, mouth open in a soundless wail of apology.

He then went quiet, lost somewhere in his mind's eye. 'Your father,' he said softly to Nonhle. 'He ruined me. Nearly destroyed everything.' Just as quickly, he became indignant. Arms swung wildly around the room to take in each wall, lined with baskets and bottles. 'He is a jealous, spiteful man. Wanted to be the only one who made something of himself. But,' he said, peering at Nonhle out of the corner of his eye, 'now he will lose something important. Just like me.'

Suddenly, Nonhle knew, on the fringes of her fuzzy mind, why she was here. A memory of herself perched on her father's knee, his best friend sitting opposite them on a fallen trunk, emerged from the fog. And then she recalled Mthunzi's unexpected visit to the house, and months later, her father accused of a crime he would never commit. It all connected. Mthunzi's years of anger finally playing itself out.

Jesus, she prayed. There would be no proving Samson's innocence if she didn't get off this mountain alive.

The tokoloshe moved like a crab behind them, blocking any chance of an escape through the open door. He grabbed Zodwa by the shoulders and hauled the terrified woman to her feet. Mthunzi bent forward to bring his face in line with hers.

'Ndodakazi,' he said, stopping to giggle into her mucous stained face. 'It is time. Your request has been granted.'

'Makhosi!' she cried. 'What are you doing?'

Nonhle watched Zodwa's body shake violently. There had been a plan, and it was going very wrong.

Mthunzi rose to his full height. 'Zodwa Shezi,' he intoned. 'You have been summoned by the ancestors. It is their will that you take the life of your cousin, Nonhle Ngubane, to undo the betrayal committed against me by Samson Ngubane.'

'Hayi, Baba. No!' wailed Zodwa.

She spun away from Mthunzi's face and into the waiting arms of the tokoloshe. They struggled together, but the tokoloshe had power in its stance. It clamped vice-like hands around Zodwa's arms, turning her back towards Mthunzi. Mthunzi stooped to pick up the knife, its long blade resting across his two open palms, and moved towards Zodwa.

Mthunzi tried to hand the knife over to Zodwa, her eyes rolling in her head as she comprehended what he wanted her to do.

'Do it!' he yelled, spit flying. He grabbed her from the tokoloshe and pulled her over to where he stood. The tokoloshe leant down and dragged Nonhle onto the mat. He pushed her down and her head cracked against the wooden headrest. She tried to fight back, but her legs were still so weak, her hands unable to fend him off. The tokoloshe straddled her stomach, her arms pinned beneath the weight of his legs. Mthunzi forced the knife into Zodwa's hand, crushing her fingers around its hilt. 'Now,' he demanded.

Zodwa's eyes welled at the weight of the knife in her hand; she looked up at Mthunzi, then down into Nonhle's stricken face. 'I can't,' she wept.

'You must!' roared Mthunzi. His wig flew, the beads tapping a furious summons.

Nonhle began to wail as Zodwa struggled against Mthunzi. He grabbed her by the back of her neck, pushing her face until it was centimetres from Nonhle's. Tears and spit mingled as the two women cried out, Nonhle's torso bucking under the tokoloshe's weight. With one last look at Nonhle, Zodwa gave an unholy shriek, rising as she pushed back against Mthunzi. The knife swung through the air, its blade scraped across the tokoloshe's mask, then connected with Mthunzi's throat as she turned to face him, a spray of crimson falling across her.

Time stopped as Zodwa, Nonhle and the tokoloshe stared at Mthunzi in mute horror. The isangoma's fingers tried to clamp the cleanly sliced edges of skin together, but could find no purchase as the warm, sticky liquid poured out. He fell to his knees, his body slumped before Nonhle as if begging for mercy.

Zodwa, still holding the knife in her hands, turned to look at the tokoloshe.

'*Phuma,*' she hissed, jabbing the knife in its direction. 'Get out now, before I kill you.'

27: I'm done
2nd December 2012

Dutch was in a complete state. A small travel bag lay open on his bed, and he lobbed items of clothing into it with one hand, while speaking into the phone at his ear.

'I'm done, Bento! Lucky's gone too far this time!' he shouted. 'Did you know about this ridiculous plan of his?' Dutch rifled through his safe for his passport and foreign exchange as he listened to Bento trying to placate him. 'I don't care!' Dutch was becoming increasingly agitated by Bento's lack of concern. 'I'm the one stuck here having to field questions by the police about the SIM card, and why the CCTV cameras conveniently weren't working that night. I'm the one who's lying through my teeth. You think Lucky cares about me? I'm going to get caught out, while he's probably already on his way to you. Soon he'll be drinking your expensive whiskey out of a crystal tumbler!'

The sound of determined feet had Dutch dashing to the window. He pulled the curtain back a fraction and saw Senzo heading in his direction.

'Damnit!' he exclaimed in frustration, then he dropped the call. He pulled the bag towards him, stuffed everything inside, and hauled it under the bed. He smoothed the bedspread hastily and kicked the safe door closed. He cast his eyes around the room one last time, then opened the door before Senzo could knock.

'Senzo!' he smiled at the large man before him. 'I would have come to you at reception. You should have had them call me.' He closed the door behind him, and he tried to move past Senzo. 'Let's go to my office, they can bring us drinks there.'

Senzo didn't move. 'What were you doing at Jika Jika Tavern last night?' he asked, catching Dutch off-guard.

'Jika?' he shrugged. 'What do you think ... a few beers, some pool, maybe a girl. You have a problem with that?' An uneasiness crept up on Dutch. 'How do you know, anyway?'

'We've been watching that place for months now,' said Senzo. 'It's interesting what goes on in there ... but I think you know that already.'

Dutch rose to his full height in indignation. 'What exactly are you implying?' he demanded.

Senzo stepped forward, closing the gap between them. 'Something about this case has been bothering me; and today, I figured out what it was. It's you.'

Dutch had somehow become trapped between his door and Senzo, and the veneer of sweat on his skin turned icy cold at Senzo's words.

'But it's not just this case. I think it's been going on longer than that. You arrived in Mevamhlope two years ago, right? And, around that time poaching began to increase in our area, and then we began to hear the name Lucky Mhlongo.'

The moth in Dutch's chest began to flap its wings in earnest. 'Are you suggesting that I know Lucky Mhlongo?' he stammered. There was no possible way that they could link him to Lucky. They'd never visited Jika at the same time or been seen together in town. When they met up, it was somewhere remote, like a bird hide at Mkuze Game Reserve.

Senzo stood back and gave Dutch an odd smile. 'We'll find out soon enough. We received some news after you left. Karel should be bringing Lucky into the station right about now,' he said, looking at his watch. He slipped his phone from his pocket and checked his messages. 'Yes,' he said, with a nod. 'They've got him in a holding cell.'

Dutch could not stop it. He felt the moth rocket up his throat and explode from his mouth. With it came a confession carefully constructed by Bento two years ago, should Lucky ever prove to be more of a liability, than an asset.

***

The police vehicles slowed down to navigate the road that had grown treacherous as the final curtain of night fell. With headlights on high beam, now and again, the ghostly form of a startled animal was captured in mid-flight. The sky was a dome of scattered planets and stars, the milky way trapping energy and light in a frozen mist. Samson sat in the passenger seat, his body hunched in silent vigil, broken only to direct Karel up the mountain towards Mthunzi's home.

The thick silence in the car was broken by a sudden outburst from Karel, his knuckles white on the steering wheel. 'For foks sake!' he growled through gritted teeth, as the wheel was yanked to the right. 'Of all the bladdy places to live! How does he make any bladdy money if no one can get to him!'

Karel had been fuming the whole way up. No, if he was honest with himself, he'd been fuming since that bladdy meeting, what with all the interference and people, not policemen, mind you; insisting that they knew how to do his job. Bladdy Thomas McKenzie, in the back seat forcing his way into the car, like some lovesick boyfriend. Surely not! And Senzo! racing off to, *what*? Arrest a man Karel considered to be a good friend?

Karel thumped the wheel again, then cast an eye towards the man in the seat next to him. At least he'd been right about Samson revealing the name of the sangoma. Not quite the story he'd been expecting, but it had at least got them this far. Karel had been amazed at how quickly Samson's tune had changed when they told him about Nonhle. That silent, stoic bastard had sung like a bird! When Samson told them about the arrival of the isangoma at his house, and the discovery of the ragdoll in its straitjacket of pink beads, its heart pierced by a thorn, Karel hadn't even tried to suppress an eye-roll. But then Samson revealed their relationship and the nature of the 'great betrayal', and Karel got that feeling, based on years of experience, that told him that there was truth in the man's tale. He would check that out when he got back – there'd be records of that incident, somewhere.

Karel jumped as Samson grabbed him by the arm. 'There!' Pinpricks of light appeared in the dark ahead.

Karel brought the vehicle to a stop and squinted through the windscreen. 'How far do you think we are?' He wanted to sneak up on Mthunzi.

The man was unlikely to get visitors this late at night and he would be suspicious; but then, there was nowhere for the sangoma to go. He'd have to drive past them if he wanted to escape.

'It is difficult to say in the dark, but perhaps a hundred metres or so,' Samson estimated.

28: An elaborate plan
2nd December 2012

Less than a hundred metres away, the smell of blood, urine, and fear saturated the air in the house. Nonhle lay helplessly on the floor watching Zodwa advance on the tokoloshe. She held the knife out before her, both shaking hands gripping the handle to keep the blade still.

'Get out now!' Zodwa cried. 'Before I kill you.' She lunged towards the creature, jabbing the knife in the direction of its unchanging expression.

The tokoloshe backpedalled out the open door to escape the blade. Zodwa, brandishing the knife in one hand, leant back to grab the door to lock him out. The tokoloshe grasped her by the wrist, swiftly pulling her out into the night with him. The knife fell to the floor as he manoeuvred her into a chokehold; her eyes bulged, and her nails tore at his skin. Nonhle dragged herself towards the open door and she watched helplessly as they struggled. Zodwa outweighed him by a good fifteen kilograms, his skinny frame fighting to overpower her desperation to live, and his attempt to grab the knife at the same time.

Zodwa dragged the tokoloshe a few metres away from the doorway, then her legs buckled in exhaustion. She crumpled to the floor and the tokoloshe darted back to fetch the knife where it lay. It turned back to Zodwa; knife raised above its head as it prepared to separate her head from her body. As it screamed out in fury, the twin beams of a vehicle trapped it in a ghostly scene of gothic proportions. Nonhle screamed out, tears streaming, as the vehicle, horn blaring, picked up speed and roared towards them.

The lights and noise broke the singular intent of the tokoloshe. It wasted no time in abandoning its task, sprinting around the back of the house, and down the narrow path that ran along the ridge of Intaba Yemikhovu.

***

The tokoloshe ran; its ears alert to the laboured breath of the man behind him trying to navigate the unfamiliar terrain. It heard its pursuer stumble, a curse punctuated the night, and the light from a torch bounced off the tokoloshe's body, then fell away as the man tripped and fell to his knees.

When he felt he had outrun his pursuer, Lucky wrenched the mask from his face, flinging it out into the night. As he watched it spin into the darkness, he let out a cry of frustration at how things had turned out. He ran on until the taste of copper filled his mouth, and a volley of barks rang out as hunting dogs, tied up for the night, caught his scent. On he ran until finally, the blanched spidery form of a toppled acacia came into view. Its leafless branches drooped in such a way that a woven canopy, big enough for a man to wait out the night, welcomed him.

Lucky lay under the canopy, his breath burning in his chest. He felt exactly like he had when he'd run for his life, away from Joe Cele and the baying crowd, all those years ago. He cursed himself for his stupidity. He should never have involved Mthunzi in his plan. He thought that he was being clever. He should have simply had Nkosi shot and been done with it. But no. He wanted drama. He wanted to prove that he could orchestrate an elaborate plan and get away with it, and he'd wanted to give the isangoma the parting gift of longed for revenge. Because Lucky had recently decided to engage the services of another isangoma. One who did not face a moral dilemma, every time Lucky encouraged him to go one step further away from his calling.

Things were changing for Lucky, horizons were expanding, and he needed someone with less heart, and more courage. Convincing Mthunzi to change his plans regarding Nonhle's future had been hard work; only the oversupply of the muthi that messed with Mthunzi's fragile mind had made it possible.

Thinking about Mthunzi made Lucky suck his teeth in irritation. What a waste, he thought. *Clever girl like that would have fetched a good price.*

Lucky made up his mind; he needed to keep a low profile. He would head over the border into Mozambique and make his way to Bento, or perhaps not. Bento might not be too amused at the mess Lucky had managed to create. He sent a message to one of his men to pick him up at first light, behind the local high school in the area. It would be a long wait until dawn, but he felt secure in his makeshift hiding place. He scrolled through his messages and felt his confines grow even smaller as he read the one sent from his contact at Mevamhlope police station. Dutch Müller had been brought in.

'What should I do?' the policeman asked. Lucky sat like a hare entranced by the glow of his cell phone screen.

Would Dutch keep his mouth shut? Lucky couldn't take the chance.

29: Blind to the obvious
2nd December 2012

Back at Mthunzi's homestead, Karel du Randt opened the passenger door to his vehicle and dropped heavily into the seat. His nerves were completely shot. He felt unhinged, like a madness had taken him over, leaving him buzzing and disjointed. It was as if all the scoffing and laughing he'd directed at the belief in the supernatural, held by any Zulu who made the mistake of sharing it with him, had come back to taunt him. And he'd be lying if he said that an ancient belief within himself, one he didn't know he even possessed, hadn't responded to the sight of the tokoloshe leaning over Zodwa. He tried to justify it with the way the headlights had lit up the scene, the heightened emotions in the vehicle, and the unnatural way that the tokoloshe loped off into the night. He would have sworn on his Bible that it was true, had anyone thought to ask.

The interior of the house had only added to the overall certainty that evil lived there. It was not, ironically, in the slumped figure of the lifeless sangoma. No, the evil was there, in the large number of containers filled with animal parts, that lined the walls, on shelves, under the bed in Mthunzi's home. Karel could simply not understand who, in their right mind, would inflict such agony, such misery, on an animal. He had been told that the most powerful muthi came from living beings, animal or human, who had suffered greatly. It made him want to vomit. He had been furious, and deeply disappointed when they failed to uncover even one rhino horn, or anything alluding to horn having been on the property.

He'd felt completely stupid once the mask had been retrieved. It had hit a rock in the vicinity and split itself in two. The men had shared a good laugh as the pieces were placed into an evidence bag; there was no denying that last night as the vehicle lights captured the scene, all of them, black and white alike, had believed in the power of the supernatural. Although the footprints, and physical signs of a scuffle, etched into the soil were evidence enough that two human beings had engaged in a battle for life, the mask was the confirmation each needed to breathe easier.

The door opened and Joseph Dlamini and Thomas got in, both as bleary-eyed and shattered as he was.

'The medics have checked Nonhle and Zodwa over. No major damage, but Nonhle should probably have her head checked out,' said Thomas.

'So should Zodwa,' said Joseph, with feeling.

They hadn't been able to retrieve any useful information from her. It was as if her mind had taken off down the mountain with the man in the mask. Karel was certain that it was Lucky Mhlongo, but they hadn't found anything yet, to confirm it. Karel would make sure that the samples taken from under Zodwa's nails, would be kept in the file marked 'Lucky', which he kept in his top drawer. Karel sighed. The only person who could have revealed the identity of the tokoloshe had spilled that secret into the soil of his own home. Karel would just have to wait. The place was covered in fingerprint dust, and they had the vehicle that didn't belong to Mthunzi as well as the blue cooler. Karel shuddered at the thought of its intended purpose. When Nonhle revealed that they had intended to kill her, and, no doubt Zodwa, once she'd played her part, Samson had begun to cry softly. Karel immediately thought of his own two girls at home and he had to clear his throat vigorously to compose himself.

'Thomas,' he said. 'Will you take Joseph's vehicle and give the girls a lift back to town?'

'Sure,' said Thomas. 'I'll get Doc Hansen to check them out, and then take them both back to the lodge. You can come and interview them again there if necessary.'

Now that the adrenaline, which had kept Karel's focus solely on the task at hand, had subsided, a strong feeling of disappointment quickly replaced it.

'I just can't believe that Dutch is involved,' he said, with a sad shake of his head.

Thomas had read out Senzo's message as they made their way up the mountain. Dutch was at the police station, and Senzo had the evidence to prove that Dutch was heavily involved. Thomas was to call him as soon as they arrived back. Karel was disappointed with Dutch, but more so, with himself. This was his case to solve. How had he allowed himself to be so blind to the obvious?

The call came through as Karel took the off-ramp from the N2 towards town. Joseph could barely make out what was being said, with all the yelling and screaming happening on the other side of the line. Joseph managed to make out Senzo's voice, telling them to get themselves to the station, immediately.

Karel put his foot down as he hit Main Street, then took a sharp left. The gate of the police station was closed, and he blasted his horn repeatedly until it was pulled back to let them through. Inside, the station was complete bedlam. One of his officers sat on the floor, head in hands, while another stood over him uncertainly, panic written all over his face. Karel pushed his way towards Senzo, who stood in the doorway of the men's bathroom. Lying on the floor, was the crumpled figure of Dutch Müller; dead from a fatal bullet wound to the chest.

'What the hell happened here?' Karel roared, covering Senzo in a spray of spittle.

'Apparently,' said Senzo, looking over his shoulder at the seated officer, 'Dutch was escorted to the bathroom. When your officer turned his back, Dutch grabbed his gun. They got into a scuffle, the gun went off, and now our main witness is dead.'

Karel glared at the seated officer, whose mouth opened and closed like a beached fish.

'You!' he said to Senzo, through clenched teeth, 'had better have something good, or this ...' he said, indicating Dutch, '... is on your head.'

Senzo dipped a hand into his pocket and pulled out his phone. 'It's all on here,' he said. 'Full disclosure of his relationship with Lucky, and Samson's innocence. And, earlier I asked one of your men to put an alert out at the Mozambican borders ... just in case Lucky uses his real passport. It's unlikely, but worth a try.'

Karel stared at the phone, then at Senzo. 'Right,' he said, before turning on his heel. 'I suppose you'll be wanting my job next?'

30: You know the truth
7th December 2012

Mthunzi was unused to being alone. For the last 25-odd years, he'd had a constant companion in MaNoxolo, and then Mzamo and Zenzile had arrived, and with them had come bickering, anger, and resentment. Now, he was surrounded by complete silence, which sat like a shroud of mist over a valley floor. It was rather nice. It had taken a few days for Mthunzi to come to terms with his earthly demise, and he felt only a cold hatred for the man whose selfish ambitions had caused his death.

***

The crucial conversation between Lucky and Mthunzi, which had purposefully not included Zodwa Shezi, had taken place on the mountain the morning of Mthunzi's death. Lucky had arrived at first light, banging violently on the door. Mthunzi opened it with a wide yawn, and Lucky pushed his way in, then dropped a large blue cooler box at Mthunzi's feet.

Lucky sat down heavily onto the leather sofa and filled Mthunzi in on the latest developments. He had received a call from Dutch, the night before, revealing that Samson Ngubane's daughter had been snooping around Jika Jika Tavern. Lucky had stayed up all night contemplating how best to handle this unexpected problem. Mthunzi had never seen Lucky so agitated. For a man who appeared to take most things in his stride, he was very concerned that Nonhle was somehow going to connect him to the incident at The Last Outpost. If she managed that, then the past two years growing his rhino poaching business, and keeping a low profile, would be ruined. Lucky wasn't prepared to risk it. Something had to be done, and quickly.

The news had shaken Mthunzi to his core. This had not been part of the plan. He ran around the room in a fit of worry, endless questions tripping off his tongue.

What should we do? How can we stop her?

'All that planning ... for nothing!' he cried. Mthunzi glared at Lucky and wiped beads of sweat from his forehead with a facecloth. 'This is your fault,' he shouted. 'You are selfish! I could have done this on my own, but you had to serve yourself as usual!'

'Hawu, Mthunzi! I was trying to help you. Moan, moan, moan. That's all you do. What have you done? Nothing!' Lucky flopped back onto the threadbare couch, in indignation.

Mthunzi gave him a dirty look. 'I was waiting,' he said, gloomily. 'The ancestors had to agree.'

'Aaai,' said Lucky, flicking his hand, and clicking his tongue at Mthunzi in irritation. 'Sometimes a man needs to take matters into his own hands.' He launched himself into a seated position, elbows resting on his knees. 'You know,' he said, craftily. 'If you want to make Samson suffer, there's only one way.'

'What's that,' muttered Mthunzi, smarting from Lucky's rebuke.

'Open that,' Lucky said, pointing to the blue cooler box he'd brought in with him.

Mthunzi flipped the lid and looked inside. 'And...?' he shrugged. While it was filled to the brim with ice blocks, and old folded newspapers, there was nothing of value in it.

'I've been thinking,' Lucky said, slowly. 'To get your revenge on Samson, you need to take away the thing that's most important to him. The thing he lives for.'

Lucky looked at Mthunzi expectedly. Mthunzi felt a thrum of fear he couldn't quite place. He remained silent for a beat too long and Lucky sighed impatiently.

'What's the most important thing to Samson?' Lucky shouted at Mthunzi.

'His family,' he stuttered.

'Ja,' said Lucky. 'His family.'

Mthunzi opened his mouth to speak, then shut it. He didn't like the way Lucky was looking at him; like a leopard ready to pounce.

'You think too small, Mthunzi,' Lucky said. 'You're only thinking about Samson when your problem is much bigger. Nonhle is interfering where she is not meant to, asking difficult questions in public places. What happens if someone points her in your direction? Do you trust Zodwa? How'd you know she's not going to change her mind, and send them looking for you?

And if they do, all this …' he said, his arms stretched wide to encompass the hut, the boxes, and containers of dead animals, the wads of notes hidden in the roof, '… is gone. You are finished. It won't be Samson sitting in jail – it will be you. Lucky brought his hands together in a resounding clap. 'Makhosi,' he said. 'Trust yourself. You know the truth. There is only one thing to do …'

Mthunzi looked up at Lucky. 'What?' he whispered.

'Kill her.'

Mthunzi's face crumpled in on itself. 'Haibo, Lucky…' he said, shaking his head slowly from side to side.

Lucky, who had finished rolling a fat joint, handed it over to Mthunzi. 'Here,' he said.

Mthunzi took it with a shaking hand and inhaled deeply. He felt calmer with each lungful of smoke, his mind a little clearer. He peeked at Lucky through one eye and whispered cautiously, 'Who will …?' He looked at Lucky fearfully.

Lucky laughed. 'Not us, madoda!'

'Aaaai, Lucky,' Mthunzi cried. 'Come on … if not us … who?'

'Zodwa,' smiled Lucky, his gold tooth catching the light. 'We are going to get Zodwa to kill her cousin. But we won't tell her until it is time.'

Mthunzi felt sick and sought out the eyes of his ancestors. Surely they would not agree to such a permanent and drastic solution? His eyes swung from one side of the room to the other, from MaNoxolo to Mzamo and Zenzile, and back again. But then, something in the air changed, and Mthunzi's eyes were drawn back to Mzamo's. Before he could stop himself he turned to Lucky and said, 'What will we do with the body?'

Lucky grinned and pointed at the cooler box in the corner. 'We,' he said, 'are going to sell it.'

***

Mthunzi sighed with feeling. Oh, how he wished he'd not let his gaze deviate from the face of his lovely MaNoxolo. But he had, and now, now he feared he would be facing eternity, alone.

31: A place for her
7th December 2012

Nonhle watched Samson walk over to the fence line and lower himself onto the fallen marula trunk. Sunlight ran around the curve of his head, leaving a yellow halo in its wake. It had been a week since he'd been released, and he'd gone straight back to work as if nothing had happened. She poured two mugs of coffee and made her way carefully down the path and over the road to join him. He looked up as she offered him a mug.

'Ngiyabonga, my child,' he said, before taking a sip.

She joined him on the trunk, and they watched the gentle wind ruffle the crest of hair that ran between the head and tail of a nyala bull. Two oxpeckers jockeyed and squabbled for position, over a clump of ticks, on the nyala's left ear.

'How do you do it, Baba?' she asked finally, taking in the relaxed position of his body.

Although they had spoken of what had happened, she had found herself becoming increasingly frustrated at his complete lack of anger or resentment.

'Do what my child?' he said, looking at her.

'Remain so calm. So … peaceful. Aren't you angry?'

She was. Angry on his behalf. Angry at Mthunzi, at Zodwa. At everyone who had believed that he was guilty and did little to help him. To help her.

Samson gave her a smile that turned only the corners of his mouth. 'No,' he said. 'I am not angry. I think perhaps that I am sad, sad that things should end in such a manner for Mthunzi.'

'Sad! For him!' she cried, spilling her coffee in her frustration. 'Baba, I don't understand. He tried to ruin you! He tried to kill me. How can you be sad?'

Samson took one of his daughter's hands in his. She felt the rough skin – as comforting to her – as rubbing the blunt end of his little finger was to him.

'I am sad because I understand now that I should have done more for Mthunzi. I was angry with him for such a long time. Even though I am a Christian; I held on to that anger. I knew that I should make peace with him, but my heart was hardened towards him. Always, when I thought about going up there, my mind would take me back to that house. To those dead animals and to the choices he made.'

'Baba,' she said, squeezing his hand. 'You can't blame yourself. Mthunzi was a grown man. He made those choices.'

'It is not guilt I feel ... but regret. He was a lonely man, called to a lonely life. I could have tried harder to make his world less small.'

'Do you think that he would have forgiven you? That notebook they found in Mthunzi's home was awful. He was obsessed with getting his revenge, Baba.'

'Perhaps,' he shrugged, 'but that would not have been important. He would have known that I had forgiven him.' She leant over, her head resting on his shoulder. He placed his hand upon her head, and asked, 'So, my child. What about you?'

It was a good question. One to add to the growing list of questions that occupied her mind at night, when she couldn't sleep because she could not get the scene at Mthunzi's house, out of her head. Although she had been booked off work, she had seen more of Thomas McKenzie now, than when she was at the lodge. He would come and fetch her every second afternoon, and they'd drive into the reserve, a cooler bag on the seat behind them. On each trip, he took a different route, and she was becoming familiar with the lay of the land. At night, she would imagine herself as a bird, soaring high in the thermals, scanning the veld below for food. She could picture the position of the water holes and the thin animal tracks, and dirt roads, that connected them, the sweep of yellow and green that made up the fever tree forest; and the lodge, sitting on the hill – a king surveying its kingdom.

Thomas had invited Senzo to join them on one of their drives, and to both their surprise, he had said yes. They'd sat in the back of the game vehicle overlooking McKenzie's dam, watching as the sun set the clouds on fire, and discussed the outcome of the case. Dutch's body had been repatriated back to Germany. His confession pinning the blame squarely on Lucky Mhlongo who had disappeared without a trace.

The two adult poachers had been sent to Empangeni prison, and within a week, Nkosi was dead. Cause of death: a bicycle spoke to the back of the neck. It seemed so unbelievably unfair. The one person who truly deserved to go to jail, or die, in Senzo's opinion, was Lucky. But typically, like so many bosses who took advantage of their disadvantaged workforce, he was running free; no doubt having skipped the country to lie low until it was safe to resurface. The second phone they found on Dutch contained two numbers; the first went straight to voicemail, and the second was answered by an old Mozambican woman who swore like a soldier, in Portuguese, then refused to pick up their repeated calls.

When Nonhle looked at Thomas and Senzo, she knew for certain that she wanted to be out there, with them, doing something to make a difference. She wanted to be in the communities, listening and observing, asking the right questions, and hearing the real answers.

Could she be a voice for those that didn't feel they had one?

Nonhle laughed softly at the audacity of her thoughts; and then she thought of Samson and the fact that, although she was woefully unprepared, and the wrong person for the job, she had tried, and now he was home safe. Maybe there was a place for her out here, doing something meaningful.

She looked at her father who waited patiently for her response, his eyes closed to the sunlight that bathed his face. She noticed a thin line of moisture trembling along each lid. Then the sound of chipping and chirping could be heard in the tree above them.

'Can you guess, Baba?' she asked, giving him a soft nudge. Although each morning that week they'd stood under the large flame tree that reached over the house, Baba had not asked her to close her eyes, and guess what birds played in the branches above.

He gave a low chuckle, the first since his return, and wiped his eyes. 'It is a little bee-eater, ngane yami.'

The Leopard in the Lala
Book Two in The Poacher's Moon Crime Series

It's been a year since Nonhle Ngubane was held hostage on a windswept mountain by two crooked and murderous men. She's settled into her new job at The Last Outpost Lodge, and her greatest concern is whether the man she loves, feels the same way.

While she contemplates matters of the heart, the rhino poaching war continues to escalate and kingpins are partnering with corrupt judges. Her friends, Thomas McKenzie and Senzo Mdletshe, find themselves fighting a daily battle to keep the poachers at bay.

Then Nonhle discovers that leopard populations are also under attack. While their skins are worn with pride as a symbol of power and royalty across the African continent, farmers destroy those leopards they consider to be a threat to their livestock.

When a university acquaintance unexpectedly arrives in Zululand, Nonhle finds herself involved in a case that brings the past roaring back into her present.

Letter of thanks

Writing Down at Jika Jika Tavern was an eight-year journey of stops and starts, bursts of inspiration, and attacks of doubt. I remember clearly when the journey started. I was in year one of my Anthropology PhD., but knew, overwhelmingly, that while I wanted to conduct research and write, I wanted to write creatively about my experiences in the field, and the game farm my family was involved in. I deregistered from university, took a short course in creative writing, and the journey to Jika Jika Tavern began. For more on how this story came to life, read the section at the end of this letter of thanks.

As in all of life's activities, we rarely journey alone, so there are many travellers I must thank for walking this road with me.

My mom, Geraldine; who isn't here to read the completed work, but was there when the very first thoughts of the story came to life. Thank you for not making a fuss when I ditched my studies, and for encouraging the storyteller in me. You are loved and missed.

My husband, Grant; what a luck I got! You are a wonder and my greatest earthly gift. Thank you for listening carefully, unravelling plot knots, the multiple read-throughs, and catching the inconsistencies. Mostly, thank you for loving me and believing in me.

My dad, Don, the consummate storyteller, who ensured the tradition of Irish storytelling lived on in his South African daughters. We are the daughters of a man who pulled a sinking ship across Durban harbour, with only his teeth; who ferried a tower of sick farm animals upon his back to the local vet. The daughters of a man who has managed to pull many a leg. If you ever get the chance, read his memoir, The Life and Times of Mrs McCarthy's Second Eldest Son.

My sisters, Cara McCarthy and Niamh Target, who have always supported me in my somewhat unusual choices in life. Thank you for a childhood of drama, song and dance, and a solid friendship spanning three continents.

Sibongile, Portia, Nonhle and Namhla; our unconventional family life together has been another wonderful gift. You are my only family in this country, and I am grateful for the three generations of Seshanges in my life.

Sizah Mtshali, thank you for your friendship, and your partnership in rural development work. Those long hours in the car, and quiet evenings in the bush, opened the door for genuine conversations around culture, and the challenges of being both Zulu and Christian. Thank you for listening, advising, translating words and phrases, and encouraging me to tell this story.

To author, Elana Bregin. Your writing workshop in the beautiful Ixopo Valley helped me to take myself and my craft more seriously. Thank you for reading the first draft, providing invaluable suggestions, and supporting me in the self-publishing process.

To the early readers and wonderful friends: Kirsten Van Heerden (only a best friend could listen to every version of this story with patience and enthusiasm), Kirsten Hoppe, Kim Ward, and Annemarie Pletscher, thank you for joining the journey at different points along the way, and giving your honest feedback and edits. Sindiswa Ntlangulela, I am so glad you approached me in the parking lot that day! Thank you for your friendship, and for providing cultural fact-checking, translation of words and phrases, and for also telling me when I've applied my white lens to a particular situation.

And then to those experts in the field, those passionate individuals, those who've answered the call placed upon their lives to make a difference, and change the world:

Cath Jakins, who interviewed convicted rhino poachers at a prison in KwaZulu-Natal, to better understand the drivers behind poaching in the province. I don't think I'd have the guts to walk into a South African prison and ask the difficult questions. Well done!

Steve McCurrach, a pilot, who provides his services during anti-poaching raids and rhino de-horning expeditions (amongst other amazing conservation projects). He both manages to fly and take spectacular photographs of these events. The anti-poaching world is, understandably, difficult to gain access to, so Steve's insight and experiences gave me enough to work with, without giving away any sensitive information.

Wayne Stead, who now works with my husband, and kindly shared his experiences in the anti-poaching unit at Hluhluwe-Imfolozi Game reserve. Wayne set up the K9 unit there, and managed operations, training staff and dogs to ensure the accurate prosecution of arrested suspects. It's the little details that give a story authenticity, and I am thankful to Wayne for that.

Dr. VVO Mkhize, renowned traditional healer and author of many books written about African spirituality, and founder of the Umsamo Institute in Pietermaritzburg. Being both white and Christian, writing about a traditional healer was never going to be easy. However, as many rhino poaching incidents have involved izangoma, including one on the farm neighbouring ours, the character needed to be portrayed authentically but also sensitively. I knew, from the start, that Mthunzi was not going to be the stereotypical one-dimensional isanomga as often portrayed in tabloid newspapers: a greedy, devious, unfeeling character, interested only in money and personal gain. I wanted to understand why someone who felt called to a life of healing, would turn to a life of crime. The first step, however, was learning about African traditional beliefs and the healer's call to 'do no harm'. Thank you for allowing me into your world, Dr. Mkhize, and also for allowing me to creatively explore Mthunzi's relationship with his ancestors. Any errors in my portrayal of Mthunzi, as a healer, are mine alone.

And to those who prefer to remain nameless. When researching the rhino poaching aspect of this book, it became very apparent that few people involved in anti-poaching were keen to share information, experiences, or their names (especially not to an unknown writer). And for good reason; a great deal of what goes on is not meant for public knowledge. To those who were able to share, I am extremely grateful.

I am most thankful for my deep faith in God, and for all he has done in my life, including, ensuring that my Irish parents, who met in Switzerland, moved to South Africa. I truly believe it was divinely orchestrated, and I am thankful that I get to call this country, home.

Author's Notes

You don't find the story; the story finds you.

I can clearly remember when the story of Down at Jika Jika Tavern found me. Although I had started toying with the idea of writing a novel in 2012 (after deregistering from my PhD), I wasn't doing it very well. I had the main character but was fumbling with the plot. I had a notebook full of possible scenes, but no storyline to convincingly pull it all together. It was only in 2014 that the story transitioned from a set of stand-alone chapters to a book with a working plot. It finally began to take shape, thanks to a series of events, the first of which took place on New Year's Eve, 2013.

The man who shoots without moonlight

That evening, while sitting on the veranda at the game farm my parents were involved in, my friend Amy and I heard a gunshot out on the reserve. The cacophony of night sounds: the high pitched singing of reed frogs, the incessant buzz of flying insects, the witchy cackle of a nightjar, ceased abruptly. We all stood stock-still until the orchestra resumed its nightly concert. But Amy and I were convinced; poachers were in pursuit of a rhino. This assumption was based on the fact that for the past few New Years' eves, rhino had been poached on the game farm. So why should New Year's Eve 2013 be any different? Suddenly a hazy light appeared out in the dark of the reserve, and within the circle of light it cast, lay a large motionless grey lump. A fallen rhino! We were beside ourselves, both shocked and enthralled; our imaginations in overdrive as we sat in camping chairs, binoculars in hand, trying to get a better view of just exactly what was happening out there. It was a long and fruitless wait.

The next morning, we were informed that the light we'd seen was from a new quarry on the hill, and the motionless grey lump: a gravel dune. We were both disappointed at our poor investigative capabilities but also thrilled to learn that our vigil had been in vain.

As we did every morning after breakfast, we jumped into the game vehicle, eager to see what we might find out on the reserve. While driving through the veld, the scent of summer in the air, another game vehicle pulled up and indicated that we stop. In it sat a man - the quintessential ranger; one bronzed arm hanging over the side of the door frame, hair charmingly windblown. And then, he released the arrow that changed the direction of my stalled book. There had been a poaching attempt the night before, and it was rumoured that it was a former Renamo soldier, a Mozambican who could fell a rhino with one shot, and, without the aid of moonlight. Thankfully, last night, he had failed.

The image of a man walking through the bush at midnight, without the moon to guide him while he tried to locate and kill a rhino, remained with me throughout the game drive. A few days later, I navigated a 4x4 track that took me right up to the fence line of the Hluhluwe-Imfolozi Game Reserve. On the other side of the fence were a tribe of goats, and on our side, a few metres into the bush, was a grazing rhino. The vision of a boy, his entire life lived in poverty and with no hope for a future outside of his village, came to life. And I thought about the former soldier and the young boy. I thought about what might lead a person to poach a rhino; especially those that stood to lose the most, if things went awry out there in the veld, in the middle of the night.

There is much information to be found on those at the top of the poaching pyramid; we understand that greed, status, and corruption drive the industry, but so to do the desperate, the poverty-stricken, and the uneducated who, in search of a cure for a dying loved one, will place their hope in a vial of keratin. Just like every user of rhino horn does not do so out of malicious intent, surely not every poacher poaches because they are greedy, soulless, and without conscience. There are many books, articles, blogs, etc. that focus solely on the people without a conscience, who see no wrong in trading animal parts, endangered or otherwise, but not much (at the time) had focused on those in the trenches, the expendable pawns who risk life and limb for a small cut of the pie. What socio-economic drivers push people towards such a dangerous career path?

The Danger of the Single Story

As Nigerian writer, Chimamanda Adichie, warns us, there is danger in telling a single story. I wanted to write a book that, while acknowledging the terrible realities of poaching in South Africa, might give us insight into why people do the things they do. However, it's important to say that Down at Jika Jika Tavern is not a book about rhino poaching, per se. The poaching angle was a necessary driver of the plot and allowed me to explore relationships between different classes, different races, and faiths. I don't believe you can tell a story set in South Africa from one point of view; it would be sorely lacking in depth, colour, and the lived realities of others.

For most of my life, whether at the multi-cultural Catholic school I attended during the apartheid era, as a craft developer, an anthropologist, and an NPO founder in rural Zululand, I have had the privilege of working and living with people of different races, socio-economic classes, and faiths. My approach to life has been profoundly affected by the opportunity to get to know people who don't have the same story as me. It is in the daily interactions, such as cooking and eating together, whiling away the hours as you wait for workshop participants to arrive, and the long hours spent driving to remote destinations, that provide opportunities for genuine and intentional conversations to take place. It is through these conversations that understanding of the 'other' begins, serious contemplation of one's prejudices take place (both conscious and unconscious), and friendships blossom.

Before there were rhinos

But, before rhinos charged onto the scene, a tiny girl child called Nonhle arrived in my life in 2012. For five years I co-raised her with her granny at our family home. The faceless main character of my book suddenly had a name and imagined characteristics. I began writing with the intention that Nonhle, when old enough, would read a book in which the main character carried her name. A character who was strong, and clever, and conscious. Growing up I had a terrible relationship with reading. But the day I was given a book, with my very un-South African name in it, that relationship changed. No longer would I have to console myself with the only book in the library bearing my name – a book on trees. I had finally been upgraded from an Ash tree to an adventurous girl.

The story would take place in Zululand, with a game lodge as the main setting. Nonhle Ngubane, a student anthropologist, has chosen a different path. Due to an upbringing very different from her peers, she stands on the periphery, but still wants to fit in. So when the vision of the boy on the outside of the Hluhluwe-Imfolozi Game Reserve came to me, it spoke to me again of this young woman, looking in at the private game reserve where her parents worked. It made me think of all the people who live on the outskirts of places that once belonged to them, or they had unhindered access to. People who feel that more value is placed on the life of a rhino, than their own. But also of the people who bought and paid for that land, the deep connectedness they feel for it, and their fear at losing it.

Journey to Jika Jika Tavern

On a more recent trip to Zululand, I was sharing with a new friend how I had managed to come up with the content for the book. And in sharing some of the stories of the research conducted, and people met, I realised that sharing the research itself is as important as the book. So over the coming weeks, I'd like to share some of that research, introduce you to people doing phenomenal work in the field of conservation (both academic and field), take you into a South African courtroom, in the hopes of witnessing a poaching kingpin gets his just deserts, and take you on a journey to Jika Jika Tavern.

To read more articles on the behind-the-scenes research and experiences, please visit: www.ashlingmccarthy.co.za

Reading group guide

1. The main characters (Nonhle, Mthunzi, and Thomas) of Down at Jika Jika Tavern are quite diverse individuals. Did you feel you could relate to any of them, and if so, why?

2. Nonhle is a young woman who stands at the intersection of many circles: culture and faith, rural and urban, inequality and privilege. Do you identify with her position in any way?

3. As Thomas gets to know Nonhle, some of his opinions and assumptions about the lodge staff and the community are challenged. Can you think of a time when you engaged with someone who made you reassess your own opinions and assumptions about people different from you?

4. Mthunzi, the sangoma, is a good example of how good people can become corrupted by greed. Did your feelings about Mthunzi change when you realised he was being manipulated by Lucky?

5. Nonhle is a young woman called to make a serious decision about her future; does she pursue a career based on financial stability, or a career that she finds meaningful and that will benefit others. Is this something you have experienced, and if so, can you share your story with the group?

6. The issue of rhino poaching makes for heated conversations, specifically around perceptions of rhino poachers, and what should be done to those that are caught.

a. After reading the chapters of the three poachers (Nkosi, Bheki, and Mandla), and learning about their motivation to become poachers, have any opinions you may have had on the topic, changed in any way?

7. In the Author's Note, the author reflects on the danger of telling the 'single story'. Did you feel that the author successfully shared the various stories of those involved in, and affected by, poaching, social inequality, and structural poverty?

8. Since reading Down at Jika Jika Tavern, have you looked at the world and those around you, differently? If so, how?

9. Are you supportive of a meaningful cause? If so, why not share it with the group and see who else might share your passion.

10. Who would you recommend Down at Jika Jika Tavern to, and why?

Glossary

South Africa has 11 official languages, with some words being adopted across the cultural groups. South African conversations can be spoken in a predominant language (such as isiZulu), but littered with words in English, Afrikaans, Sotho, to name just a few.

The translation of words and phrases below are given in English, then followed by the language of origin. A brief description is given, based on context.

Abelungu	White people. isiZulu.
Ag!	Afrikaans. Pronounced with a long drawn out word, like achtung used to express irritation or resignation.
Amadlozi	Ancestors. isiZulu. In Zulu culture and spiritualism, the amadlozi are ancestors (the living dead).
Amasi	A meal that's made up of sour milk and meali meal. isiZulu.
Bakkie	A light truck. Afrikaans. Similar to a UTE in Australia.
Bladdy	Bloody. A frequently used expression used to emphasize something of interest, or irritation. Not considered a 'bad' swear word. Both bloody and bladdy are used in South Africa.
Boma	An enclosure. Kiswahili. Although usually referring to an animal enclosure, it is also used in South Africa to describe an enclosure for hosting guests, where drinks and meals are served around an open fire pit.
Bossies	Go wild. Afrikaans. A slang term meaning crazy, wild, out of control.
Braai.	Barbeque. Afrikaans. Short for braaivleis, which is to cook meat over an open fire. Not to be confused with an American gas grill barbeque.

Goli	Place of Gold. Sotho. The name for the city of Johannesburg – the city founded on gold mines.
Eina	Ouch. Afrikaans.
Eish	isiXhosa. An exclamation of disbelief or dissatisfaction. It is a term used by South Africans in general.
Fok!	Exactly what it sounds like. Afrikaans. If we said this word as kids, we'd be in BIG trouble.
Gecko	A small lizard.
Gogo	Grandmother. isiZulu.
Haibo!	An expression of surprise or disappointment. isiZulu.
Hawu!	An expression of surprise or disappointment. isiZulu.
Hayi!	An expression of surprise or disappointment. It can also mean, 'no!'. isiZulu.
Hlekabafazi	Laughing women. isiZulu name for the Green Wood Hoopoe. Hleka, is to laugh, and abafazi means women, which is exactly what these birds sound like when chattering in a tree. Although, don't go calling your grannies abafazi, as it's considered an old derogatory term.
Ibomvu	Red soil. isiZulu. Used by graduate traditional healers, and African women, to protect their skin from the sun. It is applied as a face mask and left to harden.
Idlozi	Ancestor. isiZulu. In Zulu culture and spiritualism, the amadlozi are ancestors (the living dead). Singular.
Intaba Yemikhovu	Ghost Mountain. isiZulu. A mountain range in northern KwaZulu-Natal.
Impepho	African sage or liqorice plant. isiZulu. The herb is burnt and used to invoke the ancestors. It has a calming effect.
Ingwe	Leopard. isiZulu.
Inhlawulo ceremony	Penalty paid by a man for making his

girlfriend pregnant out of wedlock. If he wants the baby to take his surname, he must pay. isiZulu.

Isangoma
An African traditional healer. isiZulu. An isangoma is a type of African healer; there are five in total. The name given is determined through the way in which he/she was possessed by the spirits. For example, an isangoma has been possessed and trained through dancing and music.

isiZulu
The Zulu language.

Isigodlo
Healing room. isiZulu. A room where the isangoma practise the art of healing and the ancestors (amadlozi) reside.

Isilo asithintwa
What's dead is dead. isiZulu. An idiom similar to 'let sleeping dogs lie'.

Inyanga
Herbalist. isiZulu. A traditional healer who heals with herbs/plants.

Izinyanga
Plural of inyanga.

Jambiya
A short curved knife with a rhino horn handle. Yemeni Arabic.

Kak
Crap. Afrikaans.

Khehla
Old man. isiZulu.

Knobkerrie
A short stick with a knob at the top. Afrikaans. Traditionally used as a weapon by the indigenous peoples of South Africa.

Kraal
An enclosure to keep cattle safe at night. isiZulu. Pronounced 'crawl' not kraaaaal.

Kuhlonishwa kabili
To get respect, one must give respect. isiZulu. A Zulu proverb.

Kwaito
A style of music similar to hip hop. If you're into music, look up kwaito artists: M'du Masilela or Mandoza.

Lekker
Good, pleasant. Afrikaans.

Liebling
Darling. German.

Makhosi
King. isiZulu. A respectful term used when addressing an isangoma.

Maskandi	Zulu folk music. isiZulu. The word actually derives from the Afrikaans word, musicant. The guitar is main instrument. Look up artists such as Khuzani and Mroza (who sang at my wedding in 2017).
Meisie	Girl. Afrikaans.
Mielie	Maize. Afrikaans.
Mfana	Boy. isiZulu.
Mfo	Brother. isiZulu.
Mpundi wa dinembo	Tattoo artist. Makonde – Mozambique.
Muthi	Medicine. isiZulu. The word muthi refers to traditional medicine supplied by traditional healers. It is also a term used by South Africans in general when referring to medicine.
Ndumba	A sacred hut used for healing. isiZulu.
Ndunankulu	The big boss. isiZulu.
Ngane yami	My child, or, my baby. isiZulu. Term of endearment.
Ndodakazi	Daughter. isiZulu. Does not have to refer to a biological daughter.
Ngeke	Never. isiZulu.
Ngena	Come in, or, you may enter. isiZulu.
Ngibukeka njenge silima	Do I look stupid? isiZulu.
Ngingakusiza	Can I help you? isiZulu.
Ngiyabonga	Thank you. isiZulu.
Pantsula	A style of dance in South Africa. isiZulu.
Pap en sous	Mielie meal porridge with a sauce of diced tomatoes, onions and spices. Afrikaans.
Phuma!	Get out! isiZulu.
Rooibos tea	Red bush tea. Afrikaans. A uniquely South African herbal tea.
Sangoma	Traditional Healer. The incorrect English way of referring to an isangoma. Usually pronounced san-go-ma.
Sanibonani	Hello. isiZulu. Translates as 'I see you'. Plural.
Sawubona	Hello. isiZulu. Singular.
Shesha, manje	Hurry, now. isiZulu.

Shisa nyama	Translates as 'burnt meat'. isiZulu. It really refers to meat cooked over an open flame.
Sis	Gross. Afrikaans. An expression of disgust.
Sisi	Sister. isiZulu. Used when greeting a female of your own age.
Sjambok	Leather whip. Afrikaans.
Spaza shop	An informal trading store.
Thula	Shut up. isiZulu.
Tokoloshe	A mischievous or evil spirit looking to make trouble. isiZulu.
Tsotsi	A street thug. Sotho.
Ucikicane	The little finger. isiZulu.
Umbhulelo	A form of witchcraft. isiZulu. The intention is to make the person very ill or die.
Umcako	White mineral lime. isiZulu. The white version of ibomvu (red lime).
Umngani wami	My friend. isiZulu.
Umhlonyane ceremony	A coming of age ceremony for girls when they reach puberty. isiZulu. Similar to a sweet sixteen.
Umlungu	White man. isiZulu name for a white person.
Umngani wami	My friend. isiZulu.
Umthakathi	A witch. isiZulu. Involved in the art of witchcraft and dark magic.
Ungubani igama lakho	What is your name? isiZulu.
Unjani?	How are you? isiZulu.
Unkulunkulu uzokusiza	God will help us. isiZulu.
Uyaphi?	Where are you going? isiZulu.
Wena	You. isiZulu.
Yah! Madoda	Yes! Men. A South African phrase of exclamation.
Yebo	Yes. isiZulu.
Yirre!	Lord! Afrikaans. When we were growing up, we were not allowed to say Yirre!
Ziduphunga	They smell. isiZulu. A rude term for the police; similar to calling the police pigs, in English. It can also mean stupid people.

DOWN AT JIKA JIKA TAVERN

Printed in Great Britain
by Amazon

27855271R00124